Primitives in Peril

JOSH LANGSTON

Books by Josh Langston

A Little Primitive
A Little More Primitive
A Primitive in Paradise
Primitives in Peril
Resurrection Blues
Treason, Treason!
Greeley
The 12,000-Year-Old Whisper
Zeus's Cookbook
Oh, Bits!
Voices
Garden Clubbed
A Season Gone to the Dogs

With Barbara Galler-Smith

Druids
Captives
Warriors
Under Saint Owain's Rock

Textbooks on Writing

Write Naked!
The Naked Truth
The Naked Novelist
Naked Notes

Dedication

It's hard to write books about little people without thinking of the little people in my own life. So, once again, I'm thinking of the grandkids who make my life, and that of my bride, complete: Alexis, Annabelle, Nicolaus, Knox, and Adam.

Nobody could ask for a more diverse, yet loving, pack of carnivores. Go get 'em, gang!

And, if you ever get around to reading this, please know that you've been in my thoughts all your lives. You are not just loved; you are adored.

—Pop

Chapter One

*"The rude awakening I got was that this country
can determine the fate of anyone by using
propaganda on a public that is hungry for lies."*
–Bushwick Bill

By the time Leonard Pilcher reached his 23rd birthday, he could count each of his significant accomplishments on one hand, with four fingers to spare. Leonard's one noteworthy achievement consisted of earning a bachelor's degree in archeology from Southern Montana State University. This he accomplished without leaving his parent's home on weekends, participating in an authentically scientific archeological dig, or losing his virginity. Though not the biggest loser on campus, Leonard's impact on student life remained minimal, as did his hopes for the future.

Lacking anything resembling a social life, Leonard took part in every lame venture proposed by his mentor and faculty advisor, Simon Dole, associate professor of paleoanthropology. Leonard knew those who accompanied Dole on his alleged research forays would almost certainly end up in a bar where they would discuss whether or not the "expedition" (Dole's term) could be deemed a success.

Along the way, Leonard had seen a little primitive art on rock walls and examined a few items alleged to be ancient artifacts. But mostly he just hauled gear for Professor Dole. Leonard had no misconceptions about his appeal to the females who signed up for such projects. They all had far more interest in Dole than in anything he investigated or anywhere he went.

While Dole's good looks could qualify him for the lead role in a James Bond movie, Leonard's looks would forever relegate him to the role of an extra, most likely a garbage collector or a street sweeper. Dole's looks and charm had a profound impact on the coeds in his academic circle, and they eagerly volunteered to aid him in his field work.

For Leonard, simply being part of Dole's company would land him a spot in a booth with attractive females. That they didn't care whether or not he continued to draw breath didn't bother him in the least. He'd be seen with them; that was enough.

Until one particular trip a few months earlier.

That outing, in nearby Wyoming, had ostensibly been to search for evidence of Indian artifacts and/or remnants of Native American culture in the Cloud Peak Wilderness area of the Bighorn National Forest. Professor Dole had been quite cagey in discussing his reasons for going there, but it seemed obvious that most of those reasons were responses to the demands of a female reporter from the *Cheyenne Times*.

During the post-excursion get-together, Dole and the reporter put their heads together and ignored Leonard and the other grad students. Leonard, however, did not ignore them. Though he couldn't make out everything they said, he was able to glean enough to know their just concluded outing had nothing to do with Indian artifacts. Instead, it had everything to do with Indians. Very, very small ones.

~*~

Randi Rhoades had no doubts about the lengths to which her boss, Timothy Archer, the Chief Executive Officer of Puck Productions, would go to see that his new resort property would be a success. And while his primary interest was financial, Randi suspected he had nearly as much interest in notoriety. In his world, that which made Puck unique, made him unique as well. In Randi's mind, Archer could be described in many ways, but unique didn't make her list.

His latest venture, Puck's Paradise, a sprawling five-star resort on the island of Kauai in

Hawaii, had opened the previous year to rave reviews. Though the opening had been seriously delayed owing to staffing problems, a terrorist plot, and a nationwide pandemic, things were operating smoothly now. At least, that had been Randi's impression. Her hopes that she could focus on other corporate issues died with a single phone call.

"Hello?" she said.

"Rhoades?"

"Yes, sir?"

"I thought we had an understanding."

Randi squinted at the speaker phone on her desk. "What's this about, Mr. Archer?"

"After all our lengthy discussions about the Menehune and how phenomenal it would be to employ some if only they weren't just a native fantasy."

"I'm not following you."

"It turns out they *aren't* just a Polynesian fantasy. What angers me is that you knew, and didn't tell me."

Randi could feel another Archer-induced headache coming on. "I'm sorry," she said, "but I still don't know what you're talking about."

"I know you're not stupid, so stop acting like it. My new security chief at the resort sent me still photos taken from surveillance footage during last year's... unpleasantness."

Oh, shit! I had no idea they were operational. "I don't recall seeing any such photos. That's really not my area of—"

"Don't try to bullshit your way out of this, Rhoades! You lied to me."

"What, exactly, is in those photos, sir? I swear I'm not aware of anything—"

"You wouldn't have had to see them. There are photos of you, among other people, including that damned cowboy you had me hire."

"Nate Sheffield?"

"Yeah, him. I saw you and his wedding party on the beach."

"And?"

"And right there, among the gathering, stood a tiny human. Little more than knee high."

"Are you sure it wasn't a child?" she asked. "I don't recall—"

"Sweet Jesus, Rhoades! Do I hafta paint you a damned wall mural? That little yahoo is one of the Menehune! Where'd you find him? I want him working at the resort. Him and any others like him."

"Sir, I think—"

"Your duck and dive crap won't work on me, Rhoades. I'm not in the mood. That damned resort came in late and way over budget. Then the godforsaken virus from China had us lock down everything. Do you have any idea how much that cost?"

Randi squirmed. "The timing could not have been worse, I know."

"That's the understatement of the century. But, finally, we're past all that, and now I need something that will draw patrons out of the woodwork. We'll have to raise our rates to make up for the prolonged shortfall, to say nothing of construction costs and ongoing liabilities."

"And you think having a few little people working on the property will make a difference?"

"You bet your ass I do. And I expect you to round that little guy up, dress him like a native, and have him report to work by the first of next month."

"I— I can't imagine where I'd even start to—"

"Spare me, Rhoades. Get me as many of those little people as possible. If there's one, there's bound to be more."

"But—"

"Just do it! If you can't, I'll find someone who can. And I suspect they'll be able to handle all your other duties as well."

Archer hung up before she could protest further.

Randi eased back in her chair, her headache in full flower. Working for Timothy Archer had never been her idea of a dream job, but she'd had little to say about it. Archer's political connections made it possible for her to get a low-profile but high-paying job with Puck Productions. Her former position with a little-known group inside the National Security Agency had to be abandoned. The job with Puck allowed her to engage in one last security-related operation.

Since then, she'd grown accustomed to a fat paycheck and profoundly gratifying "extras." In short, she loved her new job's rewards, if not the job itself. Dealing with Tim Archer was the absolute worst part of it.

Reluctantly, she punched the call button for her secretary. "Fran?"

"Yes'm?"

"See if you can get Nate Sheffield on the line. He was in Wyoming the last time he checked in."

Mato, also known to his clan as Black Otter, sat motionless on a boulder which grew increasingly more uncomfortable. Making matters worse, his mate, the diminutive female known as Reyna, would not leave him in peace. She seemed intent on making him miserable by doubting every word of explanation he offered for his recent absence.

"You refuse to believe the truth," he said. "Would you rather I lie?"

"You already have." She all but spat the words.

Mato rubbed his head, then looked away.

Reyna moved just far enough to center herself once again in his line of sight. "Why would anyone *believe* you? You say you have been to a vast forest in the middle of an island ringed by mountains, but you do not know where it is or how you got there. You claim to have ridden inside a great flying bubble, unlike the anything anyone has ever seen."

"The giants called it a bah-limp. Some of them, anyway."

Reyna pursed her lips in dismay. "I think it only flies inside your head, Mato. I think devils have eaten your brains. You no longer know the difference between what is real and what we tell babies to help them sleep."

Frustrated, Mato clenched his fists. "I went with giants. You know the ones—Tori and Nate, Cal and Maggie—they are your friends, too. Shadow was there as well." He wondered briefly where the huge dog was sleeping.

"*Friends?* Pah!" This time she did spit. "Giants and dogs. Nothing but trouble. You have a family now, a child. Your place is here, with us. But...."

"But what?"

"I do not want our child to hear your stupid stories about another band of the People living on an island in the middle of a lake so vast you cannot see the shorelines."

"It is called an ocean," Mato said.

"Oh-shun." Reyna groaned. "Another giant word."

"It is the truth!"

"So, thanks to the giants' magic, you can fly?"

"It is not magic," Mato said. "And you know I am right. They have clever machines. Very clever. You have seen some—the box with moving pictures, and music, and even voices. You have ridden in the machines which carry them about on their hard, black paths. They do not use spells or spirit words. These things are just tools. Like ours, only... better."

"Better for them, perhaps," Reyna said, frowning. "We have no need of them."

"So, you are content to freeze in the winter and melt in summer? You have no desire to see what exists beyond our mountains? The world is—"

"Right here!" Reyna said, her voice rising. "This is our world! This cave! And what little is left of our hunting grounds now that there are so many giants around. We never saw so many before you wandered off the first time."

"So, it is my fault the giants have come?"

Reyna didn't answer. She merely crossed her arms and turned away.

"Then maybe if I go away again, they will leave the People alone. Is that what you want?"

"I did not say that."

"But it is what you meant."

Reyna remained silent.

"Maybe I should just leave," he said.

"Maybe you should. And take that dog of yours with you."

~*~

Nate Sheffield carried his dishes to the sink in Tori's kitchen, which amounted to a short length of countertop, a refrigerator, and a stove. The kitchen, like the living room, bedroom, and study were all part of the same cramped space. The building had been constructed shortly after the Civil War by one of Tori's relatives whose work she chronicled in her first novel. Though she'd had extensive remodeling done on the house, it remained a tight squeeze for two adults and, occasionally, one extremely large dog.

The renovation had occurred a couple years before she met Nate, whom she'd ultimately married. Sharing the house had been Nate's idea, but he'd begun to have second thoughts about the wisdom of it. The sale of his own home generated much of the money they needed to build a new place on Tori's land, and while Tori pitched in where she could, the hands-on construction of their home fell largely to Nate.

They were both learning a great deal more about construction than either of them had ever dreamed possible, and Nate had grown increasingly disheartened by it.

"Look at it this way," Tori said as she rinsed off the plates after their late breakfast, "at least you're not in New York anymore."

"True."

"And you have to admit, there are certain benefits to being here with me." Glancing over her shoulder, she batted her eyelids at him and wiggled her bottom.

Nate chuckled and hugged her from behind, his unshaven jaw resting against her smooth cheek. "*'Benefits?'* That's the best you can come up with? I thought you were a writer." He slid his hands up under her soft, thin T-shirt and caressed her.

She reached behind and did some exploration of her own. "The subject popped up so quickly I didn't have time to ponder it." She made a purring sound. "Seems like something else may have popped up as well."

"Indeed," he whispered.

11

She eased away from his embrace. "Too bad you have to go work on the house."

"Wait. What? You're gonna leave me like this?"

She turned and kissed him on the nose. "Yep. Now saddle up yer cute little ass and go build us a castle."

"It's a ranch."

"That's what I said." She giggled then adopted a faux British accent. "And make sure it has a proper boudoir, with room for a much bigger bed. I'm really tired of sleeping in the library." She pronounced the final word "lie-bur-ree."

"What library?"

She pointed at the disheveled sheets and blankets on the mattress. "See that bed? It's in the library. You can tell 'cause there's a fireplace located conveniently nearby."

"If that's the case, then the bed is also located in the foyer, the dining room, and the walk-in closet."

"Ah, but the loo is all by its ownsome." She dried her hands on a towel and waltzed toward the bathroom. "I'll finish up after my shower. You just trundle out to the job site. I'll check on you later."

Nate watched her sashay into the only portion of the house she'd had added before she moved in. The door closed behind her with a click.

"I'd be all too happy, ma'am," Nate said, loud enough for her to hear, "if you'd allow me to assist you in the shower."

"I'm sure you would, cowboy. But I'm quite capable of taking care of myself."

"Yeah, but—"

Nate stared down at his cell phone as it rang. He didn't recognize the number, but since it originated in the local area code, he answered it with an unenthusiastic "H'lo?"

"This is Arron Johannsen, Chairman of the Board of Commissioners in Big Horn County," said a low male voice. "I'm trying to reach Nathan Sheffield."

"That's me," Nate said. "What can I do for you?"

"We'd like to talk to you about a possible job opening."

"Doing what?" Nate asked, praying it had nothing to do with construction.

"We're looking for someone to assist the rangers up in the national park. Is that something you might be interested in?"

"Maybe." Nate scratched his jaw and gazed at the closed bathroom door. He could hear the shower running and knew Tori wouldn't be able to hear his conversation; since his run-in with mob types during their stay in Hawaii, she'd made it clear she didn't want him to remain in the security trade claiming it was too dangerous. "What's involved?"

"Nothing major, I'm sure," Johannsen said. "We don't have a huge police force, though it's a might larger than Washakie County's."

Nate couldn't help but grin. "That wouldn't take much."

"We got your name from one of the rangers who work in the park. Maybe you know her; Margaret Scott?"

"Maggie?" Nate chuckled. "Yeah, we're friends. It figures she'd try to get me a job."

"Well, you came highly recommended," the commissioner said.

"You still haven't told me what the job entails."

"Right. Uhm, technically, you'd be a deputy sheriff, like you were before in Washakie County."

"*Technically?*"

"Yeah. See, your primary role would be to coordinate with the rangers and look into any mischief that goes on in the park."

Nate couldn't restrain his skepticism. "What kinda mischief, exactly?"

"Oh, I dunno. Little stuff, mostly. You know, dealing with folks who break park rules."

"Like littering?"

"Sure, but not just that. See, the rangers tell us they've had way more visitors than in the past, especially in the Cloud Peak Wilderness area. And many of them are flat out ignoring the rules. We've got campfire issues, motorized vehicles—"

"Aren't they prohibited in the Cloud Peak?"

"Among other places. But there just aren't enough rangers to patrol everywhere, all the time."

Nate snorted. "And you think adding one deputy sheriff to the roster is going to make a difference?"

"No, of course not. But one genuine lawman can have an impact, especially if the rangers can hand off the more serious violators and concentrate on the majority of visitors, people who respect what the park is all about and follow the rules."

The commissioner paused, allowing Nate to consider his response. When he didn't speak up right away, Johannsen added, "The job's yours if you're interested. We've got a partial grant from the federal government to fund the position. Don't know how long that'll last, but it's good for a year or so anyhow."

Just then Tori stuck her head out through the bathroom door. She pretended to put a phone to her ear then raised both palms in a silent query.

Nate held up his hand in a stand-by gesture then returned his focus to the phone. "Lemme give it some thought," he said. "I'll call you back later today."

"Don't dally too long," Johannsen said. "We'd like to get this squared away pronto."

"I understand," Nate said and rang off.

"Who was that?" Tori asked.

"Quite possibly a knight in shining armor."

~*~

The framed photo on the wall of Simon Dole's office completely captured Leonard Pilcher's attention. Not only that, it captured his imagination.

"A lovely example of primitive art," Dole said, glancing at his academic protégé.

"Primitive in what sense?" Leonard asked. "It's not ancient. Birch trees don't live that long, so the bark carving had to have been done in the past few years."

Dole nodded. "I agree. I was referring to the simplicity of it, which to me, is reminiscent of some cave paintings I've seen."

Leonard opted not to respond, though he completely disagreed. The image carved into the birch bark was that of a pretty young woman, possibly of Polynesian descent. He decided to change the subject. "This is the first time I've seen this photo. I didn't realize you'd taken shots of anything but footprints in the snow during our last

16

excursion."

Dole laughed. "I took quite a few of those, plus a handful of that carving. Finally got around to having one printed and framed. It's quite a conversation piece."

"That was the best trip of yours I've been on," Leonard said. "I'd love to see the rest of the pictures you took."

"There's not much to see." Dole eased back in his padded chair and stretched. "But, I'm sure that's not why you dropped by. How're you doing on your dissertation?"

"I'm making progress. It's just slow." He paused, wondering how to get back to the photo topic without seeming too obvious. A tap on the framed photo of the bark carving gave him an idea. "What would be my chances of finding this carving on my own?"

Dole shook his head. "You're thinking of hiking up into the Cloud Peak on your own? No guide? That's a bad idea. Besides, what's so special about the bark carving? The other grad students who went with us didn't think it was a carving at all."

"Yeah, but—"

"They both thought it was a freakish act of nature, like seeing a face in a mountainside or the shape of an animal in the limbs of an oak."

Leonard held his ground. "I'd like to study it

more carefully. There's got to be a way to determine if it's actually a carving."

"I doubt you'd need an expert for that," Dole said, smiling. "The bigger question is whether or not you'll be able to find it again."

"This is a digital imagine, isn't it?"

"Yes. So?"

"So, the location information should be stored with the original photo."

Dole squinted at him. "It was in the Cloud Peak Wilder—"

"Yes, of course. But the *precise* location, the GPS location, should be recorded in the image's metadata." Leonard eyed him with suspicion. "You didn't tamper with the image, did you? Copy it to another device, or—"

"One of my students worked on it for me," Dole said. "You'll have to ask her."

"You don't have the original?"

"I'm sure I do, but—"

"Then that's all I need. Can you email a copy of it to me?"

"I suppose."

"Great! Then I'll get out of your hair."

Dole's face registered relief at the suggestion of Leonard's departure. It was a look the grad student had seen all too often.

A tested warrior and the People's primary seer, Mato knew the kinds of devilment the Spirits would provide if he gave in to his anger, but he had little experience with emotional pain. Had he not earned the trust of his clan, or at least his mate? Had he not proven himself well enough or often enough? Did he truly need to leave his people, his mate, and his child because *they* lacked the ability to see the truth in his words?

"I am not a liar!" he yelled as he stood at the mouth of the cave which led to the People's winter lair. Most of the clan had already moved in, since the weather would soon turn. In this, their deepest cave shelter, the spaces available offered more than just an escape from the worst of the weather. It provided niches where families could separate themselves and enjoy a degree of privacy. That privacy did not survive loud arguments, however, and despite occupying the space furthest from the central fire, everyone inside could hear Mato and Reyna's voices echoing through the rock-walled spaces.

Mato forced himself to relax his jaws lest he grind his teeth flat. There had to be a way to demonstrate that everything he'd told them was true. What made it even more frustrating was the knowledge that if someone else had boasted of such adventures, Mato would have denounced them as deranged, too. What he needed was proof. But what could he provide that would convince them he hadn't been making things up?

Shadow, the massive canine he shared with the giant named Tori, sat beside him. Mato wished the animal could say something, for he had also participated in the adventure, at least in part. But that was just silly; dogs only communicated with other dogs.

If only he could present just one of the island's Menehune, in person, to the clan. That would do it, assuming he could ever convince one to leave their tropical paradise. He continued to concentrate until he recalled Ivan, the giant among giants with whom he'd flown the bah-limp to save his wounded friend, Nate. But delivering Ivan wouldn't work either. He knew the People well; they'd scatter at the first sight of the enormous man.

If a solution existed at all, it would require help from the giants, for what he experienced took place in their world, a place about which the People knew nothing.

Mato placed his arm around Shadow's huge neck. The dog turned toward him, his massive tongue ready to slather the little warrior. Mato backed away, grinning. "A bath? Now? Not this time, my friend. Maybe when we reach Tori's home." He looked up at darkening skies. "Provided we can make it before the snow comes."

Chapter Two

*"In the older folklore, faeries were frightening beings.
In fact, it was such a bad idea to get their attention
that people would use flattering euphemisms for
them such as 'the people of peace,' 'the little people,'
and 'the good neighbors.'"* –Holly Black

"You're a hard man to reach."

Nate instantly recognized the cultured tone of Miranda Rhoades, better known as "Randi," the statuesque redhead who had recruited him as head of security for the construction of Puck Paradise, the high-end resort recently opened on the island of Kauai in Hawaii.

"That sorta depends on who's lookin' for me," he said, turning the speaker on before putting his phone in the cradle on the dashboard of his truck. He was hauling the last load of lumber he needed for framing the house.

"Is that your way of saying you don't want to talk to me?"

Nate thought he could hear a shade of poutiness in her voice, something he couldn't imagine Randi employing under normal circumstances. "I'm always willing to chat with beautiful women, just not while I'm trying to romance the gal I live with."

"Ah, yes. Tori. How's she doing?"

"Great. Except—"

"Uh oh, here it comes."

"She wants me to build her a house."

"So, what's the problem? You should have plenty of money after the settlement you got from Puck Productions. And I understand you sold your old house. So, just find a contractor and—"

"When I said she wants *me* to build it, that's *exactly* what she meant. She wants me to do anything and everything that doesn't require a license."

Randi whistled. "And you're good with that?"

"Actually, no. I can hammer a nail with the best of 'em, and I know how to use a saw and a screwdriver, but I'm no carpenter."

"I get it," Randi said. "You'd rather shoot people."

"Hm. Funny you should say that. A couple folks do actually come to mind."

"There's only one I can think of." Randi's

22

laugh contained little mirth. "Tim Archer."

"Your boss? The head Pucker himself?"

Nate smiled when he heard Randi snort, then added, "So, what's he done this time?"

"He saw some footage of your wedding taken by a security camera—"

"I thought you said those cameras weren't in operation yet."

"You're right," Randi said. "That's exactly what I told you, but I was wrong, and I'm sorry. Anyway, Archer saw something in the video he wants me to look into."

"Go on."

"He saw your little Indian friend, the one I smuggled into and out of the hospital in Hawaii. Matt, right?"

"Mato," Nate said, exhaling with a sigh. "I was afraid you might say something like that. I don't suppose we could pass him off as a child."

"I tried, but Archer wasn't buying. He's angry at me for not saying anything about the little guy. He wants to know if there are any more like him."

Nate felt a rapidly growing sense of dread. "What'd you tell him?"

"He didn't let me say much of anything. He wants me to round up Mato and any others like him and fly them all out to Kauai."

"And then?"

She paused for a breath while Nate held his. "He wants to dress 'em up like Menehune," she said, "and put them to work at the resort."

Nate burst out laughing. "Seriously? He wants to *hire* Mato?"

"And any others like him."

Nate could barely contain himself. "I'm sorry, but that's gotta be the dumbest damned thing I've ever heard. Although it strikes me as even dumber that someone like Archer could believe a mysterious race of tiny Polynesians lives all over Hawaii, even though no one's ever seen one."

"Had anyone ever seen Mato or his people before you did?"

He shrugged. "Maybe. You may find this hard to believe, but someone on the Lewis and Clark expedition interviewed folks living out this way who told them about a tribe of Indians who stood about eighteen inches tall."

"Mato's taller than that," Randi said.

"And so is his true love, a little beauty named Reyna."

"Don't get weird on me."

Nate pressed on. "Archer doesn't know the first thing about Mato, and I'm fairly certain Mato has no concept of what a 'job' is. I can't imagine even trying to explain it to him."

"C'mon, Nate. What's so hard to understand about a job? It's not that—"

"Complicated?"

"Yeah."

"Try explaining it to someone who's lived his entire life in the Stone Age. He has no concept of things like 'money' or 'supervisor.' I cringe at the thought of how he might react to criticism from some cranky management type. He'd most likely whip out his trusty blowgun and send a poison dart up the boss's butt."

Randi giggled. "I'd love to see the look on Archer's face if that happened to him."

"Right up until the moment he either passed out or—"

"Or what?"

"Died."

"Ouch."

Nate pursed his lips and exhaled through his nose. "Yep. It depends on how fresh the poison is. As I recall, snake venom is one of the ingredients."

"Well, I'd still like to talk to him about it. Archer won't rest until I get back to him. He wants this pretty badly, and I imagine he'd pay dearly."

"It won't be easy," Nate said. "I can't

guarantee I'll even be able to find Mato, let alone his clan. He went home right after we returned from Hawaii. It's not like I can call him. The closest thing to a cell phone he has are smoke signals, and I'm a little rusty when it comes to them."

"I wish you'd stayed on as head of security after the resort opened," Randi said.

"Nah. My contract was up. I was eager to get back to Wyoming where I belong. Besides, when my attorney filed suit over the shooting incident, I figured that would be the end of any chance I'd ever work for Puck again."

"Maybe not. Still—"

"The settlement was a whopper, as I'm sure you know, so I didn't feel like I was burning any bridges. But I left that job as much for Tori as for myself. She put a happy face on our wedding, but she's been reluctant to let me out of her sight ever since."

Randi chuckled. "So, it's not your phenomenal building skills she's interested in. She wants you where she can see you."

"I 'spect so."

"In any case, I've got to talk to Mato. I'll be flying out later this week in fact. I've got some things to do at the California theme park, but after that I want to come out and see you and your friends."

"And Mato?"

"Most especially Mato."

Nate shook his head though she couldn't see him. "I can't promise anything, but I'll see what I can do about finding him. If nothing else, it'll give me a break from my construction job."

"I hope that won't cause too many problems," Randi said, her tone apologetic.

"We'll see."

~*~

Leonard Pilcher approached the headquarters of The Cloud Peak Pro with a good deal of apprehension. The small, ancient log cabin "headquarters" appeared anything but stable; its timbers were primeval, and the material used to fill the gaps between the logs had seen better days. Much of it lay on the ground. Though tempted to peek inside through one of the resulting holes, Leonard instead walked to the front entrance.

A hand-lettered sign hung from a nail in the center of the door. He squinted at the message:

NO ANSWER? CHECK THE OUTHOUSE.
IF I AIN'T IN THERE, COME BACK LATER
J. KRANTZ

Leonard prayed Jedediah Krantz was in the cabin, waiting for him. He held his breath and knocked on the door.

"It's open!" someone inside yelled. The voice was low and gruff, the way Leonard might have imagined a bear would sound if it could talk. He pushed on the door, but it wouldn't open.

"Give it a shove!" shouted the man inside.

Leonard shouldered the solid wood door until it gave way, creaking on hinges that likely hadn't seen oil since Texas joined the Union.

"C'mon in. Don't be shy."

Leonard gazed at a man lounging in front of a cast iron stove, his feet resting on a straight back chair. The room smelled of woodsmoke and cigarettes tinged with other aromas he chose not to identify. The speaker, presumably Jedediah Krantz, looked like a refugee from the California Gold Rush, rough as a pine cone and as civilized as a rabid woodchuck.

An ancient wooden desk dominated the room which, besides the stove and two chairs, held no other furniture. Nor would there have been room since most of the remaining space sported either camping gear or rodeo memorabilia clumped in piles.

The man pulled his booted feet from the chair, sat upright, and waved Leonard toward the remaining vacant seat. "I'm Jed Krantz, son. Who would you be?"

Leonard introduced himself while trying not to be too obvious in examining the wooden seat for anything that might attach itself to his clothing. Mostly satisfied, he sat down.

"How kin I hep ya?" Jed asked.

"I need a guide, Mister Krantz," Leonard began. "You see—"

"Call me Jed, son. I don't much hold with that 'mister' stuff." Krantz opened a small pouch of chewing tobacco, pinched off a wad of shredded brown plant material, and shoved it in his mouth. He worked it into position with his tongue and an index finger before continuing. "A guide, huh? Up in the Big Horn?"

"The Cloud Peak Wilderness, actually."

Krantz eyed him critically. "You got a horse?"

"Uh, no."

"Have ya ever *ridden* one?"

"Well—"

"I mean, other than the merry-go-round kind?"

Ordinarily, Leonard would have found such an assertion offensive and demeaning. But, considering he'd just wandered into an outpost of the Wild West in all its 19th century buckskin bluster, he just shrugged. "I haven't ridden since I was a child." He didn't add that the horse was actually a pony led around a small circle by someone with a firm grip on the animal's halter.

Krantz squinted at him. "So, you figger to *hike* up in there?"

"I thought maybe a Jeep or—"

"Not allowed," the old timer said. "How far up you wanna go?"

Leonard swallowed. "I'm not sure exactly. I was there once, earlier in the year, as part of a team. Basically, I just followed along. We drove in and parked, then hiked. Seemed like it took forever. I've got the GPS coordinates."

"Gee—pee—ef, eh? I don't know much 'bout that fancy stuff. I know the trails, though, like the back o' my hands."

A quick glance at the namesake hands caused Leonard to shiver. The dry, cracked, and calloused skin on Krantz's hands gave them a distinctly topographical look.

"I can find the coordinates on a map," Leonard said. "The Internet makes that pretty easy."

"I kin read a map, son. You jes' mark the spot you wanna go to, and I kin git ya there." He paused long enough to grab a well-stained coffee mug from the top of the pot-bellied stove and ejected a stream of brown saliva into it.

His stomach churning, Leonard wondered if he'd completely lost his mind just talking to Krantz.

"I got a couple mounts," Krantz said. "They ain't pretty, and they sure wouldn't make it in a rodeo, but I reckon they'll survive another trip into the mountains. We'll trailer 'em in as far as we can, then ride the rest of the way."

"As I recall, the area I need to get to is pretty steep and heavily wooded."

"You just leave that to me. I'll git ya where ya wanna go." Krantz scratched his grizzled jaw. "Whatcha lookin' for up there? Gold?" He eyed his visitor with suspicion. "You don't look like much of a prospector."

Leonard forced a laugh. "You wouldn't believe me if I told you."

"Try me, son. I've heard plenty of crazy shit. I doubt you kin top it."

"I'm mostly interested in the wildlife," Leonard said, hoping not to sound too cagey.

"Antelope? Bear?"

"Smaller stuff, actually."

"Beaver? 'Coon?"

"Something like that, yeah."

Krantz let fly with another stream of tobacco-stained saliva. "It'd help, son, if you'd just quit jackin' me around and tell me what you hope to find. It's gold, ain't it?"

Leonard shook his head. "No. It's... There's a carving up there I want to see. I don't know who did it or how long ago it was done, but it's of a pretty girl."

"Pardon my sayin' so, but yer talkin' about spending a butt load of cash for that. Is she nekkid?"

"What? No. It's just her face. 'Cause I wouldn't—"

Krantz held up his hand to silence his visitor. "Listen, kid, I don't really care what you hope to find up there. I just hate to see you waste my time and your money."

"Can you get me there and back in one piece?" Leonard asked.

"Sure."

"What'll it cost?"

"You wanna spend the night up there?" Krantz asked.

"Not if I don't have to."

"Fair 'nuff." The old cowboy eased back in his chair, his hands folded across his lap. He looked straight at Leonard for a long moment. "And yer not lookin' fer gold, eh. How's twenty-five hun'erd sound?"

"It sounds high. Way too high," Leonard said, hoping to appear a seasoned bargainer. "Is that for two days or three?"

"Three?" Krantz laughed. "If you cain't find whut yer lookin' for in two days, you ain't gonna find it at all."

"I can't afford that much." Leonard shook

his head and admitted the truth. "I could maybe go a thousand, but I'd have to pay you in chunks."

After a pause, Krantz asked, "How much kin you pay me up front?"

"A couple hundred. I've gotta buy books for—"

Krantz waved off any response, worked the tobacco wad in his cheek, then nodded. "When ya wanna git started?"

~*~

Stone Fist could barely contain his glee after listening to Reyna and Mato argue. Everyone knew, except possibly Reyna, that Stone Fist had his eye on Mato's mate. And now it seemed the two would part ways, thus creating an opportunity for the young hunter to take Mato's place. And why not? Stone Fist was bigger, stronger, and unburdened by a gigantic dog or connections to the giants. Reyna's newfound belief that Mato was a liar made the situation especially sweet.

Though he tried not to appear too interested, Stone Fist had inched closer to the contentious pair while they had words. Their young child, a boy not yet old enough to have earned a name, lay swaddled in cloth given to Mato by his flatland friends. Reyna, it seemed, also had some connections with the over-sized people, many of whom invaded the People's land and despoiled it—more in the past wheel of seasons than ever before.

Stone Fist had often argued that the People should do something to make the giants pay, but his arguments fell on deaf ears. Winter Woman, especially, reveled in silencing him. The thought made him scowl. The oldest of the elders, she would die soon, or so he hoped. His own mother, Gray Feather, could easily become the clan's new leader, and if so, Stone Fist would also rise in importance. Once that happened, and with Mato gone, Reyna would be foolish not to accept his advances.

"Oh, there you are," Reyna said. "I was just outside looking for Mato. Have you seen him?"

Stone Fist snorted. "Why would I waste my time chasing liars?"

Reyna narrowed her eyes at him.

"That is what you called him, is it not?" he asked. "Everyone could hear you screaming at him."

"I do not scream."

"Of course not. It must be my ears. I hear the tiniest sounds."

"Like words exchanged between a couple?"

"I can hear a butterfly fart."

Reyna made a face, turned away, and exhaled over her shoulder. "You disgust me."

"Where are you going?"

"To find Mato. I am not finished talking to

him."

"Who will watch your little one while you are gone?"

Reyna turned to face him. "He sleeps now, and I will not be away for long."

"You cannot know that. Mato could be anywhere."

"He has not been gone that long," Reyna said. "Besides, I could track that stupid dog of his in the dark."

"As could I," Stone Fist said. "You need to stay with your baby. I will look for Mato." He thought Reyna appeared relieved by his words.

"Thank you," she said.

"You can make it up to me later."

Again, Reyna squinted at him. "How, exactly?"

"Do not worry," he said. "I will think of something."

~*~

"You got a new *job?*"

The look on Tori's face confirmed Nate's worst fears; she didn't like the news, nor did it require much imagination to know he'd have a tough time talking his way through to a happy solution. "Well, uh... Yeah."

"And you didn't bother to mention a word

about it to me? *Before* you agreed to it?" Tori crossed her arms and glared at him. Her stance immediately reminded him of his failings as a child which led to a similar expression on his mother's face.

"It wasn't exactly a snap decision," he said, stopping himself from shuffling his feet like an adolescent. "I gave it a lot of thought. Really. But my heart is in law enforcement. It's who I am."

"So, you're going back to being a cop?"

"Sort of. I'll be helping the rangers up in the Cloud Peak. I'll be working with Maggie some of the time."

"It can't be a money issue," Tori said. "Between the settlement you got from Puck and the royalties from my books, we're in good shape." She shrugged her shoulders as if mystified. "So, who's going to work on our house while you're out playing lawman?"

"We'll hire somebody. C'mon Tori, almost anybody knows more about construction than I do. If we want a place we can actually live in, we need to find a contractor."

"I thought we were making great progress," Tori said. "And besides, having you around makes me feel a lot safer, especially since Mato took Shadow with him. We don't even know if the poor dog is still alive. He was my... He was the *only* protection I had back before we got married."

Nate squinted at her. "You don't feel safe out here? You've got a shotgun, and I know for a fact you're quite capable of using it. And nobody's gonna sneak up on you coming down that miserable track we call a driveway."

"It's not that. It's... I just need you here, that's all. And it's not really about...."

"What?"

"You getting shot. You almost *died* on your last stupid security job! You were in that hospital in Hawaii, and that horrible little man wanted me to give away your heart and lungs and kidneys and God only knows what else, and I—"

When sniffing and sobbing prevented her from going on, Nate closed the gap between them and pulled her into his arms. "Babe, listen. Nothing's going to happen to me. The danger level I'll experience on this new job is like... I dunno, like being a meter maid."

"Oh, bull," she said. "You don't know that." She pulled away from him and backed up against the kitchen counter, a frown darkening her features.

"I'll be fine. I swear."

She wasn't smiling. "Maybe you need to think about it a little more."

"What d'ya mean?"

"I mean it's real easy for you to stand in here, nice and warm with dinner almost on the table, and tell me everything's gonna be okay when you don't actually know anything about your new job. You act like you're some kinda modern day Wild Bill Hickok. But may I remind you he got shot in the head?"

"Hey now, that's not fair."

"I imagine Wild Bill's wife said the same thing."

"Aw criminy, Tori. I—"

"I think you need to give this job some more thought. A helluva lot more."

"How 'bout we both just sleep on it tonight," he said.

"Fair enough." She walked to the front door and opened it. "But you aren't sleeping on it in here."

~*~

Randi Rhoades sat in the back seat of a Rolls Royce Phantom limousine alongside Tim Archer, the CEO of Puck Productions. Despite the spacious accommodations in the luxury vehicle, she wished she could edge farther from her boss.

"I just thought you'd like to see how the other half live," Archer joked.

"I don't have envy issues," she said. "I don't care what clubs you belong to or how you spend your free time."

"See? That's part of your problem, Rhoades.

You're now one of my closest associates, and yet you know nothing about my personal life."

Randi turned away and looked out the window. They were headed toward the San Gabriel Mountains. The area they passed through had been devastated by brush fires.

"Appalling view, no?" Archer said, his voice void of sympathy.

"Yeah," she said. "I feel for the people who had to abandon the area."

"I'm sure they had insurance."

She glanced at him, trying hard not to let her expression reveal what she really thought of him. *If I didn't love this job, and the ridiculous salary he's paying me, I'd choke his pompous ass to death right here and now.*

"So," she continued, tamping down her homicidal instincts, "what was it you needed to discuss with me way the hell out here? You already made it clear what you want me to do. So, why couldn't we handle whatever this is about by phone."

"I wanted you to see this," he said, gesturing lazily toward their destination. The closer they got, the better the vegetation looked.

"Swell."

"Considering your background in... security issues, you'll appreciate that I've found this vehicle to be the most secure meeting place I have."

"Okay," she said, unsure of where he was going.

"Now, I've given some more thought to my demands about the little fellow I saw on the security footage from the resort. I don't suppose you know his name, do you?"

"It's Mato."

"Right. And I presume there are more of his kind where he comes from?"

"That's my guess, but I really don't know. I spoke to Nate about—"

"*Nate?*"

"He handled security at the new resort during the final phases of construction."

"Ah, yes. When a terrorist 'borrowed' my billion-dollar airship?"

Randi tried to hide her anger. "He nearly died trying to protect that stupid thing."

"He had a job to do; he screwed it up."

"Do you want to hear what I have to say, or would you prefer to discuss things you know nothing about?"

That sat him back a bit, and Randi reveled in a minor victory. He couldn't fire her without consulting her former NSA bosses, and she had every confidence they'd back her up.

Archer waved it off. "Listen. I've been giving

this whole thing a lot more thought, and I realize I may have been a little hasty."

"Hasty?"

"Yes. I admit I hadn't taken into account some of the potential issues at stake."

"Like what?"

"Well, for openers, you responded to my phone call with a memo in which you suggested this Mato character may not be entirely civilized."

"Based on what I've heard from Nate, that's an understatement."

"But," said Archer, "what it suggests to me is an opportunity. If Mato and his people are living in primitive conditions, what reason would they have to decline an invitation to live in relative luxury? I mean, think of the amenities Puck could provide— food, housing, medical and dental care, education. The list goes on."

"And you're willing to foot the bill for all that?"

"The corporation would," Archer said. "I can make that happen in my sleep."

"And all those people have to do is come to work for you?"

"Yes. That's it. That's all."

"And wear those ridiculous costumes?"

"Well," he said with a shrug, "we might need

to find a little wiggle room there."

"As I told you before," Randi said, "I'll do what I can."

Archer put both hands on her forearm, and she struggled to hold any reaction in check.

"I'm counting on you," he said.

Chapter Three

"I actually don't think there is machismo in America, unless it's the cowboy type—the silent, smoking brooder." –Rosecrans Baldwin

Reyna wondered if her infant son would ever grow old enough to wipe his own behind. It seemed as though she had to clean him up a hundred times a day, and she had grown weary of dealing with the remarks from the tribe about the smells *they* had to deal with. It was enough to make her envy the way the giants dealt with such things. They had machines to wash their clothing. They had water which magically appeared *inside* their homes. They had so much clothing, they could change into something new every day for months, if not longer.

"Reyna, I need to talk with you."

Reyna looked up at the voice of Winter Woman, the People's leader. "Yes, Grandmother. What is it?"

The aging tribal leader sighed. "I long for the day when you will take over for me. I am old, and tired."

Reyna frowned. "What are you talking about?"

"Can you leave your little one for a time? I want to speak with you about something."

"Matc is not here right now," Reyna said. "Stone Fist is out looking for him."

"Stone Fist?" She made a face. "He is as bad as—" She paused. "He still thinks like a child. All he knows is what he wants."

"Can we not talk right here?" Reyna finished wrapping her child in a soft, child-sized blanket which the giant Tori had given her. It did not escape Winter Woman's notice.

"I wish we had more blankets like that one," the old woman said. "These winters grow colder every year."

"It is warm enough in here," Reyna said.

"I suppose, but would it not be nice to live outside, in the fresh air? Would it not be nice to smell like something other than the smoke from our campfires? Would it not be nice if we could see where we are going? These caves are so dark! I did not mind so much when I was young, I could carry a torch; I could find my way, but now?" She shook her head. "Like I said. I am old. I stumble. I do not have the strength I once had."

"How can I help?" Reyna asked. "What is really troubling you?"

"A child."

Reyna gasped and quickly put a hand on her infant. "But—"

"Not your child," Winter Woman said, shaking her head. "An older one, but not yet fully grown. She is barely past her first moon time." She paused again. "I pray the Spirits allow her to live long enough for another."

"Is she sick?"

"No. But like most young ones, she thinks she will live forever. She takes terrible risks, but the People do not try to stop her. Instead, they urge her on."

Reyna suddenly realized who the clan's leader referred to. "You mean Ember, don't you?"

Winter Woman nodded. "It shames me to say this, but I have done nothing to stop her either. I have grown accustomed to the magic she brings us. I know it is wrong, but—"

"Mato says it is not magic. The giants are just very clever with their tools."

"That may be true, but I worry they are clever enough to catch our little thief. In fact, I already dreamed about it happening."

Reyna knew the power of dreams, especially for the few, like Mato and Winter

45

Woman, who sometimes saw the future in them. "Not all dreams bear fruit."

Winter Woman appeared close to tears, something Reyna had never seen in her. "We must stop her, Reyna. If she continues to steal from the giants, they will take her away. Far away!"

Reyna remembered caring for Ember when she was a much younger child. Some of those memories were painful. "What would you have me do?"

"Talk to her! Explain the danger. You have lived among the giants. You know how terrible they are—how they put you in a cage. Is that what she wants? To be kept like an animal?"

"Have you spoken with her?" Reyna asked.

"I tried. But she will not listen to me. She thinks I am old and stupid because I do not praise her for bringing the giant's magic to us. She can make fire with a single little stick! She can light up a cavern at will. Most of the People are afraid to touch the things she steals, but they all share in the wonder, and they want more."

"I will do what I can," Reyna said, wondering how she might enlist Mato's help to convince the child that she wasn't just endangering herself. Her actions could lead to the giants' discovery of the People. If that happened, none of them would be safe.

~*~

Stone Fist wandered out of the cavern where the People normally spent the winter and strolled through the rugged mountain landscape in search of a pleasant spot to rest. On such a warm fall day, he knew he could find some sunshine and a bit of sheltering rock to protect him from the wind which could be strong enough at times to knock a warrior off his feet.

He had no intention of wasting his strength looking for the idiot, Mato, no matter what he'd promised Reyna. His thoughts dwelt on the young mother and the delights she could offer him if only Mato stayed away permanently.

A trio of buzzards circled lazily in the sky a short distance away toward the sun. Their quarry could not have been too close, or he would have smelled it. No doubt, something had died, most likely an animal some clumsy giant had injured. No matter how frightening their weapons, giants lacked the ability to track their prey the way the People could. Giants were slow and clumsy, even their hunters. They could barely smell themselves let alone a wounded animal, or worse, an animal intent on killing *them*.

Stone Fist often wished his spirit animal was a bear. He could use his massive talons to shred giants. The thought made him smile, almost as much as thoughts of Reyna did.

Once he found the spot he'd been looking for, he made himself comfortable and stretched out for a nap. With any luck, he would dream about

Reyna and the wonderful things she would finally do to him.

~*~

"I'm glad you're home, Mags," Cal said. He poured drinks for both of them, took a seat in front of their fireplace, and sighed.

"Hard day at the store?" Maggie asked as she hung her well-worn park ranger hat on a hook in the hallway. "It's a nice day to go out, crazy warm for fall. You probably had a store full of eager shoppers."

"I wish," he said. "But that's not what's bothering me. It's Nate. I never thought I'd see this day."

She picked up her drink, took a sip, and savored it. "I'm not following you," she said, then smiled. "But keep making me drinks like this, and I'll follow you anywhere."

Cal chuckled briefly then shook his head. "It's not just Nate. It's him *and* Tori. They had an argument, and according to Nate, she got so angry she kicked him outta the house."

"You re kidding! That's... That's insane. What were they arguing about?"

"Nate's new job. Tori wants him to work on their house instead. He'd rather do cop stuff than pound nails. If it was me—"

"Thank God it's not!"

"I know, right? I'd rather bash my thumb with a hammer than take a bullet for some ungrateful schmuck."

"So, you're taking Tori's side." Her expression *appeared* neutral.

"Not necessarily. I understand where Nate's comin' from. He needs... I dunno, a sense of adventure maybe."

"And being with Tori isn't enough?"

"Don't go puttin' words in my mouth."

She took another sip of her drink. "So, when did you talk to him?"

"Today. He wandered into the store just as I was closin' up. Said he needed an air mattress. When I asked him why, he told me about their squabble. He doesn't think she'll stay mad for long. According to him, she'll get used to the idea of him being a lawman."

"An air mattress, huh? Sounds like he's not too sure he'll be welcome back inside anytime soon. I'd better give her a call."

Cal put on his best That's A Bad Idea face, complete with a sideways glance.

Maggie frowned. "What?"

"You really think you need to get involved? They are grownups, y'know. I'm sure Nate's right. Tori'll cool down in no time, and everything will return to normal."

"That's a jinx if I ever heard one. The kiss of death for sure."

"You're just being dramatic," he said.

"And you're being just like a man." She paused and tapped her fingers on her glass. "Make that a Neanderthal."

"Hey, cavemen have feelings, too, y'know." He shook his head. "Okay, so call her. But what're you gonna say? That she's right, and you're taking her side?"

"I don't intend to take anyone's side," she said. "But I can tell her a good deal about what Nate's new job entails. I filled you in about it a couple weeks ago, but I'm not entirely sure you were listening."

"I heard ya. He's gonna be working alongside you and the other park rangers. If somebody gives you too much trouble, you'll turn 'em over to him."

"That's pretty much it. And now that the weather's turning colder, we should see the usual drop off in hikers, especially in the high country. It gets damned cold way up there. I hate to go near the Cloud Peak in the winter."

"I suppose somebody has to."

"That'd be Nate. I just hope he won't have to spend too much time there. Folks say it makes ya mean and hard to live with when you come back down."

Cal took a long pull on his drink. "No wonder Tori's pissed off."

~*~

Leonard Pilcher swallowed hard when struck by the reality of what he'd wrought. After riding with his hired guide in the old man's battered pickup, and surviving the sway of the unbalanced horse trailer rumbling along behind, they'd arrived in the foothills of a mountain range he'd last visited with Professor Dole, two other grad students, and a reporter. That trek had begun somewhere else and was made on foot.

Now he found himself staring at a mount easily the size of the one the Greeks used to sneak into the city of Troy. The animal snorted at him as if to indicate its disdain.

"He's big," said Jedediah Krantz, "but he makes up for it by bein' stupid. You'd best use a tight rein on 'im."

Leonard could only imagine what the crusty trail guide meant. Though he'd been around horses any number of times since his short, childhood ride on a pony, he'd never actually had to maneuver such a creature all by himself.

"Whatsa matter, son? I thought you were eager to git movin.'"

"I am. It's just— I'm not very good at this."

"It's easy. Just stick your toe in the stirrup, grab the saddle horn, and throw yer leg over as you pull yourself up. Nuthin' to it."

"For you, maybe," Leonard said. "Your horse is smaller. I don't suppose you've got a step stool around here somewhere."

"I don't. And even if I did, I wouldn't let you use it. There won't be any ladders where we're goin'. You might as well learn how now. Oh, and just so you know, that ain't a horse. It's a mule."

"Right. I— Uh... Never mind." Over the course of the next few minutes, Leonard managed to climb aboard the huge brown animal. Once safely in the saddle, he reached forward and patted the beast's neck. "What's his name?"

"*Her* name is Buttercup," Krantz said.

"That's nice."

"It shore wasn't my idea. I'd have named her Dumb Ass." He snorted louder than the mule. "Or worse."

Leonard made a conscious effort to avoid groaning. "You think we can do this in one day? You know, get up there and back before dark?"

"That's a long shot, son. It depends on what you plan to do. You ain't said much 'bout that yet. Is it some kinda secret or something? It's gold, ain't it?"

"It's not a secret, really. It's just— Well, see, I didn't want you to think I was crazy."

Krantz laughed. "It's a little late for that. But

if you let me in on what you aim to find, there's a good chance I can save you some time findin' it. Unless, of course, you're looking for gold. In that case, yer shit outta luck."

"Why's that? Not that I'm interested in prospecting."

Krantz's eyebrows dipped. "You think I'd take you to the gold if I knew where it was? I ain't completely nuts! If I knew where it was at, doncha think I'd be diggin' it up for myself instead of livin' in a ratty old shack, tryin' to make a livin off tourists? Geez."

"Of course; of course. I— Listen, my interest is purely... uhm... academic. I'm looking for signs of an indigenous race of people."

"You mean Indians?"

"Well, yeah, kinda."

"Kinda what? There's only one Indian reservation in the whole state, far as I know. That'd be Wind River, and it ain't anywhere near here."

Leonard gave a nod of agreement. "You're right. I'm looking for something more historical. I'm studying to be an anthropologist, and finding something like this would really make a difference in getting my doctorate."

"Like puttin' a feather in yer cap," Krantz said with a wink. "If ya catch my drift."

Leonard turned away so the old man wouldn't see him roll his eyes in exasperation. He had no intention of saying anything more about the pint-sized Indians he sought.

Krantz whistled to get his attention. "We'd best get to it then."

"Yessir," said Leonard. "Lead on."

"Don't forget what I told you about the tight reins. Otherwise, ol' Dumb Ass there will wander off in search of a barn."

~*~

Mato spent the morning with Shadow. The dog had grown better about accepting commands from him, but still raced off at times without any obvious reason. If thus engaged, Mato had little hope of calling him back before the animal did whatever he intended to do. Ill-disciplined children often behaved the same way, though their behavior ceased to be their parents' concern once they had reached their naming day.

He remembered his own vividly, and the memory of it restored thoughts of Reyna and their child. Leaving them now, on the verge of winter, seemed cowardly. And yet, if he didn't do something to prove that he hadn't lied to them, his honor would be forever tarnished, if not completely forgotten.

Reyna could be as changeable as the weather, kind and loving one moment, but irritable and demanding in the next. He rarely knew which would greet him after he'd been away. Eventually he realized the only way he could live with himself required him to venture once again into the world of the giants. Not only might he be able to cleanse his reputation, but perhaps he could bring some of the giant's gadgetry with him. After all, Ember, the little thief had developed quite a standing for one so young, and all because she dared creep among the huge humans while they slept.

Imagine what Mato himself could accomplish by aligning with humans while they were awake! Feeling reinvigorated, Mato began a search for Shadow. With any luck he might shoot something for a meal and give it to Reyna before he left.

In the distance he heard Shadow's unmistakable bark and wondered what sort of trouble the enormous dog had gotten into.

~*~

"Here's your office," Maggie said as she waved toward a corner of the cramped Ranger outpost.

"Well, looky there," Nate said, "it's got an itty-bitty desk and everything."

"And a phone," added Maggie. She turned toward the opposite end of the room and pointed. "Coffee pot's over there. We've got a fridge, too, but—" She made a face. "I don't think it's been cleaned out since Eisenhower was in office."

"I'd have thought someone would figure it

was time for a little nicer office. This isn't much of an HQ."

"It was originally a one-man shop, but we've expanded the staff to handle all the new tourists coming to the park. The original plan was to tear this place down and build something new, but they decided to put the money into hiring instead."

"More rangers?" Nate asked.

"Nope." Her pursed lips eventually worked themselves into a smile. "You."

Nate swallowed. "They aren't paying me *that* much, I promise. Though it'd be nice. Anyway I thought the money came from a federal grant of some kind."

"Yeah, well as far as I can tell, they take the money from one pocket and put it in another. But don't worry; the other rangers will forgive you... eventually."

"Good to know."

"More like 'good to hope.' Sometimes it's hard to tell with them. Coffee?"

Happy to have a change of subject, Nate readily agreed.

"You might wanna give that pot a rinse. You'd likely be the first person in a good long while to do that."

Nate walked to the coffee service and began

cleaning and straightening. Maggie pitched in beside him. "I had no idea conditions were so primitive up here," he said.

"Well, yeah, inside that's true," she agreed. "But we all know the real work gets done outside, and to be honest, there's not a soul working here who wasn't pleased to hear about you comin' on board."

Nate grinned. "Why's that? Big crime spree in the Cloud Peak?"

"Actually," Maggie said, "there is."

Though tempted to blow the assertion off with a shake of his head, Nate focused instead. "What sorta crime? Hell, what's up there anyone would want to steal? Trees? Rocks?" He paused. "I 'spect there must be some dandy mineral deposits in the area."

Maggie waved his guesses away. "It's theft. Petty theft, mostly. Campers have been coming in for... I dunno, most of the past year, complaining about stuff going missing while they're out on overnights."

"What kinda stuff?"

"Flashlights, headlamps, fire-starting kits, water bottles, snack food. You know, little stuff."

"Anything valuable?"

"Not that I recall, but I haven't taken down all the reports. It depends who's on duty when the disgruntled campers drop by." She smiled a mouthful of teeth at him. "Now, *you* get to take those reports, and—" She drummed on a countertop with both hands. "—you get to follow up on 'em!"

Nate turned at the sound of the office door opening and spied an older gentleman accompanied by what appeared to be his grandchildren. "Hey there," he called to them. "What can we do for ya?"

The old man pointed down at his feet, both of which were wrapped in ragged cloth. His pained expression spoke of both anger and ache. "You can find the little shit that put my boots in our campfire. The soles melted after they caught fire."

Nate looked immediately at the two youngsters, a boy and a girl. He guessed them both to be under ten.

"Naw," said the man. "They didn't do it. Some wiseass practical joker sneaked into our camp during the night and did it."

Nate gave him a stern look. "I'd rather you didn't use language like that in here, especially with kids around."

"Why the hell not? They've been listenin' to me piss and moan for the past several hours as we hiked down out of the mountains. My feet are killin' me!" He paused for a breath then continued. "You ever walked barefoot in the wilderness? I haven't. That's why I bought boots. I ain't no saint, and I sure don't have rubber soles on my feet."

"I'm truly sorry to hear this," Nate said. "Have you any idea who did it?"

"Not a clue. I wouldn't have woken up if not for the stink of burning rubber." He turned toward Maggie. "I'm surprised none of your people stormed the camp, too, to complain about the dark smoke."

Maggie crossed her arms and looked straight at him. "If we'd seen the smoke, we'd have come down on it like stink on—"

"Right," Nate said, guiding their visitors back toward his end of the office. "Have a seat, and let me get your statement. I wish I knew how we could make you feel better—"

"They stole my headlamp," the little girl said. "Gramp gave it to me special, for this trip, and now it's gone." She teared up before she finished the sentence.

"I expect you to look into this," the man said. "We didn't drive all this way just to be treated so badly. It ain't right, and I won't stand for it."

Nate got a description of the missing headlamp and directions to the campsite. "I promise I'll look into this," he said. "But beyond that, I can't guarantee anything. As you know, it's one huge park."

Maggie chimed in before the man started ranting again. "How 'bout I give you three a lift to your car? You've likely had your fill of hiking for today."

The man squinted at her then seemed to relent. "Yeah. That'd be great. My feet hurt so bad, I'm a little concerned about driving."

"Then before we go, why don't you let me look at 'em. We've got a top o' the line first aid kit handy. You're welcome to anything you need."

As Nate watched Maggie tend to the man, he tried to imagine what might possess someone to toss another's boots in a campfire. What kind of idiot would think something like that was funny?

He looked back at the two children huddled close to their grandfather and wondered if he and Tori would ever have kids of their own.

Chapter Four

*"I decided, 'Well, I'll be a forest ranger!' Because I
thought, 'I'll get to go out in the woods. I'll be in the
forest, and I can sit in a tower and watch for forest fires
and play my guitar. That's what I want to do!' Well, I
was an idiot, of course."* —Keith Carradine

Reyna left her son in Winter Woman's care
and went looking for the child who called herself
"Smoke." It didn't take long; the girl appeared to be
playing the role of elder, sitting in front of a small
group of youngsters and a handful of adults.

"He was old and fat," the girl said. "I could
hear him snore from far away. He had two young
giants with him, but I do not know how they could
sleep with all that noise."

She then mimicked the sleeping giant,
snorting and groaning like some blighted animal.
Her audience found that hilarious and urged her
on.

"What did you take from him?" asked one.

"He had nothing of interest to me," she said. "His smell kept me at a distance. I thought I had nearly fallen into a cache of rotten meat." Again, her audience rewarded her with laughter.

"But when I got close to the two young ones, I found this." Smoke held up something which Reyna thought resembled an odd belt. The girl fastened it around her waist and fumbled on the underside of it. Suddenly, a bright light burst from the center of the belt, frightening several who had gathered to listen to her.

"Magic!" cried one of the older observers.

"The Spirits live in it!" gasped another.

The younger members of the small crowd laughed at their elders and cheered the adventuresome girl.

"Do not be afraid," Smoke said. "Giants wear these on their heads to see in the dark. The giants are just... clever. Very clever. They know how to make things, and they have many secrets. I have learned some of them, like how to make the little sun shine." She tapped the object around her waist with her thumb. "I wish all their secrets were so easy to unravel. One thing I know for certain; that which gives them power also makes them weak."

"What do you mean?" Reyna asked, stepping forward and drawing the attention of the compact mob. "What sort of weakness have you seen?"

62

The girl shook her hair back over her shoulders and smiled as if enlightened. "Giants depend on their tools and clothing too much. If they lose their moccasins, they cannot walk very far or very fast. They wrap themselves in heavy furs at night, and while those furs may keep them warm, they are also a trap. Giants cannot get up quickly and escape if a bear or a wolf comes to visit."

"Perhaps," said Reyna, "but they also have tools which can kill from a distance."

"We have bows and spears. Our poison darts can—"

"Can do some damage, yes," Reyna allowed, "but only if we get close enough to use them. The giants can maim and kill from far away."

Smoke dismissed the comment. "I have never seen such things."

"I have," Reyna said. "You have much to learn, Ember."

The girl turned dead eyes toward her. "I am called Smoke now. I have earned—"

"You have earned nothing. What these children who surround you call bravery is nothing more than stupidity. You risk your life for toys." Reyna drew herself up to her full height, a half head taller than the girl.

"You're jealous."

Reyna laughed. "Of *you?*"

63

Smoke reached behind a boulder and brought forth a deerskin loaded with items she'd stolen from the giants. "You are jealous of all this!" she said. "No one else calls these toys."

"None of you have lived among the giants as I have," Reyna said. "I was a prisoner. I thought my only escape was through death."

"And yet you still live," the girl said, a smirk fixed nastily across her face. "How do we know you are not making things up like your foolish mate? Everyone knows he is a liar. I think you are, too."

Reyna shook her head and sighed. "So young; so... stupid."

"I am done talking to you," Smoke said.

"I wish you well, Ember. But I fear you will not be with us much longer."

"My name is *Smoke*, not Ember, and I do not care what you are afraid of! I *have* no fear, but I do have dreams. One day I will lead the People."

Into what, Reyna wondered. *Into what?*

"Any luck tracking down our little warrior?" Randi asked, putting her cell phone on speaker while she drove. "Archer is acting strangely. The last time I spoke with him, he was almost pleasant, but I could tell he's still intent on turning Mato into an employee."

"The man's an idiot," Nate said.

Randi bobbed her head up and down. "Though it's unlikely either one of our phones is tapped, I reserve the right to respond to that remark at another time."

"But in answer to your question, Randi, no. I haven't seen Mato. I've made a couple trips up into the Cloud Peak, and I presume he's up there somewhere, but his people are experts at staying hidden. If they don't want to be found, no one's going to find 'em."

"That's what I was afraid of." Randi exhaled in frustration and pulled into a parking space at the Puck office complex. "Y'know, we might not be looking at this thing the right way."

"What d'ya mean?"

"Well, based on what you've told me, and on the little I know of Mato from personal experience, his people could probably use a bit of real-world technology. I know what Mato did for you to facilitate your recovery in Hawaii, but—"

"The world can't know about that," Nate said, his voice stern.

"I know; I know. But—"

Nate quickly cut her off. "I'm serious. Whatever it is in Mato's blood that generates rapid healing has to remain a secret, otherwise the world will never leave him alone. Not only that, they'll likely assume all the other members of his tribe have the same attributes in their blood.

They'll all be subject to intense efforts to coerce them into medical studies. That might not be so bad, but there are people in this world who aren't willing to play by the rules."

"Of course. And I know you're right. It's just—"

"They wouldn't hesitate to kidnap one or more of the little people, and I seriously doubt they'd bother with anything as nice as mere coercion. In fact, they've already done it."

Randi snapped her head back in surprise. "Who? How?"

"It happened a while back, and fortunately, everything turned out okay. But it was nothing short of a miracle no one died."

"I had no idea."

"We kept the whole thing a secret. We had to. The kind of people who'd do something like that..." He lowered his voice to a growl. "Let's just say they aren't interested in the betterment of mankind. All they care about is short-term gain."

"The little people would be... Well, not a golden goose, more like golden geese?" Randi's question was more statement than query.

"You got it."

Randi eased back in her seat. "But don't you think Mato's people could benefit from at least *some* of what we have to offer? Their clan is almost certainly small, otherwise someone, at some point, would have spotted them somewhere. Your wife did. Don't you wonder how they survive the brutal winters up in the high country? If one of them gets sick, they probably all get sick. And wouldn't they love to have indoor plumbing?"

"Indoor plum—"

"I doubt they have indoor *anything!*"

"Well, maybe. I really don't—"

Randi delighted in cutting him off. "They're living in the Stone Age, remember? That's what you told me."

"That may have been an exaggeration."

"I doubt it. My guess is they're living in caves."

"Well...."

"Caves, Nate! No heat, no light except from fires, and then God only knows how they handle the smoke."

"I suppose—"

"And animals! Geez. Bats and bears would likely share those caves, wouldn't they? And bobcats, wolves, coyotes, snakes, to say nothing of insects. Just thinking about it scares me to death."

"So," interjected Nate, "what are you suggesting?"

"I'm suggesting that maybe what Archer is offering isn't all that bad. What if he provided some nice housing, decent food, plus medical and dental, too? Would that be so terrible?"

Nate chuckled.

"What's so funny?"

"You are," he said. "I never thought I'd hear you get so worked up. You're always so calm and rational. Now you sound a little like Tori."

"If so, then I like her even more than I thought I did. She's a class act, Nate. You'd be a complete idiot to let her get away."

"I married her, didn't I?"

"And you think that's it? That's all you have to do?"

"Of course not."

"Good. Don't ever forget that."

"Yes, ma'am."

"And find Mato."

"I'll do my best."

~*~

Leonard Pilcher's butt hurt. Making matters worse, Jedidiah Krantz laughed when Leonard complained about it. The day-long ride convinced the graduate student he'd never again attempt to visit the Cloud Peak Wilderness area, no matter what. That decision left him wondering how he might talk Krantz into returning periodically to check the memory card in the motion-activated camera he wanted to set up.

"There it is!" Leonard announced when the tree he'd been looking for all but jumped out of the woods. He'd examined his photo of the carving so many times, he knew the spot well.

"We ain't even gone up above the tree line," Krantz replied through a mass of chewing tobacco crammed into his cheek.

"Yeah, well, this is the spot I care about. I don't need to go any higher."

"You ain't just sayin' that cause you got saddle sores, are ya?"

The grin on the crusty cowboy's face did nothing to improve Leonard's mood, and he ignored the old timer's question. "I'm getting down now. I want to find a good spot for the camera." He carefully swung his leg over the back of the saddle and lowered himself to the ground. He arched his back and rubbed his tortured flanks.

"Camera, huh? Need my help?"

"That depends," Leonard said, holding up the video recorder he intended to aim in the general direction of the carving. "Do you know anything about motion-activated cameras?"

Krantz scratched his armpit then dismounted and stood uncomfortably close to the grad student. "I've heard of 'em. Some hunters I know stash 'em here and there to see what's available—bears and bighorns mostly, trophy stuff. But you didn't tell me you wanted to hunt up here."

"I don't hunt," Leonard said. "I just want to shoot some videos."

"Of what?"

"Anything that comes near that tree." He pointed at the birch, hoping Krantz wouldn't become overly interested in the carving near the base.

The old cowboy shrugged. "Suit yerself, kid. You kin take care of that while I find us a place to camp."

Krantz's casual declaration that they'd be spending the night took Leonard by surprise. "We aren't going back today?"

"Yer the one with the sore ass. You think you can handle the ride back without givin' yer butt some time to heal?"

"It's just— I wasn't planning on it. I didn't bring a sleeping bag or anything to eat other than snacks."

"I don't much like the idea of ridin' around up here at night, especially since the weather's about to turn. And anyway, I packed two bedrolls and a little extra grub. I figured you wouldn't bring either. Hope you like sardines."

"Actually, no, I don't. Can't stand 'em," Leonard said. "Got anything else?"

"Some cheese and a little tequila. I'm willin' to share the cheese."

"That's—"

"I don't like to travel with lots of food 'cause it attracts bears." He reached into his saddlebag and extracted an ancient revolver. "This is all I brought for protection, and a bear would just laugh at it." He jammed the handgun back in its place.

Leonard swallowed. "Bears?"

"They're all over up here. Now, you go on and do whatever it is you need to do with yer camera thingy. I'll make us a fire."

"Okay, great," Leonard said before Krantz turned away. "And I need to ask you something."

"Shoot."

"How much would you charge to come up here from time to time and swap out the memory card? You'd have to get the card back to me so I can see if the camera caught anything."

"I reckon that depends on how hard it is to change the cards."

"It's simple. I can show you in two shakes."

Krantz pursed his lips and drew down his eyebrows as if deep in concentration. Eventually he responded with, "I 'spect we can work something out."

~*~

71

"This will tide you over for a while." Mato dropped the rabbit he'd killed at Reyna's feet and immediately turned to leave.

"Where are you going?"

He spoke over his shoulder. "Back to the giants. They can help me prove I am not a liar."

"How? Will you bring them here, because that is just what we need, *more* giants! Have you not spent enough time with them? Why not stay here and take care of your family?"

Mato glanced back at her before shaking his head. "I must go. I have no choice."

"You would abandon your child? *Again?*"

"That is not what I am doing."

"It feels exactly like that to me," Reyna said.

Though tempted to suggest she find someone who cared to listen to her complaints, he merely shrugged. "I will be back as soon as I can."

"Wait, Mato! Please."

Ignoring her, he walked straight to the cavern entrance where Shadow waited for him. "Time to go," he told the huge canine. "It is a long walk."

The dog seemed every bit as happy as Mato felt sad, but the little warrior refused to look back. Even if Reyna came running after him, he intended to keep going. His honor demanded no less.

Dusk and chilly winds greeted him outside the People's underground home. His eyes needed no time to adjust since the caves were even darker than the sky. He let Shadow run ahead; he had seen only one pair of giants earlier when he went hunting, and they appeared to be settling in for the night. He would not run into them.

Mato knew all the trails the People used. They shared most of them with the animals. Giants had no idea the People even existed, so they ignored any signs clan members might leave behind, or mistook them for marks of other giants' passing. Shadow would sniff at them, but rarely paused for long. Like Mato, he seemed eager to leave the high ground and reach the warmer lowlands.

The need to travel light forced Mato to carry only his bow, a quiver of arrows, and the folding knife given to him by his friend, Nate. Having no pockets, he used a leather cord to suspend the blade Nate called a "pig sticker" from his neck. He and Shadow would look for food only as a last resort since Tori would feed them well when they reached their destination.

~*~

Smoke loved the attention she earned from her encounters with giants who invaded the People's homeland. Anything she could do to discourage their return seemed reasonable. And if, by taking some of their toys, she could enhance her position within the tribe, so much the better.

73

Her career as a thief had begun innocently enough. She encountered a group of four giants— two large and two small—who hiked into the mountains and were camped beside one of the many snow melt lakes in the area. Their music had drawn Smoke closer; she had never heard anything like it, and she watched the giants from the shelter of nearby trees while they made a small fire. She thought it odd when they didn't cook over the fire. Instead, they ate something wrapped in flimsy skins which they then threw into the flames.

When all of them finally crawled into their sleeping furs—all the same beautiful color, but in two sizes—she drew closer to examine the magical device from which they had coaxed the music. It lay near the fire a short distance from the sleepers.

Earlier in the evening, the two small giants had quarreled over the object. Smoke could not tell what the argument was about, but the large female giant grew tired of the squabble and took the music-maker away. She silenced it, sent the two small ones to their sleeping furs, and left the device—which the little ones called an 'Empee-three"—out of their reach near the fire.

Smoke waited until all four were asleep, then crept up to the fire and grabbed the Empee-three for herself. It was surprisingly light to contain so many Spirits. But, she reasoned, Spirits had no weight, and therefore a container for them didn't need to be heavy.

Though more than ready to return to her

own sleeping furs on the far side of the lake, she decided to give the giants something to think about if they wished to come this way again. Setting the Empee-three on a rock where she would easily retrieve it, she hastened to a shallow portion of the lake which provided an abundance of dungweed.

Careful not to let the stiff, thorny limbs scratch her too much, she pulled an ample supply from the muddy shore and carried it silently toward the giant's camp. After one last look to ensure they still slept, Smoke piled the damp brush on top of the glowing coals in their firepit.

Sneaking back to the trees from which she began her observation, Smoke watched as the smoldering plants gave off the foul aroma for which they'd earned their name. The People had learned in ages past how hard it was to rid their clothing and anything else tainted by the smoke from the dreadful smell that accompanied it. The giants would soon learn the same lesson, a fact which stretched the girl's grin into a broad smile.

The reaction of the giants proved to be most gratifying as they were slow in waking which allowed the layer of smoke to grow. A windless night kept the fumes in a rank cloud above them. When they finally awoke, coughing while trying to hold their noses at the same time, Smoke covered her own mouth to stifle her laughter.

The memory of the trick she'd played on the dull, lumbering behemoths inspired her to adopt a more fitting name: Smoke. She had never been truly happy with the one forced on her at her naming day, Ember. It evoked thoughts of something left over, done, and dying. Smoke however, could mean many things, not the least of which was the stealth with which it could move among the unwary.

She often replayed the event in her mind to bolster her spirits during later forays among the invaders. Stealing their precious things had given her a boost in the eyes of the People and drove her to take something new and different whenever she could. Her aim remained to secure a bit of magic the giants were sure to miss.

Such thoughts occupied her mind as she came upon two male giants and their enormous animals, one of which stood taller than the biggest antlered buck. She watched, fascinated, as the older of the two giants showed something she'd never seen before to the younger one. He then returned it to a pouch on one of the leather seats they strapped to their beasts.

Whatever the thing was, Smoke wanted it.

Despite the hard ground and a bedroll that smelled strongly of Krantz's mule, Leonard eventually relaxed. Lying prone seemed to ease the pain in his hips, butt, and thighs, and while the old cowpoke's limited food supply left him hungry, he grew oddly content. For one thing, he'd never have to make this particular trip again; Krantz could do it for him. Leonard felt sure he could talk his parents into funding the sorties. His assurances that he could monetize the results and then move out on his own would work like magic. They'd be all too happy to pay. Later, he knew, he would have to return, but by then he'd have an entirely different agenda, and most likely the funds to cover his expenses.

Not even Krantz's snoring could ruin his mood. Things were finally going well. Though he had yet to fully plan how he would capitalize on his discovery of a stunningly small race of humans, Leonard knew it could lead to both wealth and fame. Who knew? He could be nominated for a Nobel prize! The key, he presumed, was in the timing. He had to have all the elements properly arranged before he said a word to anyone, including Krantz.

It wouldn't be enough to provide the world with photos. He intended to gain the trust of the little ones, learn their language, and do a treatise on their lifestyle, all of which would make him the world's only expert on them. He dreamed of a role managing their connection with civilization. Documentaries, nature shows, and commercial arrangements would all go through him. Anyone attempting to promote a particular spiritual or political agenda would likewise need his blessing, if not a receipt for his consulting fees. He drifted off to sleep with visions of fat bank accounts dancing in his head.

He had no idea how long he slept before he awoke to Krantz's gravelly voice.

"Who's out there?"

The darkness offered no reply.

"Talk to me, damnit!" Krantz groused, his voice growing steadily louder.

The light from their fire had diminished to a reddish glow, utterly unhelpful.

Krantz clicked on a flashlight and played the tight beam in the general direction of the tree with the carving some thirty yards away. "You see anything, kid?"

"Nope. Do you? What'd you hear?"

"Hard to say, 'zactly. Sounded like somebody dropped something, steel on stone, clunky. It's pretty rocky back up that way."

Leonard was impressed; he hadn't heard anything prior to Krantz's outburst. He was about to share that tidbit when the sound of gunfire shattered the still night. A single shot momentarily lit up the darkness some yards away, and Leonard instinctively dropped flat.

Meanwhile, Krantz scrambled out from under his blanket and lumbered toward the saddles, his flashlight casting a wobbly probe in front of him. After digging briefly in his saddlebag, the old curmudgeon cursed, then headed off into the gloom, his shouts of outrage convincing Leonard that his companion had lost his mind.

What sane person chased after a gunman in the dark? There could be more than one! Rather than follow Krantz's foolish charge into the unknown, Leonard pulled the blanket over his head and tried to blend in with the soil. He prayed no one would put a bullet in his head.

"Git up, you little chicken shit!" Krantz yelled, punctuating the slur with a toe to Leonard's ribs.

"Are they gone?"

"Yeah. Whoever tried to steal my gun dropped it and shot hisself, the dumb ass. Now git up and show me where you put that camera."

Leonard slipped into his running shoes and got to his feet while Krantz donned his ancient cowboy boots, shaking them out first to remove any unwanted insect life. Leonard regretted his failure to do the same thing, but since nothing bit him, he tried to act as fearlessly as Krantz.

They made their way to the tree in short order, and Leonard opened the camera case to reveal a tiny screen. He borrowed Krantz's light in order to see the buttons which would allow him to replay any video captured by the device.

When the scene unfolded in the oddly glowing shades of thermal photography, Leonard took a sharp breath and tried to keep Krantz from seeing the video. Krantz shoved him out of the way.

Chapter Five

"The Senate is the last primitive society in the world. We still worship the elders of the tribe and honor the territorial imperative." —Eugene McCarthy

Tori sat on the front step of her compact, homespun cabin waiting for Nate to return from work. He was overdue. She glanced at the partially framed building which was supposed to become their new home. The stud walls looked skeletal and only added to her depression.

Such unhappy feelings were relatively new. She had experienced fear and negative self-esteem thanks to her former husband, now deceased and unmourned, but life with Nate had changed all that. He was courteous, gentle, loving, and generous. Yet she had kicked him out of the house for the sin of not doing her bidding—kicked him out because he got a job!

What the hell is wrong with me? Nate is my whole world! How could I....

But she knew the answer; her whole world truly was Nate, and she couldn't bear the thought of losing him. It's why she wanted him to be the one who built their house, right where she could see him. Knowing where he was, and that he wasn't in any danger, had become the focal point of her existence, verging on obsession.

But that's not me! I'm not one of those women who whine and cling and— Or am I?

Suddenly her thoughts shifted in a different direction. *What if he doesn't come home? What if he decides to sleep with someone—* She couldn't finish the thought. Nate would never stray, no matter the temptation. He'd proven that by not falling for Randi Rhoades, the stunning redhead he worked with previously. Randi had turned out to be a decent person. More than decent, actually. And she had a big hand in saving Nate's life in Hawaii.

So, where was he?

A scrabbling sound shifted Tori's focus. She looked up as Shadow bounded toward her. A welcome sense of joy propelled her toward the huge dog whose unreserved show of affection left her face and neck wet from canine kisses.

Tori buried her face in the mutt's shoulder, his thick, dark fur soft and pliant, if a bit smelly.

"Where Nate?"

The voice could only have belonged to her pint-sized Indian friend, and she looked up to see him standing a few feet away. "Mato! Welcome back. Is everything okay?"

"Dog hungry," he said. "Mato hungry, too."

"Well then, come inside and let me get you something to eat." Giving Shadow one last hug and a pat on the head, she stood and ushered her visitors into the cabin.

Mato quickly searched the compact dwelling, then repeated the question he'd asked when he first arrived. "Where Nate?"

"He's working," she said. "Up in the Cloud Peak somewhere. But he should be home before long." *At least, I hope he comes home soon.* She tried not to look concerned.

"Mato wait."

Though she knew Mato's English skills were limited, Tori nonetheless attempted small talk. "What brings you here?"

Mato squinted at her, then pointed to his feet.

"Oh, right." She wanted to slap her forehead. "I get it. You walked."

"Shadow carry, but Mato—" He paused, clearly struggling to find the right word, then smiled. "Heavy. Mato heavy. Make dog go slow." He went on without a pause. "When Nate come?"

"Any time, now."

Mato looked confused.

"Soon," she repeated. "Very soon." She set a plate of cold chicken wings on the table and gestured for him to dig in. Finding something for Shadow proved more challenging since she'd long since used up the last of the dog food. Finally, she scrambled a half dozen eggs and added some scraps of leftover meat.

Shadow dug in with gusto.

"Why do you need to see Nate?"

"Why talk Nate?" Mato chewed vigorously before answering his own question. "Mato need bah-limp. Nate bring."

Tori couldn't help but smile. *This should be interesting.*

~*~

Maggie Scott looked up when the door to the ranger station opened. Two men walked in; one looked like a college student. As for the other, much older visitor, she'd seen better groomed vagrants. "Can I help you?" she asked.

"Ya know ya got a thief up in the wilderness, doncha?" asked the senior member of the duo.

"We've had some complaints," admitted Maggie. "Did someone take something from you?"

"Some damn fool tried to steal my .38."

"I presume you have a permit for it. The park has strict—"

"Listen up," the man said, his voice part bark and part rumble. "I ain't interested in no third damn degree. I'm tryin' to do my civic duty—"

"Of course," said Maggie. "And I appreciate it."

"You ain't the law anyway. Where's the deputy? I saw the sign out front, said there was a lawman inside."

"Deputy Sheffield had to leave a little early today. He didn't say why; he doesn't report to the ranger staff. But, if you'd like to file a report, I'll be happy to help you, and I'll see that Nate—Deputy Sheffield—gets it when he returns. If not today, then tomorrow for sure."

"Sheffield, huh?" Krantz's lips twisted. "Name's familiar."

"Do you want to file a report, or not?"

"All right, I guess. What d'ya need to know?"

"Your names for starters."

Maggie patiently recorded their contact information and smiled when she got confirmation that the younger one, Leonard Pilcher, was indeed a college student, though in a graduate program. The older man, Jedidiah Krantz, offered little beyond his name, address, and phone number. When she asked what he did for a living, he offered nothing.

The grad student spoke up. "I hired him. He's a—"

"I'm visitin', just like the kid here. He wanted to go up into the Cloud Peak and didn't wanna walk. I let him use my mule."

"That's decent of you," she said. Her smile went unanswered; the student wore an odd look on his face.

"So," she continued, "what can you tell me about this attempted robbery?"

"It was a little Injun brat," Krantz said, his voice dismissive. He jabbed his young companion with an elbow. "Show her."

Pilcher moved slowly, seemingly reluctant to reveal whatever it was Krantz wanted him to share. "It's a short video," he said eventually. "I doubt you'll be able to make out anything useful. In fact, looking at it's probably a complete waste of time."

"Show 'er, the damn movie!" growled Krantz.

"Okay, okay. Geez. I've got it right here on my cell. I transferred it from the camera." He stabbed his index finger at his phone, then turned the device so Maggie could see the screen.

She had seen video taken with night vision before, so the strange illumination came as no surprise. The screen revealed someone walking away from the camera who then went off screen. A short while later, the same person reappeared carrying a large revolver. From the size of the gun,

Maggie quickly realized the alleged thief was too small to be from anywhere but Mato's clan. *How would their existence remain a secret if one of these jokers released the video?*

She squinted at the image on the screen. It definitely wasn't Mato. This person was female, and she struggled to manage the weapon which was about a third of her size.

"My God," Maggie said. "That pistol is immense. What kind is it?"

The grad student scoffed. "It looks bigger than it is. Could be the lighting."

"Horse shit," said Krantz. "That Injun's just little. Now watch this next bit. I love this."

The gun slipped from the girl's arms and landed on her foot, then clattered on the rocky ground. The girl moaned and dropped down to rub her toes.

"D'ja hear the racket she made? It's what woke me up."

Maggie watched as the girl stood up, wincing, then bent over to retrieve her prize. In the process she lifted the weapon with both hands inside the trigger guard. The gun went off. The resulting flash briefly obscured the screen, and when it cleared, she was back on the ground in obvious pain.

"Oh, my Lord!" Maggie exclaimed. "Did she shoot herself?"

"Nah," said Krantz, "otherwise we'd have found more blood. There were just a few drops, and we couldn't even see them 'til daybreak. Besides, she skedaddled before I could git to where she left the gun. I think maybe she got hit by a shard of rock or something."

"You really can't see her features all that well," the grad student commented.

"Not that ya need to," Krantz observed. "How many people that small are runnin' around?"

"Can I have this video?" Maggie asked.

"You can have a *copy*," the younger man said. "I'm keeping the original."

"Of course. I understand. It's just that Deputy Sheffield needs to see this. Can you email it to me?"

"I guess." The prospect clearly didn't appeal to him.

"I insist." She dictated her email address and watched as he tapped it into his phone to make sure he didn't make any "mistakes." After verifying receipt of the missive and its attachment, she thanked him.

"You be sure and tell yer lawman I wanna press charges." Krantz threw his shoulders back and stood tall. "No snot-nose little brat's gonna git away with tryin' to rob me. We need to make an example of her. I don't care if she's one o' them indigital people."

"I think the term is '*indigenous* people.' And we don't know that she is one."

Krantz's face warped into a look of exasperation. "Just look at how she's dressed fer cryin' out loud! Ya think maybe she's a ballerina?"

"Last time I checked," Maggie said, struggling to keep the snarky tone from her voice, "'ballerina' wasn't considered an ethnicity."

"That ain't—"

"Let's not get ahead of ourselves," she concluded. "I've got your contact information, and I'll see to it that the deputy sheriff gets it along with the video. I'm sure he'll look into the matter." *And I hope he can find out if that girl's okay.*

~*~

Nate waited in the parking lot of the Worland airport. Passenger service had been discontinued a few years earlier, but private aircraft regularly used the field. He expected the Puck jet bearing Randi Rhoades to arrive soon. He checked his watch. He'd be a good hour late getting home, and if Randi was running behind... Well, he couldn't help that. Tori had been unusually emotional of late, and it concerned him, though he had no idea how he might get her turned back around. But he knew for sure that keeping her in the dark wouldn't help. He called her cell.

Tori answered on the first ring, a note of anxiety in her voice, "Hello? Nate? Are you okay?"

"I'm fine, sweetheart. I just—"

"I was getting worried, but then Mato showed up, and he— I'm rambling. Just tell me when you'll be home."

"That's why I called. See, I've decided we need—"

"Oh, God. You're not coming home, are you?" Tori sounded pitiful, utterly crestfallen. "It's all my fault. I've been such a—"

"Tori! Honey! Relax. I'm coming home as soon as I can. I had to stop in Worland to pick Randi up at the airport. I decided the three of us should go out to dinner tonight. Somewhere nice. And it'll be Randi's treat. After all, she's the one with the big expense account."

"Oh. Well...."

"Did you say Mato was there?"

"Yeah. He and Shadow showed up out of nowhere a couple hours ago. He's looking for you." Some welcome color had returned to her voice.

"Good. I've been looking for him, too. And Randi will be delighted." *I thought Tori would be pleased to get out of the house for a while, have a nice meal she doesn't have to fix. What's going on with her?*

"Where's Randi going to stay?" Tori asked. "We barely have room for you and me. And with Mato and Shadow here, too, it's going to be crowded."

89

He couldn't resist a little jab. "Does that mean I get to sleep inside tonight?"

"Aw, Nate. Of course, you can! Don't make me feel worse than I already do."

"Sorry sweetheart. Just teasin'. And Randi's got a hotel reservation in Worland. We'll drop her off after dinner, assuming she doesn't want to hurry out here and talk to Mato."

"Let's get her to put it off. I hoped we'd have a little alone time this evening. I thought—"

"Hang on; I see her. I've gotta go. We'll be there in no time." He clicked off and started the engine, then stuck his arm out the window and waved to get Randi's attention. She waved back when she saw him and headed in his direction.

Nate held the door open for her when she reached the truck.

She smiled before getting in. "As I recall, we sent a limo for you and your gang."

"Sorry, mi'lady. The Bentley's in the shop," Nate said, failing miserably at producing a British accent. "Besides, I hate puttin' on airs. Go on; get in. Where's your luggage?"

"The flight crew's taking our stuff and checking us into the hotel. I didn't want to waste any time. I'm eager to have a chat with Mato. I presume you found him."

"Sorta. I know where he is. But I thought we could grab dinner somewhere first. I want to swing by the house and get Tori."

Randi checked her watch. "I'm not sure—"

"Mato's with Tori," Nate said.

"Then what're we doing here?"

During the ride to the remote homestead, Randi asked if Tori had changed her mind about having him build their new house.

"It's hard to say. I spent a couple nights sleeping out on the deck."

"Ouch."

"It wasn't bad." He tossed off any negatives with a wave of his hand. "Clear nights, star-filled skies."

"Sounds romantic."

"Not if you're sleeping solo." He shook his head. "I just don't get it. It's like she's changed overnight. She's not the Victoria I fell in love with. But don't get me wrong. I still love her! She's just makin' it a little harder is all."

"She's just worried about you. You should have seen her when you were in the hospital with that gunshot wound back in Hawaii. You weren't the only one whose survival seemed in question."

"Hey, I was the one got shot, remember?"

Randi chuckled. "But she was the one who stayed awake the whole time you were laid up, unconscious. She had to make the decisions about—"

"Yeah. I know. She keeps reminding me."

"She's crazy about you, Nate."

"Crazy is the right word for it."

"C'mon. It can't be all that bad." She grew silent and looked out at the broad open landscape with its gentle hills and distant mountains. "I'm no doctor, but it sounds to me like it could be hormonal."

Nate's eyebrows contracted. "What d'ya mean?"

"Let's just say there are times in a woman's life when she can be a little more emotional than usual."

"Sure, sure. But this seems more extreme."

Randi remained quiet for a moment then asked, "Is she pregnant by any chance?"

~*~

Reyna responded quickly to Winter Woman's summons, hurrying through the cavern enclave with her infant son on her hip. "What is the matter?" she asked when she reached the elder's circle.

"Ember is hurt. She has a wound of some kind," the tribal leader said. "Stone Fist will bring her here."

Reyna watched as Winter Woman assessed

her collection of herbs. "Does she have a wound we must wrap?" Reyna asked, evaluating the small cloth blanket she'd been given by the giants. It would yield an abundance of bandages.

"We will see soon enough," Winter Woman said. She tilted her head toward a warrior who carried the girl in his arms as if she weighed no more than the baby on Reyna's hip.

"Ember," Reyna said, "what happened?"

The girl's eyes narrowed as she stared at Reyna. "You know my name. Use it if you wish to have an answer."

Winter Woman shooed Stone Fist away and set about investigating the extent of the girl's injury. She paused only briefly to admonish her. "Know your place, child, and remember that words have lives."

The elder removed the girl's moccasins, then held a torch above her feet to get a better look. One foot was badly bruised, the other was covered in blood.

Smoke grimaced as Winter Woman probed for the source of the blood. "It's my leg, not my foot," the girl said.

Winter Woman rolled up the girl's pantleg to reveal a gash in her calf. "How did this happen?" the elder asked.

Smoke's lips twisted, and she remained silent.

"Well?"

"I do not know."

"What?"

The girl began to cry. "I do not know! The giants did it! With their magic. I— I do not know why or how.'

"It is one thing to lie to me," Reyna said. "It is quite another when a child lies to our leader. Try harder to explain this."

"I do not need to explain anything to you. I am—" Smoke's voice shifted from words to wails as Winter Woman probed the cut on her leg.

"Silence," the elder snapped. "You will live, but only if you stop trying to annoy the giants. If you persist, they will come looking for you, for all of us. And then none of us will survive."

The girl sniffed once more, then palmed the tears from her eyes. Her look of despair turned into one of determination.

Reyna cut off a portion of the baby blanket and gave it to Winter Woman who used it to hold a poultice in place. She ignored the girl's wince of pain when she applied it, tying it in place with thin leather straps. "It will only sting for a short time."

The elder then reached into her voluminous clothing and produced a small leather pouch which she opened and held in one hand. She extracted a pinch of powder from it. "Open your mouth," she said.

"Why?"

Winter Woman frowned at her. "Do as you are told!"

"It will help ease the pain," Reyna said, forcing a smile.

The girl dutifully opened her mouth, and Winter Woman sprinkled the powder on her tongue.

"It has no taste," Smoke said.

The elder tightened the draw strings on the little bag and handed it to the girl. "Do not use more than a pinch, or it will put you to sleep. Use too much, and you will never wake up." She glared down at her patient. "Do you understand?"

"Yes, grandmother," she said. "And thank you for taking care of me."

Winter Woman packed up her potions. "Well, someone needs to."

~*~

Leonard approached the office of his faculty advisor, Simon Dole, with cautious optimism. The video he had of the tiny Indian proved that Dole had not been wasting his time when he and his reporter friend dragged Leonard and two other students on what had, at first, seemed the wildest of goose chases. Leonard firmly believed the girl in the video represented a member of a previously unknown branch of the *homo sapiens* family tree. He also believed he could waste no time in laying claim to the discovery. He hoped Dole would be content to have his name footnoted in the thesis Leonard had already begun to compose.

Not surprisingly, two female students were already in the professor's office, a half hour before classes were scheduled. Dole, nattily dressed as always, sat at his desk with a coed on each corner, as if he had been awaiting Leonard's arrival.

"Come in," Dole said, giving Leonard a good-natured wave. "Have a seat, if you can find one."

"I need to talk to you about my thesis," Leonard began. "I've made a huge—"

"Hold on a sec, will you?" Dole smiled at each of the two young women. "It looks like I have some work to do, ladies. Would you excuse us, please? I doubt this will take long."

Leonard tried to appear nonchalant as the two girls slowly departed, each one having bestowed what he'd call "come hither" looks upon Dole. The man seemed immune to such things, which left Leonard even more envious of him. He wondered how Dole and Krantz might react to each other, then figured such a meeting was unlikely to occur in his lifetime.

"So, you've settled on a topic," Dole said when they were finally alone.

"Yes, I have, and I think it's unique."

Dole chuckled. "Really? I've no idea what you mean by that. There's a great deal of intellectual territory one might explore in a thesis."

"I've made a discovery," Leonard said, "and I have reason to believe it's groundbreaking."

"*Groundbreaking?* Oh my. Oh my, indeed," Dole said, still smiling. "Fill me in."

"I'm sure you're familiar with the recent discovery of small, human-like remains on the Indonesian island of Flores."

"Oh, yes. *Homo floresiensis*. A curious find, and as I recall, the subject of much conjecture. The argument being that such creatures were more chimp-like than human, based on brain size."

Leonard shrugged. "What if I told you I had proof of an even smaller human species?"

The look on Dole's face struck him as suspicious. "Is this some kind of joke?"

"No sir."

"You say you have proof? Like what? Bones? Artifacts?"

"Video."

Dole squinted at him. "Video of what?"

"Of one of... *them.*"

Dole was about to respond when his phone rang. He gave Leonard a raised palm and the command, "Stand by," while he answered the call.

Leonard squirmed as he waited for the instructor to finish. Eventually, he did, then checked his watch. "I'm afraid I have to run."

"But—"

"I know, I know. We've a great deal more to discuss. But for now, I want you to leave this video of yours with me."

"I'd rather—"

"Just email it to me. You have my address, don't you?"

"Of course, but—"

"Then it's settled. I'll need some time to vet the material, and then we can talk some more. I hate to do this to you, but I really do need to scoot."

Leonard eased out of the way as Dole left the room and hurried down the hallway and out of sight. The idiot was gone before Leonard had a chance to tell him he also had a blood sample.

~*~

Reyna had ignored Stone Fist, even after he traversed the length of the main cavern carrying the stripling who called herself Smoke. He doubted anyone else in the clan could have accomplished the same feat. Mato would have collapsed under the weight, and if he had, Reyna would surely have fawned over him. The thought made him growl his discontent.

How could she be so foolish? Could she not see that he was superior to Mato in every way? Except for lying. Mato clearly excelled in that!

If a feat of strength made no impression on her, what else could he do? She still had most of the rabbit Mato had left for her. The meat had been smoked and the pelt stretched on a twig frame. She kept the baby at her breast and worked alongside Winter Woman. He would likely need to set himself on fire just to get her attention.

Of course, there were other females in the cavern. Reyna was not the only one, but she was clearly the most desirable. The woman-child Smoke was almost at the age where she would be available, but she had built a following, of sorts. All the younger males hungered after her; she could take her pick. Of course, if he made it known that she might entertain him, she would surely ignore all the others. That thought assuaged his ego enough to almost get over Reyna's snub.

Almost.

There had to be something he could do to prove himself. Unfortunately, Reyna had given no indication that she cared what he did. She was focused on her child, on Winter Woman, and on the injured Smoke.

Stone Fist felt certain the girl had gotten hurt as a result of her stupid attempts to steal from the giants. Only a complete fool would continue such pursuits once the giants became aware of them. If he could figure out exactly what happened, since the girl was unwilling to admit her failure, he might gain the attention he sought by explaining it to the elders, Reyna included. If possible, he could cast his version of events in Smoke's favor. What could it hurt?

But he couldn't even begin to look into Smoke's encounter without first getting more information. Where had it occurred, and how, exactly, had the giants hurt her?

He waited until Winter Woman ushered Reyna away from the girl who lay upon a bed of rushes, resting.

Stone Fist crept close, and keeping his voice low, began his interrogation.

Chapter Six

"Here's a news flash: scientists can be wrong. That's no big deal (unless the scientist is you), since research is self-correcting. Consequently, most errors by scientists become historical curiosities, with little long-term importance." —Seth Shostak

Mato had the volume turned up on his favorite tune, "Sweet Home Alabama." Tori didn't seem to mind, and they both sang along with the music. The words didn't make a great deal of sense to Mato, but he liked the overall sound. It's what had attracted him to Tori's house long ago. So much had happened since then, and much of it was unpleasant. Some, however, had turned out well.

Rediscovering the sacred cavern on top of which sat Tori's cabin was the most important, although he'd been unable to show it to any of the People besides Reyna. That remained a sore spot for him. Winter Woman, especially, needed to see it. The problem had been convincing her to make the journey. Her fear of the giants seemed to infect

101

the entire clan. It would be good for all of them to make a pilgrimage.

His mind drifted back to his time in Hawaii, and he smiled. That had certainly been an enlightening adventure. He had discovered another branch of the People, normal sized, not giants. And he could never forget his ride in the mysterious bah-limp!

If only the People had the chance to ride in it, they would finally believe him and know that he only spoke the truth. And, if given the chance, he might prove to Stone Fist and all the others that the gigantic machine really did crawl through the sky. That might best be done by tossing the brute out a window and letting him fly back to the ground.

Such thoughts always put Mato in a good mood.

Shadow alerted both Mato and Tori to the approach of a vehicle. The giants had so many different kinds, they were hard to sort based on sound. Shadow didn't care. He reacted the same way to all of them with a cross between pleasure and pandemonium. If nothing else, it put everyone on alert.

Tori smiled for the first time since he and the dog arrived. That was good, Mato concluded; she needed to smile more often. Nate had that power.

He also had the power to summon the bah-limp.

Tori opened the cabin door and released the great hound. He bounded through the opening and raced toward the truck which lumbered down the rutted, boulder-strewn driveway.

Mato stepped outside with Tori to greet the arrivals. He recognized them both, though he was surprised to see the female giant with fiery red hair. He had thought of her often since his brief encounter with her at the healing place where Nate was taken when he was hurt. His mind wandered briefly, accompanied by a note of sadness that the redheaded giant was not his size.

"Hi, babe!" called Nate.

Tori responded with, "Hey back atcha. I'm dressed and ready to go."

"Oops," said Randi.

"Yeah. About that," Nate began.

Randi held up two flat boxes. "We brought pizza!" Her squinty smile suggested the offering might not be accepted with great joy.

"Oh," said Tori. "Hi, Randi."

"I'm sorry, hon." Nate hurried to her. "But Randi was eager to talk to Mato, and I got the impression when we were on the phone that Mato was eager to talk to me."

Nate continued, but Mato had turned his attention to Randi and the aromas emanating from the two boxes she carried into the house. Mato trailed close behind. When she deposited her burden on the kitchen counter, he clambered up in a chair, lifted the lid from the top box, and inhaled deeply.

Randi grinned. "I hoped you'd like pizza. Nate couldn't remember if you'd had it before."

Mato attempted to pick up a slice, but its size made it utterly unwieldly.

"Let me cut that for you," Randi said and then began looking for a knife to make good on her offer.

"There," said Mato, pointing to the drawer which held Tori's knives along with several other tools for which he could find little or no use. A knife made sense; hands took care of almost everything else.

Randi deftly reduced the size of Mato's slice which he proceeded to consume without further preamble.

"I have a proposition for you," Randi said, holding a full-sized slice inches from her mouth.

Her lips seemed unusually bright. Mato liked that. He stared at her and chewed.

"Would you like a job?"

Mato held up two fistfuls of melted cheese and sliced pepperoni. A bit of mushroom dangled from his chin. "Mato have." He couldn't imagine what a "job" tasted like, but it didn't matter. It couldn't possibly compare with what he already held in his hands.

Randi laughed. "It's not food. It's..." She shrugged and took a huge bite of her pizza.

Nate and Tori entered the cabin holding hands. They appeared much more interested in each other than the food on the table. Giants, Mato recalled, could be very strange. The People never failed to eat when food was available. But, if the two giants didn't want to join in, it simply meant more for him and Shadow who lurked beneath the table. Mato let the dog lick his fingers before diving back into the flat boxes for more.

Randi looked at Nate, her lips twisted to one side. "Our little friend seems to think a job is something to eat."

"I wondered how you were going to get that idea across."

She started over. "Mato, do your people have much food?"

He chewed for a while before answering. "No pizza. Birds. Fish. Er... rabbit," it took a moment to remember the giants' word for the long-eared creature.

"Would they like to have as much food as they could eat whenever they were hungry?"

Mato contemplated the question, not wanting to embarrass the redheaded giant by pointing out how stupid it was. "Sometimes no food. Winter hard. Hungry."

"I can change that. Good food. Always. Any

105

time."

If he understood her words, then she had to be weak-minded. Good food, all the time? It was not possible. And yet, he recollected that when they were all on the island, the giants never hunted for their food. The more he thought about it, the more puzzled he became. Tori never hunted for food either. She went somewhere to get it, but she never came home covered in dirt or the blood of whatever prey she had to clean.

Though tempted to credit magic for such abundance, Mato knew better. Their machines made it possible, not their skill with blade or bow. "How?"

"If you do something for me, I will give you food," Randi said.

Suddenly it became all too clear to him. "I kill someone?"

Once again, Randi turned to Nate. "This may take longer than I thought."

"Nate!" called Mato. "Where bah-limp?

"I dunno," he said, pointing at Randi. "Ask her."

On one thing, at least, Mato could agree with Randi. Getting answers would take longer than either of them thought.

~*~

Nate yawned. The night before had been

long, and he would gladly have gone straight to bed when they finished eating the night before. But he had to take Randi back to her hotel first, and both Tori and Mato insisted on coming along. If Mato hadn't been willing to sit in Randi's lap, they would never have gotten all four of them in the cab of his truck at the same time.

Mato and Randi's conversation proved painful, and not just for the two of them. Nate and Tori winced with each misunderstanding and tried to laugh them off, but it grew tiresome. Randi made it clear she wanted to prove to Mato's clan that Puck could provide amazing food and housing in exchange for their help at the resort. Nate couldn't tell if his pint-sized pal completely understood the proposal.

Meanwhile, Mato pressed repeatedly for Randi to bring the dirigible they'd encountered in Hawaii to the Cloud Peak Wilderness so his tribe could see it. He never managed to make clear just why he was so intent on showing off the huge flying machine. Nor could Randi get him to call it an airship instead of a "bah-limp."

Nate felt as if the following workday had begun much too early. He had been settled in his desk with a cup of coffee for all of two minutes when Maggie Scott appeared. She smiled at him, took a deep breath, and launched into a recap of the previous day's visit by the grad student and his aging companion.

"I forwarded a copy of their video to your

email," she said.

"Have you looked at it?"

She nodded. "The college kid showed it to me on his cell phone." She looked around the room to make sure no other rangers were close enough to hear her. She lowered her voice anyway. "I think it's one of Mato's people in the video."

Nate was momentarily taken aback. "Oh, that's just dandy."

"My thoughts exactly." She leaned close. "What're we gonna do?"

"Beats me. I'd like to review the thing before I try to figure out what's next."

"Fair enough," she said.

"I'll—"

The phone rang before he could finish the thought. He exhaled and picked up the receiver.

"Sherriff Sheffield?" asked a male voice.

"Deputy Sherriff," corrected Nate.

"This is Trent Cowart with the Bureau of Indian Affairs."

"You're up in Billings, aren't you? I've been up that way a few times."

"Actually," Cowart said, "I'm calling from DC. We need your help to resolve an issue that seems to have popped up overnight."

"I'm happy to do what I can," Nate said, scrolling through his email as he talked. He found the one sent by Maggie and opened the attachment.

"It seems there's a short video that's gone viral. It features what appears to be a very small, young female who's being described as Native American. Are you familiar with it?"

"I haven't seen it, yet," Nate said. "Can you send me a copy?" He didn't want to confirm or deny anything. That would come after he'd seen both Maggie's and the BIA's clips.

"Give me your email address, and I'll send it to you," Cowart said. "Call me when you've seen it. Say in... oh... twenty minutes?"

"Sure, no problem."

They both rang off and Nate clicked the Play button on his screen. The image which appeared had an eerie lighting effect he hadn't often seen, but it was clear enough for him to make out what was going on. He winced when the girl dropped the enormous handgun she was carrying on her foot, and he flinched when she clumsily picked it up and fired it a few moments later.

"Oh, geez," he said.

His comment drew Maggie back from her side of the room. "You think the kid's okay?"

"Hopefully, yes. Criminy. I don't even know where to start."

"Do you think she looks like she might be one of Mato's people?"

"Yep."

Maggie nodded. "Who was on the phone?"

"BIA. They're sending me a video clip, too." As before, he checked his mail while he talked and quickly found the electronic missive from Washington, DC. "Here 'tis."

He fired up the attached video and found himself looking at the exact same clip Maggie had provided.

"How'd the BIA get that?" she asked.

"Beats me. The guy said it had gone viral." He pursed his lips as he shook his head. "I'd love to get my hands on the yahoo that invented social media."

Maggie raised both hands, palms out. "Don't get me started. That stuff drives me nuts."

"It looks like it could be a good deal worse than that," Nate said. "I can't wait to find out what the Feds want me to do about it."

~*~

Leonard charged into Simon Dole's office waving a printout he'd copied from the Internet. Dole's office seemed roomier without the coeds who usually populated it. Not having them as witnesses gave Leonard an added spark. "Have you seen this crap?" he asked, shoving the single sheet

110

of paper toward Dole's face.

"Actually, yes, I have," Dole admitted.

Leonard snatched it back and read the heading out loud, "Leprechaun Larceny Caught on Camera." He stopped and stared at his advisor. "Real cute. Is that something you dreamed up?"

"Of course not. And believe me when I say, I had no idea one of my assistants would post that video online." Dole's voice sounded apologetic. "I'm really sorry about that. I've already had a talk with her. It'll never happen again."

"Fat lot of good it'll do me," Leonard snarled. "She had no right to post it! Who's going to take my claim seriously after my video has become an object of ridicule?"

"What claim?"

Leonard teetered on the verge of apoplexy. "What claim? *My claim!* I discovered that kid! She represents a previously unknown race."

Dole held up his hands as if he were halting traffic. "Settle down. That video proves nothing. You can't leap to such a bizarre conclusion on the basis of one grainy bit of film or one petite thief."

"Speaking of thieves, you're the guy who hired one! That's my video, taken with my camera. And now anybody with an Internet connection can look at it." He drew in a ragged breath, his eyes expanding with previously unrealized possibilities. "Or change it! Oh, dear God! That

111

happens all the time." His eyes narrowed as he leaned over Dole's desk, his face mere inches away from the professor's. "If I knew which one of your little sluts did this, I'd wring her neck."

"And that's exactly why I won't be telling you," Dole said, shifting away. "Besides, I seriously doubt it's as bad a situation as you think. It'll all blow over in no time. Anything that's a big deal on social media today will be completely forgotten tomorrow. Meanwhile, you've got a thesis to write."

Leonard grimaced, straightened, and balled up the printed sheet which he threw at Dole's head. "You damn well better hope so."

~*~

Smoke didn't volunteer anything other than what she had already told Reyna and Winter Woman. Stone Fist frowned at her when she refused to say more. "You will tell me everything I want to know," he said, his voice low and menacing.

"Or what?" The youngster appeared unafraid. She turned away, as if dismissing a nuisance.

Stone Fist put his hand on her narrow shoulder and dug his fingers into the joint, adding pressure until she begged him to stop.

"Such a great warrior," she muttered while rubbing her abused flesh.

"Tell me where you found the giants."

"Why?"

He reached for her shoulder once again, and she pulled away. "All right, all right! Leave me alone."

"Where?"

"They camped near the tree bearing the likeness of Reyna. The one Mato carved."

The warrior grunted like a boar. "Mato, the liar?"

She shrugged.

"What did you steal from the giants?"

"I have no name for it," she said. "It was cold, and hard, and heavy. I dropped it, and when I tried to pick it up, it made a great noise and belched fire. The rocks beneath it burst, and one of them cut me."

Stone Fist pressed her further. "What did you do with it? Where is it now?"

"I left it behind. It could still be there. Are you going to look for it? Do not bring it here! The magic is too powerful."

The idea of finding whatever the thing was appealed to him. If he could inspect it, he could perhaps figure out how the giants harnessed the inferno it housed. "Say nothing of this to anyone," he admonished her. "You hear me?"

Her narrowed eyes reflected her disdain. "Oh, yes, great warrior. I hear you."

"Good." He gave her a shove that left her

sprawling and made his way to the cavern opening.

Though Mato had said nothing about the carving he'd done, Reyna had been quite vocal about it. If pressed, Stone Fist would have to admit it was a good likeness. Such carvings were beyond his skill set. He could knap flints and create stout bows and straight arrows, but capturing the beauty of a female in a carving? Impossible.

But, if nothing else, he knew where the carving was, and the more he contemplated it, the more he realized how it benefitted Mato, even after he'd left his mate and child and gone back to the giants. The People could see his handiwork. They could tell he possessed a skill no others had. The realization galled Stone Fist. It wasn't enough that Mato could sometimes divine the future or that his blood carried the healing seed. That didn't give him the right to make up stories and demand that the People believe his every word. Worst of all, the stupid carving kept him in the minds of everyone, especially Reyna.

That thought finally tipped the scale. The carving had to go. Stone Fist would cut it from the tree, burn it, and use the flames to cook a meal. A grouse perhaps, or a pheasant. He smiled; Reyna would do the cooking.

~*~

Nate dialed the number for Trent Cowart and worked his way through a pair of underlings before he got the man on the line.

"So," he said, "I've seen the video, and I read the caption on the item you forwarded to me. Despite the title claiming she's a leprechaun, whoever put the clip online thinks the girl is an Indian. That doesn't make it so."

"I agree," said Cowart, "and we prefer saying 'American Indian' or 'Native American.' Indians come from India."

"Yeah, right. I know. Sorry. I've never been good at political correctness."

"You'll catch on."

"So," Nate continued. "Why call me?"

"'Cause the video was shot in your bailiwick—up in the Cloud Peak Wilderness."

Nate squinted involuntarily. "How do you know that?"

"The GPS coordinates are embedded in the file." Cowart sounded slightly distracted, and Nate could hear him shuffling paper. "I don't know anything about that area. The Cloud Peak, I mean. What little time I've spent in Wyoming was all at the Wind River Agency."

"Wind River. Those folks are Arapahoe and Shoshone, right?"

"Almost correct. They're *Eastern* Shoshone."

"And how sure are you that the kid in the video is a Native American?" Nate silently congratulated himself for getting the term right.

Though he'd grown up in Wyoming, his interaction with American Indians had been limited. He considered the two he knew to be valued friends. "I mean, she looks almost Polynesian to me."

"Like they say, looks can be deceiving. And enhancing the video didn't help," Cowart said. "Believe me we tried. Anyway, the reason I'm calling you is because it happened in your backyard. Do you know anyone that small?"

"Well...."

"I mean, c'mon. Someone that little wouldn't go unnoticed. Visitors have to check in, don't they? It's not that we think this is a big deal, but my boss got word from her boss that the BIA needs some confirmation. It seems the host of a national TV talk show played the video, and now the news media is demanding answers from us. We could use any help you can give us."

Nate stalled rather than share what little he knew. "I might be able to give you a bit more, but this is all brand new to me. It's going to take me a while to sort it all out."

"So I figured. But please, do your best, and let me know anything you dig up."

"Roger that," Nate said and rang off. He called to Maggie across the room. "Can you bring me the complaint file from the guys who came here yesterday?"

Maggie strolled over and surrendered the

file. "It's been sittin' on my desk, just waiting for you."

"I'll bet." He glanced at the contact information she'd scrawled on the single page the file contained. "Oh, crap."

"What is it?"

"Jedediah Krantz. I know him."

"Really? How?"

Nate made a clucking noise. "Because I've arrested the idiot at least a half dozen times."

~*~

Randi called Tim Archer from her hotel room. He answered on the first ring. "Tim? It's Randi. I'm calling from Wyoming. I just wanted you to know I contacted Mato, the little guy you wanted me to hire."

"Did he say yes?"

"Not exactly."

"Then why are you calling me? Geez, Randi, I thought I'd made things clear. Now listen—"

"He didn't say no, either," Randi said. "The issue isn't that simple."

"Of course, it is!" Archer growled.

"He can't agree to something he doesn't understand. I'm telling you, the little guy is coming straight out of the Stone Age."

"Nonsense. Where's he been all his life? Reservations aren't that primitive. Hell, many of them have top-drawer casinos. Restaurants. Hotels. Spas, for cryin' out loud."

"As far as I can tell, Mato and his people occupy some mountain caves in the heart of a national park designated as a wilderness area. In fact, 'wilderness' is part of the name." Randi tried to keep her voice neutral. Getting Archer's back up was all too easy, and getting him to calm down was way too hard.

"So, what are you telling me?" he asked, still miffed.

"It's complicated."

"For a cave guy? C'mon!"

"Okay, now I know this is going to sound insane, but he has a demand. He wants to take his tribe—his clan, his people—on a ride in the airship."

"That's no problem. We'll bring 'em out here, load 'em up, and—"

"They won't leave the mountains where they live," Randi said quickly, wincing as the words left her mouth.

Archer remained briefly silent. "So… What? We're supposed to fly it all the way to Wy-bloody-oming just so they can take a joy ride? Do you have any idea what that would cost? No. Absolutely not. It's out of the question."

"But what if it's the only way to convince them we'd take good care of them?"

"It's ridiculous. Absurd. What else have you offered?"

Randi polished off the last of her coffee. "I thought providing food for his tribe, as much as they want, whenever they wanted it, would be a good start."

"And?"

"He thought I was trying to bribe him."

"Well? Weren't you?"

Archer's smug chuckle rankled her. She opted not to mention Mato's offer to kill someone in exchange for all the food, even though Archer would have made a splendid target. "Call it barter. Mato and company have no concept of money as a means of exchange. These people are hunter-gatherers, not union workers."

"You say that like it's a bad thing. Being non-union, I mean."

"I'm just trying to make sure you know what we're up against. And it looks like the airship is non-negotiable."

"The hell it is!"

"But," said Randi, conspiratorially, "I had an idea about that. What if we brought the airship to the mainland and did a cross-country tour? We could visit all the major metro areas and—"

"And do fly-overs anywhere we might think of building another park," Archer said. "That'd get us back in the press on a positive note. And after the black eyes we got when building the resort on Kauai, we need it. We need all the good ink we can get."

"I didn't know you were thinking of developing another park."

"I'm not. But we don't have to tell anyone that. And who knows? We might just get an offer we can't turn down. Tax waivers, free land, whatever. A Puck park can generate the basis for a massive tourism industry. You'd be amazed what some politicians will do in response to nothing more than a rumor." He chuckled.

"So, you think it's a good idea?"

"I think," Archer said as if he'd come up with the notion, "I need to let the board chew it over."

Ranci didn't comment on the fact that Archer could get the board to do anything he wanted. As both the biggest stockholder and the CEO, he ruled the group of directors like a medieval sovereign. The fact that he hadn't summarily shot the idea down suggested he'd probably go through with it.

"So," she said, "what can I tell Mato? Can we bring the airship out here?"

"Tell him you're working on it."

Chapter Seven

"Social media is making us more anti-social."
—Tom Green

Two days had passed since Leonard discovered his video had been spread all over the Internet. Those two days had done nothing to calm him down. Simon Dole's prediction that it would all blow over and be forgotten had not proven accurate. It seemed as though every time Leonard did a search on the topic of "tiny humans," a link to his video popped up. Along with the usual denials and claims of fakery came a veritable landslide of derisive comments, typical of which were those equating the video girl's size with a lack of intellect: "She has a brain the size of a sparrow's; no wonder she nearly shot herself!"

It wasn't just the vitriol spewed on the Internet that wounded his spirit. Dole's comments about the previously unknown human species found in Indonesia had a distinctly negative effect as well. His comments were targeted at the physical size of the discovered skulls on the island of Flores. According to Dole, the Floresians were incapable of speech; their brains simply weren't big enough.

"If that were true," Leonard announced to his empty room, "elephants and whales would be the smartest creatures on the planet." He followed this with a completely unsatisfying Bronx cheer and an epithet aimed squarely at his fashion plated faculty advisor.

Leonard had read everything he could find about the vertically challenged Floresians. There was a strong possibility that the tiny race might have survived into the 16th century when Dutch traders arrived. The little people lived in caves, according to native legend.

Caves, Leonard thought. That's most likely where the video girl lived, too. The mountains in the Cloud Peak Wilderness area remained snow-covered most of the year. Anyone living up there would almost certainly have to find shelter underground. It simply made sense, not that he was prepared to do any cave exploring, although the possibility had begun to loom large in his imagination.

Was he willing to crawl into a hole in the ground if it meant he might contact the people living there? What would he say to them? What language did they speak? How might he proceed?

The ring tone on his cell phone saved him from further reflection.

"H'lo?"

"I got it."

Leonard instantly recognized Jedediah Krantz's guttural tones. "Great! I'll head over now."

"You gonna bring my money?"

"I said I would, didn't I?"

"Yeah. So, git movin'," Krantz growled. "I'm hungry. I ain't eaten a thing since yestiddy."

"You know I sold my car, right?"

"So?"

"So, that's how I'm able to pay you. I hope you can see how important this is to me."

"Yeah, sure. When ya gonna git here?"

"As soon as I can."

Leonard considered asking Simon Dole to give him a lift, then discarded the idea. The less his advisor knew about the arrangements Leonard had made, the better. He called a ride share company, promised a tip if delivered promptly, and arrived at Krantz's ramshackle headquarters just before dark.

"I won't be gone but a minute. Then you can take me back. Okay?"

The driver agreed, Leonard shouldered the dodgy door of Krantz's cabin open, and slipped inside. The aroma which greeted him was all but overpowering. He was happy not knowing its source.

They made the exchange quickly—Leonard's cash for the memory chip from the camera—and then the grad student left, as quickly as he could. It wasn't just the smell; Leonard was eager to return to his room where he could review any images his hidden camera might have captured.

Once inside the safe confines of his basement quarters, Leonard carefully plugged the memory chip into an adapter on his computer. Moments later three video files popped up.

In his haste to review the material, Leonard almost erased one of the recordings. He focused on the first of the files. It turned out to be an intimate chase between two squirrels intent on maintaining their lineage. The second file featured another, larger rodent, though Leonard wasn't entirely sure of its breed.

The final file yielded something of interest, and Leonard watched it several times before easing back in his desk chair and sighing in relief.

~*~

Maggie Scott stood by the printer in the ranger office reading the sheet of paper she'd just pulled from the machine. "Nate? There's something weird goin' on," she said.

He smiled at her. "Well, after all, it *is* a Saturday."

She stuck her tongue out at him. "I'm serious."

"Define weird," he said, and waited for something even stranger than the way Tori had been acting lately. *That*, was weird.

"We've already maxed out on visitors, and it's not even ten a.m. They're turning folks away at the gates."

"And that's weird because... why?"

Maggie turned and walked back to her desk. "Because this isn't the high season. And with temperatures dropping almost daily this time of year, it's usually the beginning of the low season."

"Coincidence?" he suggested.

"Who knows? But here's something else that's odd. Even though we've got all these extra people on the grounds, no one's signed up for guided hikes."

"I know that's your big thing," Nate said. "But I wouldn't take it personally."

"I'm not. It's just... I dunno. Weird."

"I heard you the first couple times." *And it still isn't as weird as the way Tori's been acting.* He got up to get a refill on his coffee. "Can I ask you something, Mags?"

"Sure."

"Has Tori said anything to you about maybe being pregnant?"

She chuckled. "Don't you think you'd get that news before me?"

"I'd like to think so, but...."

"But what?"

"She's been acting strange lately. Didn't want me to take this job, even though she knew I'd be working with you."

Maggie frowned at him. "Doesn't sound all that strange to me. She's just worried about you. She'll get over it."

"So, you don't think she could be pregnant? It's not a hormonal thing?"

"I don't know!" Maggie said, clearly exasperated. "I've never been pregnant. Why don't you just ask her?"

"Yeah, I probably should."

"Y'know, for a guy who's supposed to have a lot on the ball, sometimes you can be a real dumbass."

~*~

Jedidiah Krantz congratulated himself; he'd finally figured out what the wimpy college kid was up to. The old cowboy stared down at a small glass vial containing a scrap of gold about the size and shape of something he'd extracted from his nose. It lay nestled alongside several much smaller flakes of placer gold taken from a streambed. The total weight of his treasure didn't come close to an

126

ounce, and likely wouldn't have netted him enough cash for a decent restaurant meal.

Panning for gold was long and tedious work. Digging for it was worse. Neither approach suited Krantz at all. Like the college kid, he wanted an easier way to get his hands on the precious metal, and now they both knew what needed to be done.

The second video confirmed there was more than one little Indian living up in the mountains. What they both wore proved they were primitives. The college kid had studied people like that; he knew their ways. And despite his claims to the contrary, Krantz felt sure he knew the little ones had gold. Probably stolen from hardworking miners and panners.

All Krantz had to do was get his hands on one. The thought made him giggle. It wouldn't take any time at all to squeeze the information out of them, and show him exactly where they'd hidden it. He even had a good idea about where he might set a trap. It wouldn't be anything complicated, a simple snare should do it, provided he used the proper bait.

And he knew just the thing.

~*~

Stone Fist was summoned, along with the other hunters, to a gathering at the council fire. He was among the last to arrive and had to push his way through the others to take a spot in the front rank.

Winter Woman motioned for silence and surveyed those in attendance. "There will be no hunting today," she finally announced. "There are too many giants nearby. More than we have ever seen."

Stone Fist stood and waved the command off. "It does not matter. Giants are stupid. When I am hungry, I will hunt."

"They search for something," said an elder.

"Perhaps they are searching for the things Ember took from them," said another.

"Where do they look?" asked still another.

Winter Woman held up a hand. "Reyna says most are near the tree on which Mato carved her likeness."

Stone Fist laughed. "If they search for that, they will be disappointed. The carving is gone."

"What happened to it?" Reyna asked from the far side of the council fire. "Did the giants take it?"

"Yes," said Stone Fist. "I saw them carve it from the tree and take it away. Giants have no honor." He tried not to smile, though it was difficult. He had tossed the bark pieces in Reyna's cook fire when she wasn't looking.

"Why would they do that?" someone asked.

"It does not matter," Winter Woman said.

"They are too close. No one is to go out until we know they are gone. We must not allow them to find us."

"How will we know they are gone if we cannot go out and watch them?" Stone Fist asked. "Will we wait for Mato to come back and tell us?" He paused dramatically, then went on, "Or is he helping them look for us?"

The question brought a chorus of comments and complaints, a reaction that warmed his heart. If the liar ever did come home, there would be no warm welcome.

"This is our home," Stone Fist said. "If the giants will not go away, we should make them leave."

Winter Woman leaned toward him, her expression fierce. "And how would we do that? Attack them?" Her laugh sounded more like a cough. "They would kill us all."

"I would rather die fighting than starve to death." He scanned the faces of the other hunters. "Am I the only one who would protect the People? I say we fight! If we kill enough of them, they will go away and stay away."

"You are an even bigger fool than I thought," muttered Winter Woman. "You will bring their magic down upon us. You and Ember have done this. You are the reason the giants will not leave us alone."

129

"You are an old woman," Stone Fist said. Though he spoke to her, he looked out at the others gathered there. "You do not hunt. You only eat and complain. Why should we listen to you?"

"Because I am the leader," Winter Woman said, but her voice cracked, and he knew everyone heard it. She could not hide the fear in her heart or her voice.

Stone Fist crossed his arms on his chest and spoke in a clear tone, "Then it is time we chose a new leader."

~*~

"I've put together a plan I think will work," Randi said into her phone as she waited for the Puck corporate jet to take off and deliver her back to her office. "If I'm right, we'll be able to start working with Mato's people."

"It's about time," Archer responded.

"Yes, it is, time *and* money."

"Why am I not surprised?"

"I can handle the details and logistics, but I need you to get the ball rolling," Randi said.

"Before I agree to anything, I need to know how much money we're talking about."

Randi knew Archer enjoyed playing tough, but he had a hard time giving up on an idea once he'd convinced himself of its value. Having Mato's people work at his plush Hawaiian resort was just such a concept.

"I can't give you an exact figure. I'll have to work that out once the plans are made. The thing to remember is that we have to offer these folks something much nicer than what they currently have," she said. "In order to do that we have to demonstrate."

"I'm listening."

"We need to give them samples."

"Of what?" Archer asked. "The food? The costumes?"

Why did she have to spell everything out? He's supposed to be the one with the nifty imagination. "We need to show them samples of everything—housing especially. Oh! Stand by a sec. We're taking off."

Archer ignored her request, his voice competing with increased noise from the jet's engines. "Why can't they just stay in the resort? We can rope off a section until we've got something more suitable."

"If Mato is typical of these people, they'll likely be about two feet tall, tops. How are they going to be able to use housing designed for us? They couldn't even reach the light switches, let alone use countertops or appliances. They need things customized for them."

"Well…."

"Hold on, please." She waited for the jet to

level off before continuing. "Sorry. I hate take-offs. Now, where was I?"

"Customizing things."

"Right. That's the thing. Whatever we provide has to be about one third the size of the stuff we use every day."

"But—"

"Fortunately, Puck Productions is uniquely capable of producing the one thing that will be the hardest to provide—appropriate housing. The art department can whip up some designs. We can start with a cottage, maybe two bedrooms and a bath, living room and kitchen. Of course, we'll need some larger ones for the bigger families. But the craft department can handle all that. If they can build castles and spaceships, they can handle a little cottage or two. We can get chairs, beds, lamps and whatnot from companies that make dollhouse or playhouse furniture. We'll also need to work out transportation arrangements. We'll need to bring at least three different buildings out here."

"To *Wyoming?*"

"Of course! It's where they live now. They aren't going anywhere until they know that what's waiting for them is vastly superior to what they already have."

Archer grunted. "That shouldn't be hard; they're living in caves now, right?"

"That's my understanding. Mato isn't big on

providing details."

"Where is he now? Can you bring him back with you? I'd like to meet him."

"Sorry," Randi said. "No can do. He's gone back to talk to his people to try and get them to send a delegation and sample life with the giants."

"Giants?"

"Us."

"When?"

"As soon as we have something for them to sample. Say, in a couple weeks? The weather is going to get rough very soon. Everyone's going to have to push hard to get it done that fast. Thank goodness we're not talking about permanent installations. No one from the local government is going to be doing any inspections."

"You really think you can pull this off almost overnight?"

"If you tell the department heads to get on it, and they work 24/7, then yes."

"I'll make the calls," he said. "You'd better hope this works."

"It should," she said. *God willing.*

~*~

Riding in Nate's pickup truck cut the length of Mato's return journey by a huge margin. Best of all, he would reach his destination without being hungry. Even so, he carried with him some of the treats the redheaded giant had called "en-er-gee bars." They would sustain him as he returned to the clan, but there were not nearly enough for the People. With winter setting in, food would be scarce. The People would not just be hungry; they would soon be on the edge of starvation.

"Watch yourself out there," Nate had told him, but Mato found such advice of little value. How could he watch himself when he needed to be fully aware of his surroundings? There were more than the usual number of giants about, Nate had said, though he did not explain why.

As Mato worked his way toward the upper elevations where he could access the opening to the clan's underground lair, he confirmed Nate's warning. Giants were indeed plentiful, though they seemed to congregate in the general vicinity of the carving he'd done of Reyna. That, he recalled with sadness, was back when she respected him. But, with any luck, he would once again rise in her estimation, along with the rest of the People, provided they took his advice. Unfortunately, that would not be automatic.

It is not Reyna I must convince. It is Winter Woman. She leads. If I can make her see the wisdom of my words, then perhaps no one will die this winter.

And that would be a first. The very young and the very old faced the greatest danger. His own child might go into the ground even before he had earned a name.

The thought made him move faster. He skirted the giants along the way with little effort. He knew how to traverse the woods and fields without making a sound. The light blanket of snow made it slightly more difficult, but the giants would surely confuse his footprints with those of animals. They always had in the past.

He reached into the sling he had fashioned into a carrying pouch. Randi, the redheaded giant, had given him something she called a "flip-fon." She had demonstrated its magic—*no* he reminded himself; it *wasn't* magic. The giants called it *tek-na-lo-gee*, a word he had practiced many times in order to prepare the People for it. She had demonstrated how he might use the device. It held two images: the redheaded woman and his friend Nate. If he wished to speak with either of the giants, he need only press on their image. The flip-fon would do the rest.

Mato recalled when something similar occurred during his adventure on the bah-limp, so he felt reasonably well prepared. Flip-fons were free of evil Spirits, provided it worked at all. The towering redhead had warned him that under certain conditions the device might not work, but he must not discard it. Instead, he should move to another location and try again.

His biggest concern was not whether the flip-fon would function. The challenge ahead involved convincing Winter Woman and the tribal elders that they should leave their winter quarters and travel with him to Tori's cabin. Getting there would be extremely difficult, even if Randi and Nate could bring the gigantic bah-limp to the entrance of the People's cave.

In addition to the flip-fon, Randi had given him something she called a "bro-shur" which somehow captured detailed images of the place where they had all stayed in Hawaii. Mato wasn't quite sure what good it would do, but she insisted he show it to everyone in the clan. If nothing else, it contained an image of the bah-limp, something he found all but impossible to describe.

If there was one thing that might sway his reluctant clan, it was the possibility of visiting the sacred cavern beneath Tori's home. Since he and Reyna had both described it in detail, the People seemed to believe them. It still gnawed at him that they didn't believe him when he spoke of his adventures in Hawaii.

He shrugged off the problems of the future and focused on the present. He found a route favored by deer, and worked his way through the rapidly thinning trees. When he observed something lying in the path ahead, he slowed his steps and concentrated on the sounds and smells around him. It was no time to become careless.

The object on the ground was vaguely familiar; Nate carried something similar in a stiff, leather harness attached to his belt. He recognized it as a weapon only giants could make. But, he asked himself, why would they have left it on the ground?

He reached down to investigate further only to hear a slight whirring sound before something violently constricted both of his legs and yanked him, upside down, into the air. He felt his head smack firmly against the ground, and the world turned black.

~*~

Tori eased back in her desk chair. Together with the personal computer now on her kitchen counter/office, it was a concession to her flagging career as a novelist. She held her cell phone in her left hand, the index finger of her right hand poised over the "Call" button on the screen. Nate would likely be irritated that she'd phoned him in the middle of the day, but she couldn't help it.

At least, that's what she told herself.

She had spent most of the morning fiddling around on social media rather than working on her new book, a project she now doubted would ever be finished. The distractions in her life had never seemed more demanding. It wasn't just an occasional game of solitaire, or the rare, if pleasant, opportunity to respond to a fan letter. She *needed* diversions to keep her from worrying about Nate.

It seemed obvious. He carried a gun, and therefore certain people—criminals and miscreants—considered him a target. Nate poo-

poohed the idea, of course, but he was the one who got shot in Hawaii. He was the one who nearly died.

So, why the hell wasn't he the one obsessed about his safety?

It was so completely tiring.

And unavoidable.

She stabbed the "Call" button and waited for him to respond.

"Hey babe," he said a moment later. "What's up?"

"I'm sorry to bother you, but I've been reading some stuff online I thought you'd want to know about."

"Ah, yes. The gospel according to Google."

"Whatever." She stared up at the cabin's ceiling, knowing he couldn't see the look on her face, but assuming he'd imagine it. "Listen up, ya big lug. There's some strange stuff floating around online about tiny little people."

"Really? I thought all the seriously deranged kooks were already up here. I'm shocked to hear some of them are still sitting at their computers. Maggie says they're called leprechaun hunters."

"Do you want to hear what they have to say?"

"Not really."

"You'll love this one." She read the header: "We finally know what to call them."

"Call who?" Nate asked.

"The little people." Tori tried not to sound impatient.

"That covers a lot of folks. There are 'little people' all over the world. And not just kids."

"C'mon, Nate! You know what I mean. I'm talkin' about Mato's people. They don't have genetic issues."

"You *know* that?"

"Are you gonna let me read this article, or not?"

"Sorry, hon. Please read. Go ahead."

Tori cleared her throat. "According to one source—"

"On the Internet."

She ignored him. "—the proper name for these itsy-bitsy humans in the Cloud Peak—"

Nate stopped her. "They've pinpointed the Cloud Peak? Specifically?"

"Yes. You'd be amazed at all the hubbub. It's bizarre. And some of the theories are totally bonkers."

"Worse than the leprechaun claim? Gimme a f'rinstance."

"I'm trying! Geez. Okay, the proper name for these tiny humans in the Cloud Peak? Are you ready?"

"Get on with it!"

"Lillipindians."

After a momentary pause, Nate said, "Come again?"

"Lillipindians. Apparently, it's a cross between Jonathan Swift's Lilliputians from 'Gulliver's Travels' and Native Americans: Indians—Lillipindians."

"That's off the wall crazy."

"It gets worse."

"Stop."

"I'm serious. How does 'Mindians' grab ya? Mini-Indians? Mindians, right? And there are pages of comments explaining how Mato's people are descended from ancient astronauts stranded on Earth eons ago."

"No."

"Oh, yes! And they built the pyramids, too. I'm not kidding. Others say they're somehow related to Big Foot. Mutations, or something. There's mention of radon. If you're exposed to enough of that you'll shrink evidently, assuming you don't just die on the spot."

"So, any crackpot on Earth can suggest any totally outlandish nonsense as 'the truth,' and people log on to agree?"

Tori nodded, then realized Nate couldn't see her. "Pretty much, yeah."

"That's insane."

"It's social media."

"*Mindians and Lillipindians?*"

"Or ancient astronauts. Little Foot, maybe? Little Feet, I guess. Take your pick."

Nate exhaled wearily. "There's no hope for humanity, is there?"

"I'm thinkin' not." Tori smiled. It was good to know Nate was still... Nate. "You gonna be home on time for dinner?"

"Wouldn't miss it for anything, darlin'. Not for anything in the world."

~*~

Leonard remained irritated with his alleged mentor and faculty adviser. *How could someone with that much education remain so contemptuous of a branch of humanity?* The simple truth seemed to be that Simon Dole had no more empathy than Jedediah Krantz. Both were cut from redneck cloth. The only difference seemed to be that Dole's fabric had been laundered.

The second video had confirmed, for Leonard at least, that some number of extraordinarily small human beings were living in primitive conditions in the heart of the Cloud Peak

Wilderness. He had watched the video of a tiny, animal skin-clad man, scraping bark from a birch tree. The bark in question had been carved to resemble a young woman. He had no doubt the image he'd seen in Dole's office was of the exact same carving.

Why the little man defaced the artwork would likely remain a mystery, though Leonard maintained the hope that he might ask him one day. Communication with him would be interesting at best. More than likely, it would be a more demanding task than Leonard was prepared to accept. At the very least, it would require the services of a linguist, someone with skills he could only imagine.

The starting point, he decided, would be to see how other primitive people had been treated when contemporary society impinged on them and their lifestyle. He had no problem doing the research and was eager to embark on it. Working it into his Master's thesis wouldn't be a problem, assuming Professor Dole—henceforth Professor *Joe Bob*—didn't get in the way.

Eventually, however, he'd have to return to the Cloud Peak, find a way to contact the tribe living there, and convince them they could trust him to look out for their interests.

He prayed he was up to the challenge.

Chapter Eight

"As long as people have been making little people,
they've wanted to know how not to." —Nancy Gibbs

Stone Fist left the cavern smiling, though he'd left the clan's leader wearing the opposite expression. He travelled alone, intending nothing more than a simple scouting mission. No one doubted the giants had invaded their homeland, but he wanted to see if any of them were vulnerable. If he and the other hunters could sneak up on them, they might be able to drive them away. If nothing else, they could make the giants' visit extremely uncomfortable.

Rather than carry a hunting bow, Stone Fist opted to carry only a supply of the sharp-pointed darts dipped in the sleeping paste they used for smaller game. Hunters propelled the darts through a hollow reed. Though only effective at close range, he doubted he'd have any difficulty getting close enough to his targets to use them. Besides, a bow could prove cumbersome when one needed to move silently through the underbrush.

He had no specific destination in mind at first, then turned his steps toward the tree he'd stripped of Mato's handiwork. There was no guarantee giants would be near it, but it seemed a more likely place than any other.

He was not disappointed. The immense beings, all of whom brought gigantic beasts on which to ride, clustered in several spots. Though they laughed and joked among themselves, it seemed obvious they were intent on finding something, though what that might be, Stone Fist had no clue.

By sticking to game trails and paths hidden in the woods, he moved silently and carefully toward his destination. It wasn't long before he heard a commotion. Dropping to the ground, he proceeded even more cautiously than before, making his way forward like a squirrel or a rabbit. He stopped when he came upon the source of all the noise: an old giant prancing like a fool and waving his hands in the air like someone possessed. The object of his delight soon became apparent.

Stone Fist could hardly believe it. Mato dangled by his feet two body lengths above the earth. Swaying in the gentle breeze, he made no attempt to free himself which only made the giant laugh more. Though tempted to join the giant's celebration, Stone Fist held his place, determined to watch before taking any action.

The wind shifted direction, and he caught the giant's scent for the first time. How Mato had fallen victim to the intruder puzzled him since the vile aroma of the whiskered brute should have warned him away.

Something lay in the dirt directly beneath the dangling warrior, but Stone Fist couldn't identify it, at first. Slowly, however, he came to the realization that it was likely the object Smoke had attempted to steal, or one similar to it. He had seen giants wield such things and remembered vividly how frightened he had been when one of them unleashed the fire within it. The noise was astonishingly loud, but having heard it, he understood what caused similar noises he'd heard in the distance when giants were hunting.

None of that explained how Mato could have been so foolish as to have been snared. The apparatus was simple and consisted of a rope attached to a bent tree limb. A loop in the free end of the rope had been hidden in the plant debris in the path. When Mato stepped in it to inspect the object on the ground—the bait in the trap—the giant had released whatever held the limb bent. The People had often used similar devices, though Stone Fist much preferred arrows or darts. He lacked the patience to wait for his prey to come to him.

Mato looked as though he'd been hit with one of his own darts, dangling helplessly, arms toward the ground. Stone Fist considered helping him. Distracting the giant, or simply disabling him with a poisoned dart, would have been child's play. Climbing the tree to cut or untie the rope holding Mato prisoner would also have been relatively easy. Almost any of the People could have done it. Even if Mato failed to wake up, Stone Fist could have dragged him to a place of safety, a spot the giant would never find.

While Stone Fist considered his options, the giant wandered away which gave Stone Fist time to examine his helpless clansman more closely. That's when he saw Mato's coveted "fol-ding" knife dangling from a cord around his neck.

How often had Mato demonstrated the clever device the giants had given him? Enough times to make Stone Fist sick with envy. But now it could be his All he had to do was pull the cord over Mato's jaw and it would fall to the ground.

Why let the giants have it back?

Stone Fist wasted no time debating the issue. The knife would now be his, and Mato was on his own. If he loved the giants so much, he could just go back to them.

A noise alerted Stone Fist to nearby activity; the giant had returned leading a horse. Stone Fist remained out of sight as the giant fumbled more rope from a leather pouch and tied Mato up with it, still suspended in mid-air.

Stone Fist relished the moment. The great and beloved Mato—hunter, husband, and seer—

needed his help. Stone Fist smiled at him and waved goodbye.

Then he slipped away as quietly as he'd come.

~*~

By the time Randi arrived back in her west coast office, work had already begun on the housing units she told Archer they needed. Rather than draft something entirely new, the design team had chosen to scale down house plans to which they had ready access. They chose designs which could be modularized and built in the warehouse where most of Puck's movie set construction took place. Final assembly of the three cottages would occur on-site, and the necessary workers would be sent along with the building components.

The only delays, at least in the very early stages, were caused by staff questioning why such small buildings were required. The explanation that they would house children didn't seem to satisfy. Any objections to the work were quickly quashed when Tim Archer's name was invoked. What Archer wanted; Archer almost always got.

With the housing issue largely resolved, Randi turned her attention to the other needs: home furnishings, clothing, and food.

The first two items were relatively easy to address. Because she had never been interested in dolls, even as a child, the market for dollhouse furniture in various scales came as a pleasant surprise. But rather than spend her own time picking out lamps, tables, seating, art, and knick-knacks with which to fully furnish and humanize the cottages she turned the chore over to the experts in Puck's design department. She felt confident Mato's people would be thoroughly impressed.

Clothing was a different issue, largely because she had only a vague idea of the number of people she would have to dress. Their ages, she assumed, would range from infant to seasoned citizen. If dollhouse makers could supply furnishings, she reasoned, then those who made the dolls could supply clothing.

The array of clothing options stymied her. There was simply no way she could find age-appropriate outfits for people who normally dressed in animal skins and God-only-knew what else. War paint?

Rather than waste her time guessing, she put in an order for children's sweatsuits. Because she ordered them from Puck retail shops, she not only got them at cost, but in a variety of colors and sizes. Since each of the sweatshirts featured a cartoon character from an animated Puck production, she prayed Mato's people wouldn't be offended.

She didn't worry too much about getting good fits. Mato's people could roll up sleeves and/or pantlegs with ease. She also bought outerwear, though most was designed for toddlers as all she had to go on was a height range of 20 to 26 inches. These had to come from a different supplier, and she paid a premium to have them shipped express.

What the hell, at least they'll be warm, well fed, and housed in high fashion. That, she hoped, would be enough.

The last item on her agenda was food, and she felt stumped at first. Their diet, she guessed, would qualify as prehistoric, absolutely full-on hunter-gather. She further assumed it was heavy on meats. They very likely didn't know much about vegetables, and her frantic online search didn't reveal anything of value for what she needed to provide.

Screw it! I'll go with comfort food. Everybody likes that, and as long as they're coming to us to get it, we can make damn sure it has ingredients that'll make them smile, serving after serving.

She had given thought to providing food they could take with them when they returned to their caves, in the event they didn't immediately sign up for a trip to Puck's extravagant Hawaiian resort. And, if her efforts to sway the clan's leadership proved successful, they'd still have to return home and convince the rest of Mato's people to join them. That alone would be a good trick. Therefore, she had to completely overwhelm their leadership with the benefits of accepting Puck's offer. If necessary, she could have a food truck airlifted to their front door and keep up a steady supply of tacos, burgers, pizza, and ice cream.

Randi s goal could be nothing less than overwhelmingly swaying the tiny tribe. Mato seemed to think the airship alone was enough to seal the deal. Randi wasn't so sure. But then, she'd never had to deal with cave people before.

~*~

Smoke rubbed her bruised shoulder and watched Stone Fist saunter away. He had shoved her hard enough to push her off her sleeping mat, but she managed to stay on. The nearby cavern wall provided a convenient, though hard and cold end to the abrupt, sideways journey on which he'd sent her. In the process, she dropped the little pouch Winter Woman had given her, and she scrambled to recover it. The only thoughts coursing through her young brain were those of revenge. She found herself willing to do anything she could to diminish the self-important hunter in the eyes of the clan.

She got up and hurried after him. The powder the clan leader gave her had worked, greatly reducing the pain in her leg. She would keep it close at hand. If she could focus on her anger at Stone Fist, she hoped to ignore the wound she'd received when attempting to steal from the old giant and his companion. That encounter had taught her a valuable lesson—observe first, then steal; know enough about what you're taking to ensure you don't kill yourself with it.

There remained a great deal of mystery connected to the giants. She knew that much, even if she didn't believe that everything mysterious about them came from magic.

Stone Fist, she concluded, wasn't terribly good at moving undetected. Smoke, on the other hand, excelled at it. He never knew she trailed him even though her limp might have given her away to someone truly skilled, like Mato.

Though she had no idea what his destination might be, she pursued him doggedly, never once giving herself away. Surprisingly, he worked his way toward the portrait tree, the one on which Mato had carved the image of his mate, Reyna. Smoke envied her. She could have chosen any of the available bachelors in the clan. She chose Mato, and did so for obvious reasons. There was no doubt in Smoke's mind that one day he would lead the clan. It didn't matter that for as long as anyone remembered, the People had been led by females. Mato was different. Not only was he an amazing hunter, he could see into the future. And not only that, he had the skill to create images of what he foresaw.

Stone Fist suffered mightily by comparison. He had an advantage in height and weight, and he might have even been able to move faster than Mato. But he could never have moved as quietly. And as for dreams, those he had went no further than the grunts and rumblings he shared with the People while sleeping. If Stone Fist fell off a mountain and landed head-first in the flatlands below, no one would miss him, with the possible exception of his mother. And even she might welcome his absence.

Traveling overland and simultaneously remaining out of sight proved difficult, but Smoke managed it somehow. Stone Fist had no idea she followed in his footsteps. Eventually, the conceited fool nearly stumbled into poor Mato, who hung upside-down in the middle of the deer track. He appeared unconscious, swinging gently, his arms dangling earthward.

In the distance, an ancient giant cavorted as if possessed by demons. Stone Fist saw him and ducked to avoid detection. Smoke remained in hiding the entire time. Neither the giant nor the hunter suspected her presence.

Eventually, the giant moved away. Smoke assumed Stone Fist would free Mato from the trap when he approached the giant's dangling victim. After he removed something from around Mato's neck, Smoke assumed he would haul Mato to safety. Instead, the cocky hunter merely smiled, waved goodbye, and crept away.

Smoke couldn't believe it. No one abandoned a clan member unless a rescue attempt meant certain death for both. Stone Fist could have cut Mato's bonds and hidden with him in the underbrush. The giant had already walked away, out of sight! Yet Stone Fist made no effort to intervene. None at all! Smoke felt the outrage build inside. *What was he thinking?*

And then she guessed what probably motivated him—jealousy. Mato was everything Stone Fist would never be, and more.

Smoke scrambled toward the helpless hunter, only to stop when the giant who had captured him reappeared leading one of the massive animals on which they often rode. She dropped to the ground behind a boulder and waited while the giant cut Mato down, put a gag in his mouth, and bound him with a rope. Before he left, he picked up the very object she had tried to steal. Good riddance, she thought. With any luck it would explode and injure him.

She watched as Mato was carried away, then noticed something the giant had missed: Mato's haversack lay hidden by a shrub. With the fearsome creature's back turned toward her, she dashed out and grabbed it, then hurried back to her hiding place.

The giant neither heard nor saw her.

Smoke looked inside the leather bag and fingered the objects within. There were small rectangular objects encased in something smooth and clear. She had seen giants tear off that skin and eat what was inside. She recognized nuts and grains but not the dark brown substance which appeared to hold it all together.

She also found a slightly larger object which the giants often carried. Sometimes they talked into them. At other times they held them close to their eyes or at arm's length. It made little sense to her, but the giants obviously valued them. She had never been able to steal one, and here Mato had one of his own! She slipped it into her own pouch along with the squarish chunks of food. The only other thing in Mato's bag was something thin and colorful. Composed of flat, shiny skin folded upon itself, the thing bore beautiful images and the curious marks the giants often inscribed on their possessions. That, too, went into her pouch, neatly secured while she prepared to track the giant.

Still hidden, she watched as the giant rolled Mato in a heavy blanket then tied him, belly down, on the back of a large animal before climbing atop a second, similar beast.

She had no idea where the oversized old man might be headed, but she had no intention of letting him carry Mato away without some form of resistance. If they ever caught a member of the clan, she had often been told, the giants would eat them. Unlike the cowardly Stone Fist, she vowed not to let that happen to Mato.

Nate had held off calling Trent Cowart at the Bureau of Indian Affairs. His reasoning seemed appropriate since he had very little to report other than an unusual increase in tourists who wanted to visit the Cloud Peak.

"You think they're looking for that girl? The

one in the video?"

"Could be," Nate said. "I've spoken with some of the rangers, but they're reluctant to give any credence to the possibility that there are more people like her up there. They just don't believe it's possible. They've had to turn away a lot of people. They don't want to let too many in."

"I get that," Cowart said. "But to be honest, I was hoping you'd learned a little more about that kid. If nothing else, did she get hurt when the gun went off?"

"I wish I knew."

"Have you investigated the scene?"

"No," Nate admitted. "But I intend to."

"Don't you think it'd be a good idea to get cracking?"

Nate grimaced. "It's not like I don't have anything to do. I'm the only law enforcement officer around."

"I'm sure that's true, and I apologize if I stepped over the line. I didn't mean to tell you how to do your job. It's just that I'm getting a good bit of heat from above, and there isn't much I can do about it."

"Apology accepted," Nate said. *I'm getting heat from above, too. Thank you, Tori.*

"Although...."

Crap. Here it comes.

"...it might be in your best interests to think seriously about helping us out. You never know when you might need to call on Uncle Sam for a bit of assistance in return."

Blackmail? From the Fed? Nate shook his head in disgust. "I'll do that."

"Help out? Investigate?" Cowart sounded hopeful.

"I'll think seriously about it. And if I have time, I might just ride up there and look around."

"Great! Let me know what you find."

"Roger that."

Nate hung up the phone and eased back in his chair. It made a noise that could have been interpreted as a complaint.

"BIA?" asked Maggie from across the room.

"Yeah."

"They aren't all buttheads, y'know."

"I know. I guess I'm letting my problems with Tori cloud my thinking. I know I need to ride up there and look around before the snow covers everything."

"Up in the Peak where that goofy video was shot?"

"Yep."

"Then you'd best get a move on. There's a serious winter storm headed our way."

~*~

The first thing Mato noticed, aside from his aching head, was the gritty cloth in his mouth and the smell of the animal on which he lay. Though he could move his head, the resulting pain provided all the discouragement he needed. Unfortunately, his head was the only part of his body he could move.

He had been bundled in something dark and scratchy, but if he craned his neck—something he forced himself to do—he could detect daylight. The sounds he heard were limited to that of horses' hooves and an occasional cough.

The aroma coming from the blanket, or whatever it was he'd been wrapped in, completely blocked out all others. His stomach hurt from the constant jarring, and he wanted desperately to stretch his arms and legs. More than anything, however, he yearned to kill whomever had trussed him up and tied him to one of the giants' beasts. That, of course, would have to wait until he got himself free, a goal to which he committed himself.

He had no idea how long he'd been unconscious or how long he'd been trussed and transported. Though tempted to cry out and demand his release, he knew better. Anyone who would do what had been done to him, had no intention of letting him go free. They had other plans, whoever they were. He doubted they would offer anything of benefit.

With any luck, his captor may not have discovered his knife or the talking device the stunning redheaded giant had given him. Both had been in his haversack. He'd carried no additional weapons, no sleeping paste, no bow, no spear. He had only his wits and two bars of chocolate.

Spirits willing, that would be enough. The People's lives depended on it.

~*~

Tori knew Nate would not appreciate yet another phone call from her while he was working, but the news she wanted to share with him was too important. It simply couldn't wait.

"Nate?"

"Hey, babe," he said.

"I hope this isn't a bad time, but—"

"Actually, hon, it is. I'm about to head out."

"Out? Home?"

"No," he said. "I've gotta zip up into the Cloud Peak for a bit. Not sure how long that'll take."

"Geez, Nate! Have you heard the weather reports? There's a snow storm coming. You can't go up into the mountains! Are you crazy?"

"I don't have any choice. I've got to—"

"Of course you have a choice! And what about me? What about—"

"Sweetheart, as much as I'd like to continue

158

this conversation, I can't afford the time. I have to go. Now. Seriously."

Tori desperately sought something she might say which would alter his plans, but she came up empty. "Can you please wait just one little bit? There's something I need to tell you."

"I'm afraid it'll have to wait, darlin'. I'll call you as soon as I can."

"From the Peak? There's no cell phone service up there! It's a barren goddamn wilderness!"

"I know; I know. But I'll be fine. Mags is coming with me. It appears there are a couple hikers up there who didn't have the good sense to clear out. We've gotta find 'em before they get snowed in."

"What if *you* get snowed in?"

"I'll be fine. Don't worry about me. I'll call you as soon as I get back."

"Tonight?"

"Hopefully."

"*Hopefully?*" Tori swallowed hard. "What the hell does that mean?"

"It means I have to play things by ear. I don't know how long it'll take to find the hikers, and if there's time, I also need to investigate the spot where that little Indian girl nearly shot herself."

Tori forced herself to calm down. The task

proved difficult. "Promise me you'll be careful."

"I promise," he said.

Tori groaned. "I swear, if you die up there, I'll never forgive you."

Nate chuckled, then said, "I love you. I'll talk to you soon."

When he clicked off, Tori threw her phone on the bed and muttered, "You'd better not die up there, you jerk! I don't want to raise our child all by myself."

~*~

Smoke kept careful watch on the giant who had captured Mato. He never stopped humming as he tied his captive in place, mounted his own animal, and prepared to leave. The humming, while stupid, kept him from being alert to other sounds.

She had felt a jolt of panic when the giant produced a second large animal on which he rode. How could she possibly keep up with such huge beasts, especially if they moved at any pace quicker than a walk? Her injured leg already ached from the time she'd spent tracking Stone Fist, and the prospect of running after the giant who'd captured Mato was daunting.

The giant stuffed something in his mouth and poked it deeper into his cheek. If squirrels had fingers, they might do the same thing she thought. The brief smile she'd given herself dissolved when the giant began to ride away. The beast on which he'd secured Mato bore a line he tied to his own beast. They headed toward a well-marked trail which she presumed would take him out of the People's territory. Mato was doomed unless she helped him; she had no choice but to follow.

Though the sky had turned dark with angry, snow-laden clouds, the giant appeared to be in no great hurry to leave the area. His animal plodded along, its head bobbing up and down with every other step. The weather also seemed to have chased most of the other giants away. The People knew how to survive in heavy snow; they'd done it for generations uncounted. Giants, however, needed their magic to survive bad weather.

She almost pitied them. Such thoughts would get her nowhere, she knew, and so she contemplated how she might rescue Mato if given the chance. Despite not coming up with anything useful, the mental exercise helped her to avoid thinking about her injured limb.

Because it was much wider and more heavily traveled than the deer paths the People used, the giant's trail offered few hiding places. Though she risked being seen, Smoke followed behind, but at a distance. Mato's captor never looked back. Instead, he merely watched the trail ahead, ignoring even the splendor of the mountain terrain surrounding them.

As they ventured into lower elevations, plants became more abundant and would have provided the cover she needed if the giant ever stopped or looked back. He didn't. His focus seemed to be limited to riding and spitting. The latter activity forced him to turn his head to the side, but Smoke remained far enough behind that he didn't see her, even when she had nothing to shelter her from view.

When they reached a stream, the giant allowed his animals to drink from it. That gave Smoke a much-needed break from her pursuit. She checked the bandage on her leg, pleased that it hadn't bled too much.

The giant nearly surprised her when he dismounted and ambled a few steps from the trail. While he relieved himself in the woods, she cursed herself for not having a plan to break Mato free. She didn't have long to berate herself as the giant returned to his beasts and resumed his journey.

Still grumbling to herself, Smoke followed along behind.

Chapter Nine

*"Freedom is what you do with what's been done
to you."* —Jean-Paul Sartre

Leonard finished his initial study of the primitive tribes discovered in recent years. Sadly, the outcomes differed little from those of primitive people discovered by "civilized" people from Europe and elsewhere going back centuries to Columbus, Magellan, and the conquistadores. None of it was good, at least for the natives.

History records that the population of entire islands in the Caribbean had been wiped out by disease brought by explorers, invading troops, and those intent on saving souls. They had no idea they carried germs and viruses for which the indigenous people had no immunity.

One could reason, as Leonard did, that during and after the Age of Exploration, few if any knew much about the transmission of disease. And yet, the exact same thing happened in the late 20th and early 21st centuries to previously unknown tribes living in Peru, Brazil, several South Pacific Islands, and a remote portion of western Australia.

The introduction of civilization to those groups resulted in an average population decline of 42 percent, all due to premature deaths.

It didn't require a genius mentality to realize that the little people living in the Cloud Peak could be massacred simply through contact with everyday folk. And based on what he learned from social media, quite a number of them were intent on making that contact.

No, check that. They're not everyday folks. They're everyday idiots. Morons!

And they had to be stopped.

But how could he, an individual who clearly lacked funds, be the one to make a difference? How could he stop people too stupid to realize the harm they could cause?

"Not could cause," he declared to his empty room. "*Will* cause."

The little ones did have something going for them: the weather. With winter coming on, like an express train according to the current forecast, most of the social media morons interested in finding the primitives would abandon their immediate plans or risk being stranded in the Big Horn Mountain Range during a blizzard. Those too stupid to avoid the weather deserved their conversion from peeps to popsicles.

In the meantime, he had to do something else; he had to prepare for the spring and summer. With warmer weather, the idiots were liable to gather in even larger numbers. They would have the entire winter to make their plans, prepare to travel, and thereby condemn a sizeable number of innocents to death by disease.

The little ones had to be protected. They mattered as much as anyone else on the planet, maybe more so as they hadn't hurt anyone. They'd done nothing to harm the environment either.

And then it hit him—a slogan. Why it hadn't occurred to him sooner he didn't know. That was immaterial. He had it now, and he said it out loud, testing the sound and feel of it. Some might think a slogan was a waste of time, but he knew better. People tended to rally around slogans and had for as long as there had been people to rally.

"Remember the Alamo!"

"Better dead than Red!"

"Save the whales!"

They all worked, to one extent or another, and he imagined there were hundreds if not thousands of others. He intended to add one more. He wrote it out in large letters in the center of a sheet of typing paper and smiled.

~*~

"I couldn't help but overhear what you told

Tori about going up into the Cloud Peak," Maggie said. "I can't imagine what you'd find up there that would matter, even if the weather weren't an issue."

Nate had already donned his hat and heavy coat. "You're probably right, but damn it all, I have to do what I—" He fell silent when Maggie put on her own heavy coat and buttoned it up.

"You leavin' early?" he asked.

"Hardly. I'm going with you."

He squinted at her in confusion. "You just said going up there amounted to a fool's errand."

She shook her head. "Well, it is, though I didn't use those exact words."

"Then, why—"

"Because I have a *good* reason to go up there, and I want you to go with me."

Intrigued, he urged her to go on. If she was serious, his little white lie to Tori about Maggie going with him would suddenly become true.

And Maggie obliged. "According to the registrations on file, there are still three visitors up there: two hikers and a guy on horseback."

"So?"

"We can't leave them up there with a big storm coming. Normally, I round up an extra ranger or two, but we're short staffed today." She frowned at him. "So, you coming or not?"

"Sure. And who knows, maybe I'll have time to check out the spot where that video was shot."

"Do you really think there's anything there to find?"

"I doubt it. But if nothing else, it'll give me something to report to the BIA." He watched as Maggie loaded a backpack. "Geez. You look like you're prepping for a vacation."

"Better safe than—"

"Gotcha. Are we riding or hiking?"

"That depends," she said, "since you're the only one with a horse handy. Here's the thing: I'm not a fan of riding double, and we're likely to get caught in snow. Do you want to take your horse where you can't see what it might be stepping on?"

"I'd rather not." He looked down at his boots, glad that he hadn't worn street shoes. "Is there anything you need me to carry? That pack looks heavy."

She gave him a smile. "It's not too bad. Bulky stuff mostly, not heavy. But I'd feel a lot better if we brought some extra food along, in case we have to stay up there a while." She pointed to a storage closet. "We've got MREs stashed in there. Why don't you grab some?"

Nate hadn't dined on a government-issued, ready-to-eat meal since he left the service. His memories of such repasts weren't pleasant. "*MREs?*" He made a face.

"The vegetarian ones aren't too bad. Neither is the Mexican stuff."

"Sez who?"

"It's either MREs, or you don't eat. Me? I'm okay with 'em."

"Hey, I'm not—"

"C'mon, Nate. Let's get moving. I don't wanna spend the night up there if I don't have to, and I don't want to worry Cal."

"What's there to worry about? It's just another trail ride. Only, you know, without the ride." With that he walked to the storage closet to grab some MREs for the trip.

~*~

Bound in a blanket that smelled of horse sweat and forced to lie belly-down on the back of such a beast only added to Mato's woes. His head still hurt, and he'd lost most of the feeling in his hands and feet. Whatever his captor had used to tie him up had not loosened up during the journey. His jaws ached from the wad of cloth in his mouth. Swallowing had become all but impossible. Mato could not recall a time when he felt more miserable. But rather than dwell on his wretched state, he concentrated on what he might do to the giant who had gotten ahold of him.

His options seemed limited owing to their size difference. But Mato was cunning, and his captor had no idea what he might be capable of.

168

The obvious answer would have been to stab the giant with a knife dipped in the sleeping paste that hunters among the People often used. Unfortunately, he hadn't planned to do any hunting and didn't bring any with him. His goal had simply been to return to the cavern and relay the redheaded giant's offer, a trip interrupted due to no fault of his own. Nonetheless, it was a trip he needed to complete as soon as possible.

Figuring out how to kill his captor would have to wait until he worked out some way to get free. He hadn't come up with any options when he heard a familiar voice: Nate's.

If he could just get the man's attention, his freedom was assured. Not only that, but Nate would likely help him dispatch the giant who had tied him up. Death seemed far too good an ending for him.

Mato tried to yell Nate's name, but he could barely hear himself. When nothing happened, he tried again.

And again.

~*~

Smoke could not remember a time when she had felt so worn and tired. Her leg ached, and her breath came in short gasps. She had all but abandoned her efforts to remain hidden in favor of just keeping up with the giant who had Mato. But even at that, she had fallen behind and prayed the Spirits might have pity on her. If only they would make him slow down, or better yet, stop and let his animals rest. Then she could rest, too.

In the distance, beyond the rider with his captured prey, two giants appeared, and they were walking toward him. When the giant she had been following slowed to talk with them, Smoke quickly stepped off the trail. Though it forced her to slow down even more, she continued to advance under the shelter provided by rocks, shrubs, and trees.

Eventually she drew close enough to the three giants to hear them talk. She had no idea what they said since she'd always been told giants spoke only gibberish. How they could understand each other remained a mystery. The People brushed it off as just more magic, but Smoke knew better, and she listened as closely as she could.

What she heard from the giants as they prepared to part company provided little information. What she heard coming from atop the back of the larger of the two beasts was Mato's voice, though heavily muffled. She had to strain to hear it, which merely proved giants didn't hear well. She counted that as an advantage, if only a small one.

All too soon the two giants on foot continued on their way, and the mounted giant did the same. Smoke waited until none of them could see her, then once again left the safety of the undergrowth to follow and hopefully save Mato.

~*~

Nate had always enjoyed Maggie's company. She and Cal were undoubtedly his best friends; Tori's, too. They'd survived some adventures, thanks to Mato and his tiny mate, Reyna, but those affairs only brought the four of them closer together. That knowledge alone would have been enough for him to agree to have her go with him when she told him about the "maybe missing" park visitors.

They encountered one of the three as they trudged uphill toward the area the hikers had designated on their registration form. Nate recognized Jedidiah Krantz immediately.

"Jedidiah! As I live and breathe."

"Howdy, Sheriff. What brings you all the way up here? Huntin' tax cheats?"

"That'd be a new low for you, wouldn't it?" Nate gave Krantz a once-over stopping at the bundle tied to the back of his mule. "What's in there?"

Krantz shrugged. "The usual shit. Campin' gear. A tent and what-not. Why? You wanna inspect it?"

"Actually—"

"You got a warrant?"

Nate exhaled slowly and deliberately, hoping to maintain his temper. "I dunno. You think I should get one?"

"Nah," Krantz said. "Go ahead. Knock yerself

171

out. But just unnerstand, there ain't nothin' in there you ain't seen a bazillion times. And you'll have to bundle it all up again when yer done. Don't 'spect me to help. I already done it once."

Nate tried to read the man's expression, but he couldn't tell if the old reprobate was lying.

"Did you see anyone else up there?" Maggie asked, pointing behind him. "We're looking for a couple of hikers." She dragged a sheet of paper from one of the many pockets in her coat, unfolded it, and ran her finger down the page. "Their names are Charles and Buddy Grogan."

Krantz took a moment to relieve himself of a mouthful of coffee-colored saliva. "Never heard of 'em. But then, I don't have much truck with hikers. They're all kinda... I dunno. They put me in mind of those fancy yahoos that wear goofy helmets and skin tight outfits when they ride their rich ass bikes. Sissy pants, all of 'em. Know what I mean?"

Nate gave him a nod; he'd had similar feelings from time to time, especially when trying to drive in New York City. More often than not, the bikers there pissed him off, and there were times he worried they might piss *on* him. "Well, did you see *anybody* up there?" Nate asked.

Krantz shook his head. "Not today. Not a soul." He paused as if giving some random thought a bit of deep consideration. "You lookin' for anybody in particular?"

"Just the two I mentioned," Maggie said.

"Then, no. I've been alone the whole time."

Something about that struck Nate as pure dog squeeze, but he let it go. The three of them chit-chatted for a while longer until Maggie insisted on continuing their hike. They waved goodbye to Krantz, and he went on his way.

"I don't trust that guy," Nate said. "At all."

"Just 'cause you've arrested him?"

Nate sniffed in derision. "'Cause he's a liar, a cheat, and an all-around, world-class scumbag."

"You make him sound like he's on the Most Wanted List," Maggie said.

"Trust me; he ain't on anyone's list. *Nobody* wants that guy."

They hiked on for what seemed like hours. The sun had begun to set, and they hadn't caught a glimpse of any hikers, much less evidence there had been any. He glanced at Mags. "Could those two Grogan guys have left the park without anyone knowing?"

"Sure," Maggie said. "We require visitors to register their plans 'cause we don't want to let too many people into the wilderness area at any one time. The thing is, looking at a registration form and talking to someone face-to-face are two very different things. Nothing's guaranteed. But at this time of year, it's easy to look in the parking areas, and see if anybody's left a vehicle behind."

"Yeah," snorted Nate, "but there must be a couple dozen entry points!"

"Twenty, actually. But it's not too big a deal to monitor them. Right now, we're pretty sure the Grogans are still in the park."

"Do you always mount search parties like this?"

Maggie shook her head. "No, not very often. But...."

When she didn't continue, Nate said, "But what?"

"Well, the storm that's headed this way could be a real stem-winder."

He chuckled. "You sound just like Cal."

"Well, he's lived through more than a couple of 'em. He can look at the sky and give you a pretty decent weather forecast."

"What'd he say about this one?"

Mags maintained a serious expression. "He said it was gonna be 'one mean sonovabitch.'"

~*~

Tori kept telling herself Nate was okay. She didn't need to call him. She didn't need to ask Mags if he was all right. She didn't need to do anything. She just needed to wait.

Shadow lay beside her where she sat on the floor in front of the fireplace. Nate had been good enough to restock their supply of firewood before he ran off to play nature cop. Without disturbing the dog, she tossed a small log on the fire she'd started when she saw the first snowflake hit the window of their front door. It was quickly followed by many more. Though the wind had yet to howl, she knew that would come soon, too.

The outrageously large mutt she shared with Mato put his head in her lap, a move which precluded her getting up. She fondled the dog's huge, floppy ears with one hand and gripped her cell phone in the other.

There had to be *someone* she could call.

Maggie's husband Cal beat her to it. "Hey kid. Thought I'd check and see if you'd heard anything from our nature buffs. I sure hope they wore their long johns. It's gonna be pretty damn cold up in the mountains."

"It's pretty damn cold down here," Tori answered. "I'm worried about them."

"Yeah. Me, too." There was a long moment of silence before he continued. "You know Maggie's been through this before, right? She knows what she's doing up there. Been at it a long time."

"I know. But Nate—"

"Will be just fine. They'll take care of each other."

Tori sniffed. "You make it sound so… What? Cozy? They aren't gonna get cozy, are they?"

175

"C'mon, Tori! Whad'ya think? They're friends is all. And if they have to cuddle to keep warm, then so be it. Have a little faith."

"You're right," she said. "But sometimes... Especially now... I dunno."

Cal cleared his throat. "I have no idea what you're talking about, assuming your talking about anything at all. It's damn near impossible to tell. You gals use some kinda code that ol' cowboys like me can't decipher."

Tori smiled at that. "I was hoping to tell Nate before anyone else."

"Oh, hell. Don't tell me you up and got yourself knocked up!"

"Yeah."

He chuckled. "I just don't understand why it took so long."

Though tempted to tell him the process required frequent and rigorous practice, she bit her tongue. "It's not like we planned it or anything. We just kinda let it happen."

"Well, good for you. And I've gotta tell ya, I'm more than a little bit jealous. Maggie and me, we'd love to have little ones. But the truth is, we're just too damn old."

"I don't believe that for a minute," Tori said. "I'll bet—"

"It's water over, under, and around the dam,

darlin'. Believe me. If we had a kid now... Well, they'd probably need to add a page to that goofy records book."

"The *Guinness* book?"

"Yeah. It's named after some Irish beer, right?"

She giggled. "I don't think so, and besides, I doubt you'd qualify. You wouldn't want to be in there for being the oldest parents on record, would you?"

"I dunno. Maybe. I'd have to run it by Maggie."

"I'll bet you would!"

They both fell silent.

"You still there?" she asked.

"Yeah."

"You're worried, too, aren't you?"

"Yeah," he said. "Real worried."

~*~

Simon Dole turned his gaze toward the ceiling the moment Leonard Pilcher entered his office. "I really wish you'd make an appointment like everyone else."

Leonard had grown tired of his supposed mentor's superior attitude. "I might if you hadn't allowed one of your assistants to sabotage my project."

"Oh, dear Lord. Must we go over all that again?" Dole shook his head. "What do you really want?"

"A little guidance would be nice. And as I understand it, that's something you're supposed to provide."

"It would help if I knew what you were talking about," Dole said, his expression neutral.

"I've had an idea, one which will impact my thesis. It's going to require some effort, but I think it's worthwhile."

Dole pursed his lips in exasperation. "Do you still believe there's a tribe of tiny people living out in the wilderness? Primitives no one has actually seen or heard? Do you have any idea how idiotic that notion is? There's a very good chance that the committee will reject your idea, whether you've enlarged your plans or not. Have you given any thought to that?"

Leonard squinted at him. "Now you're planning to derail my project altogether?" He was about to go on when a new thought struck him, one that seemed to make perfect sense. "You want it all for yourself, don't you?"

"What on Earth are you talking about?"

"I told you I could prove there are people living up there. I have conclusive evidence, and there's no way I'll share it with you or anyone else before I'm ready." Leonard felt better with every word. He'd never believed in himself more than in that moment.

"So, what do you want from me?" Dole asked. "My blessing? My help? My advice and counsel after you've accused me of trying to steal your ideas, and your—" He laughed. "Your *fame?* Puh-leeze."

"I'm going to start a movement," Leonard said. "As my faculty advisor, I thought you might want a heads-up. I guess I was wrong."

"Not at all," Dole said. "You came to the right place. You just didn't do it the right way. But, now that you're here, and you've already interrupted my schedule, you might as well go ahead and tell me what's on your mind. What sort of movement are you going to initiate?"

Leonard couldn't tell if Dole was sincere or not. The possibility that he might still hunger for Leonard's project remained a reality. "The problem is simple; the solution isn't."

"I'm all ears."

"The existence of primitives living in the Cloud Peak Wilderness has already been leaked to social media."

"I don't wish to—"

"Allow me to finish," Leonard said. "The problem is that those who live up there have done so in isolation. They've not been exposed to the germs, viruses, pathogens, and diseases the rest of us have lived with forever."

Dole sat back and steepled his fingers. "And you think that as soon as we start mixing with them, they'll contract all our ailments and die. Right?"

"Yes."

"And how do you intend to address the issue? What's going to propel this movement of yours?"

"I'll start with a slogan. It's simple, but it's direct." Leonard put his hands on his hips. He felt empowered.

"What's the slogan?"

Leonard cleared his throat, then spoke the three words in a firm, confident tone: "Little lives matter."

Dole remained expressionless for a moment, then asked, "To whom?"

~*~

Finally, after what seemed like a lifetime, the giant Smoke had been following, stopped. Though the Spirits had not intervened on her behalf, she thanked them anyway for ending her agonizing journey to the base of the mountains. She had never left the mountains before and had never been so far from home.

The long walk on a sore leg would have been hard enough in good weather, but falling snow had added a dreadful complication. Footing became difficult, and while remaining out of sight had grown simple due to the distance between them, she arrived at the stopping point thoroughly cold, wet, and miserable.

For the first time in her young life, she stood in the presence of some of the giants' wizardry—devices used to transport them, *and their beasts of burden!* The sheer size of them would have left her awestruck if not for her overriding concern for Mato. His captor unloaded everything the beasts carried into the back of one such machine. Then he brought the animals to a second conveyance and loaded them inside.

Smoke used the opportunity to crawl into the back of the first machine. She found a hiding place underneath the materials the giant had just dumped there. Mato lay close beside her, though he had no idea she was there. She remained quiet, hoping the giant would ride somewhere else. If so, she intended to let Mato know his rescue was at hand.

With the giant out of sight, Smoke concentrated on staying both warm and hidden though she feared she would accomplish neither. A great noise startled her. The rumbling sounded a bit like a small avalanche and came accompanied by vibrations and the rattling of the other things surrounding her.

And then, it moved.

She let out a yelp, then clapped her hand over her mouth. If the giant heard her, she would be helpless to fight him off. She would simply join Mato as a meal for the monster.

Her pulse had quickened, and sweat stood out on her brow despite the now freezing weather. She held her breath praying the giant would keep on and not investigate her foolish cry.

When nothing happened, she forced herself to relax. She reached out and patted the blanket-wrapped Mato. "Can you hear me?" she whispered.

He responded with a muffled grunt.

"I've come to save you," she said.

Chapter Ten

"Hip is the sophistication of the wise primitive in a giant jungle." —Norman Mailer

The heavy snowfall made walking uphill even more difficult. Nate had never been a fan of hiking, and this particular trek had proven to be much harder than he anticipated. Maggie, however, trooped along as if she'd been doing it for years. Which, in fact, she had.

"Can we take a break?" Nate asked.

Maggie smiled at him. "I'd like to get a little higher if we can. This snow is only going to get deeper."

"Now there's a pleasant thought."

"And since neither of us brought skis or snowshoes, we'll just have to tough it out."

"I knew the air was thinner up here," Nate said. "I didn't realize how much harder that would make hiking. But then, I guess you're used to it."

"It sucks, doesn't it? But I get it; the scenery

183

is so phenomenal that people constantly stop to look at it."

"And breathe, right?"

"Right." She tightened the scarf around her neck. "The other reason I don't want to stop is because it'll be dark soon."

"No doubt about that."

"I packed some flashlights and a headlamp, too. But I'd rather we didn't use 'em until we have to. Finding those two hikers won't be easy in the dark."

"Where do you suppose they are?" Nate asked.

"Assuming they're still up here, I imagine they've holed up somewhere. These mountains are riddled with caves large and small, and a couple have only recently been explored. I suspect Mato and his people have one they call home. Although...."

Nate frowned at her. "What?"

"Various Indian tribes used the caves up here for centuries, and we know earlier primitive tribes inhabited the area as well. It's amazing to me that none of them ever encountered the little people."

"Maybe they did and just didn't know how to record the fact."

Maggie shrugged. "Anyway, I know of a cave

near where we're heading. If we have to, we can shelter in it."

"And make a fire?"

"Sure, if there's any firewood left. And there should be. A couple of my ranger friends know about the spot, too, but it isn't listed anywhere. We try to stash deadfall in there when we can, just in case. And today feels like one of those cases."

Nate tried to look serious. "You're keeping secrets from the paying public?"

"Oh, hell yes," Maggie said then came to an abrupt halt. "You hear that?"

"Somebody yelling?"

"Yeah. C'mon, let's get moving. I just hope they aren't in trouble."

Mato assumed he'd been tossed in a truck like Nate's. If only it had been Nate's, he'd be safe. Though he had struggled against his bonds, he'd made no progress; they remained tight.

Tired and angry, he could think of little else but exacting his revenge on the giant who'd trapped him. He might not be able to do more than bite him, but if that was the limit, he swore to take as many chunks as he could before he died.

He felt the lightest of touches through the heavy blanket and thought he heard a voice, a female voice, *speaking in the tongue of the People.*

185

But, he reasoned, that couldn't be! No one in the clan could have known about his predicament. He tried to respond, but the gag in his mouth kept him from making words. He hoped his grunts and struggles would convey something—that he remained alive, if nothing else.

Comforted by the simple message that someone had come to his rescue, Mato tried to figure out who it might be. Certainly not Reyna; she had vowed not to leave the cavern. And it definitely couldn't have been Winter Woman; the voice was too young. Who else was there?

He found no solution for the mystery and could do nothing more than wait for his rescue to unfold. That proved difficult. He couldn't understand why whoever had come to save him didn't just cut his bonds and release him.

~*~

Work had progressed on schedule, for the most part, and Randi had been assured everything would be ready for transport on the appointed day. Only one member of the team voiced a concern: the weather might cause delays about which they could do nothing.

"Let's focus on the things we *can* control, okay?" she had told him. "We'll leave the rest up to Mother Nature."

And yet, the comment continued to gnaw at her. There was no doubt they'd picked a lousy time of year to try and pull off something like this, but

Tim Archer could not be dissuaded. Acts of God did not fit anywhere in his timetables, and Randi knew better than to even mention it.

She had been assured that *Puck Two*, the larger and even more opulent dirigible used to ferry passengers from the Honolulu airport to the resort on Kauai, would be ready. The transpacific flight would take several days, and required modifications to the passenger cabin so the crews would be able to live comfortably onboard.

A call to the Flight Coordinator had been scheduled earlier but had been put off, by him, several times. Randi's patience had grown hair thin. She stabbed the button on her cell phone for his direct line.

"This is Captain Bradley."

"So, you're actually in the office today?"

"Well, I—"

"This is Miranda Rhoades."

"Oh. Yes. Hello, Ms. Rhoades."

"Why do I get the impression you've been dodging my calls, Mr. Bradley?"

"It's Captain Brad—"

"If you keep putting me off, it's going to be '*Retired* Captain Bradley.' Do you read me?"

"Yes ma'am. And I apologize for the delays, truly. It's just that we've been quite busy with the airship retrofit. The distance from our base in

Kauai to Los Angeles is about 600 kilometers beyond our normal range. We're having to provide for extra fuel."

"I was told that wouldn't be a problem," Randi said, still irritated.

"It wasn't me that said that. Listen, you have to realize how difficult it is—"

"I'm not interested in difficult, *Mister* Bradley. I'm interested in results, as is Mr. Archer. His name may not appear on your paycheck, but I promise you, he's the one footing the bill for your services."

Bradley cleared his throat. "You realize that *Puck Two* was built in Germany, right?"

"So?"

"We'll use three flight crews, and they'll need some sort of living accommodations when they're between shifts. Refitting the interior requires a company with sophisticated abilities."

"Are you saying such facilities aren't available in Hawaii? Last time I checked, it was part of the United States of America, one of the world's most technologically advanced countries. Or do the Germans have some mystical capabilities I don't know about?"

"I can get into the details if that's what you really want." Bradley's manner had shifted from defensive to combative.

"It's not. What I do want to know is whether

or not the airship will be in Wyoming at the designated date and time."

"Are you familiar with the phrase, 'God willing, and the Creek don't rise?'"

"Don't be cute. I know the difference between a creek and 'the Creek.'"

"Okay, fine. *Puck Two* can travel about 90 kilometers per hour, tops. If there's a strong headwind, it'll slow her down. Because of the retrofit delays, I'm assuming we won't get out of here as scheduled, but we ought to arrive within 48 hours of the original ETA."

"There now," Randi said, "that wasn't so hard, was it?"

"No, ma'am."

"New question: can it fly in winter weather?"

"Sure. Why not?"

"'Cause we'll need it to land in the Big Horn Mountains. The elevation will be well over ten thousand feet."

Bradley whistled. "Got any idea about wind in the area?"

"Not this far in advance, no. But I'm sure it'll be both windy and snowing."

"And how 'bout where we're supposed to land? Up 'til now it's been a secret, other than 'It's in Wyoming.' *Puck Two* is big. We don't need a ground crew, but we need—pardon the expression—a butt-load of space."

"Define 'butt-load.'"

"*Puck Two* is longer than a Boeing 747, and she's nearly as wide. That tends to limit landing sites. Think in terms of football fields. *That's* how much room we'll need."

Though still somewhat vexed by Bradley's attitude, she tried not to sound overly snarky. "I keep hearing that one of the great advantages of airships is that they can land just about anywhere. Great for shipping things to remote areas. You can't get much more remote than the Big Horn Mountains."

"Yes, but—"

"I'm told there are Alpine valleys up there, and large expanses of open terrain, above the tree line."

"We can't land on the side of a mountain, Ms. Rhoades. We're talking about an airship, not a helicopter."

"I'm well aware of that. But in any case, I'm coming along for the ride. I'm sure whoever is flying that thing will appreciate my input on a landing spot."

"Whatever you say, ma'am. And by the way, I'll be the lead pilot on that trip. Now, where shall we pick you up? Or do you intend to ride all the way across the Pacific?"

"I'll be waiting for you in Los Angeles. I'll provide the coordinates later."

"Of course."

"Don't let me down, Captain."

"I won't. I promise."

~*~

Still seething at Simon Dole's heartless and utterly insensitive remark, Leonard returned to his basement quarters with an even stronger commitment to his project. That Dole was unable to connect with his slogan meant nothing, except that the overhyped assistant professor of anthropology was a complete ass.

Leonard dove into the work with a passion, a drive that had previously eluded him all his life. He spent hours on as many social media platforms as he could, beginning with those that had spouted the most commentary about the little people.

Some self-proclaimed wag had merged the words mini and Indian into "Minidian," and the name seemed to have stuck. Leonard entered one conversation after another valiantly proclaiming such terminology not only racist but possibly speciest as well since those captured on video might have traveled a different evolutionary path.

His conjecture was largely ridiculed, and more than a few of his most recent contacts "unfriended" him when they realized his platform had a decidedly narrow focus. Nevertheless, he did manage to attract some followers and built a mailing list of those who were like-minded.

The problem, he realized, would fully arise when he would need them the most. Declaring one's beliefs was one thing; acting on them was quite another. And, when the time was right, he would definitely need them to act.

~*~

Smoke had used up most of her bravado when she told Mato she had come to save him. How she would go about that remained a monumental question. If she cut the rope which kept the thick blanket around him, the giant would see it and instantly know something was amiss. She hadn't trekked all the way down from the mountains just to be foiled by a stupid mistake.

Crawling out from her hiding place in the back of the giant's rattling conveyance, she peered into the dark, ignoring the hard driven snow which stung her face and neck. They were moving fast, and from time to time she could feel the machine beneath her shift and slide. Her upbringing often required that she manage her fears, something the People lived with whenever giants roamed their lands. This situation, she told herself, was no different. So, she swallowed her dread and slipped back out of sight.

Eventually it lurched to a halt, and the noises and vibrations from the vehicle ceased. She heard several new noises as the giant went about his heinous preparations. Smoke peered over the top of the vehicle and saw the giant open two large doors. His back was turned to her, and she took the opportunity to drop down into the snow, which was already over her knees, and hide amidst a pile of things the giant had apparently discarded.

She alternately watched Mato's captor or looked for something in the pile of debris which might serve as a weapon. Neither effort provided comfort; the giant hauled Mato, still bound in the blanket, into a huge wooden shelter where he presumably lived. He left the door to it open when he returned to the vehicle to retrieve more of his belongings.

That gave her just enough time to scamper from concealment and into the building. As she ran, she appealed to the Spirits to show her where she might hide when she reached the interior.

For once, they did not fail her.

Hearing the cries of "Help!" and "Over here!" resulted in a burst of energy which Nate thought couldn't possibly have been coaxed from his weary body. Yet it proved to be substantial enough for him to hurry after Maggie as she slogged up the snow-covered trail.

The freezing white stuff had gotten progressively thicker as they worked their way further up into the mountains. If it had been daytime, and if Nate had thought to bring his skis, getting down from up there would have been fun. In the gathering darkness and continuing snowfall, a descent on foot down a snow-choked trail was out of the question.

"Thank God you guys are here," said a miserable-looking man who appeared to be in his early twenties. He wore a hoodie and a winter jacket and huddled beside another male who was similarly dressed. Snow had accumulated on both of them.

"You're the Grogans, right?" Maggie asked.

"Yeah. I'm Chuck," the first young man said before giving his partner a gentle shove. "That's Buddy, my big brother."

Maggie had her gloved hands on her hips as she stared down at the pair. "Why are you still up here? Didn't you check the weather forecast before you started your hike?"

"Well, sure, of course," Chuck said. "We didn't intend to stay up here, but Buddy screwed up his ankle. He thinks it's broken. I think he just twisted it. I tried to get him to walk on it, but—"

"It hurts, man!" Buddy exclaimed. "I can't walk on it. Hell, I can barely move it without screamin' my head off."

"Well, you can't stay here. You'll freeze to death." Maggie looked to Nate for support.

"She's right," he said. "But we can help you."

"Good. How 'bout you build a fire," Buddy

said. "I'm already half frozen."

Nate frowned at Maggie. "How far is the cave from here?"

"It's maybe ten, fifteen minutes away on a good day with clear weather. But now? If we have to carry someone?"

"Carry?" Nate quickly looked down at Buddy who appeared big enough to play on the line for a college football team. "That's not really an option."

"We could make a stretcher or something," Chuck said. "You know, with branches and stuff."

Maggie's chuckle contained little humor. "You see any trees up here? Forget it. We're too high up."

Chuck looked as if he were about to weep. "I'm not leavin' him here to die!"

"Of course not," Maggie said. "Get a grip. Let's help him up off the ground. We can take turns holding him up, one of us under each arm. He can hop on his good leg." She pointed at Chuck. "You and Nate go first. I'll lead the way."

Nate knew the voice of command when he heard it and moved quickly to the far side of the injured hiker while Chuck stood and knocked the snow off his clothing. The two then hoisted Buddy, who groaned all the way, upright.

"You're gonna be all right, man," Chuck promised him. Buddy did not respond.

Maggie dug two flashlights out of her pack and handed them to Nate and Chuck. She then slipped a headlamp over her knitted cap and switched the light on. "This way, gentlemen," she said and continued up the path.

They had to make frequent stops to accommodate Buddy who struggled to keep moving on one leg even though he was supported on both sides. The snow obscured rocks on the ground, and all three men stumbled frequently. With each such mishap, Buddy howled his pain.

"From the sounds your brother's making, one might think there's a wolf in your family tree," Nate said, hoping to lighten the mood.

"Screw you," said Buddy who, except for his groans, had said nothing since they began to assist him.

Nate grunted and shook his head. "It was a joke."

"Buddy doesn't have much of a sense of humor," said Chuck.

Nate smiled. "Imagine that. I'd never have guessed."

"You guys okay back there?" Maggie's shout barely cut through the wind, but her headlamp's beam indicated she wasn't too far in front of them.

"We're right behind ya," Nate yelled back. "So, where's this cave of yours? Little Buddy here is gettin' heavy."

196

"Hang in there," she responded. "It's just a little further along. I'd spell one of you, but finding the entrance in the dark is gonna be tricky."

Several minutes later she stopped and waited for them to catch up. She pointed to a Volkswagen-sized boulder. "Prop our patient up against that and take a rest. I'll be right back."

She paused when she saw the look on Nate's face. "What is it?"

"I was going to ask you the same thing."

"The cave entrance is only a few yards away. We'll have to crawl to get through it, but it'll be plenty roomy inside. I thought I'd go in first and make sure it isn't already occupied."

Nate felt a sudden jolt of alarm. "Occupied? By what?"

"That's what I want to find out," she said. "Wish me luck."

"Holy crap!" Nate reached for her arm, but she had already moved out of reach.

Maggie laughed. "Oh, c'mon. Relax. It's too big a space for bears. They like to curl up around their cubs and use body heat to keep their dens livable. Don't you watch nature shows on TV?"

"I guess maybe I should," Nate said, feeling useless as she slipped behind the boulder and out of sight. "Don't keep us in suspense," he yelled.

Maggie didn't answer.

~*~

Mato had learned patience as a hunter, and he needed as much as he could muster to keep calm. He needed all his senses to understand the depth of his predicament, but he could only rely upon his ears and the movement of the package he'd become

Suddenly, that package shifted, and Mato felt himself being carried somewhere. It wasn't far, and the trip ended with the bundle being dropped on the ground. He felt additional tugging and tussling before he was again picked up and unrolled onto a cold, hard, rough floor.

"I'll cut them cords off in a while," the giant said. Mato did not recognize the voice and couldn't turn his head far enough to see the giant. He sounded old.

"I'll be right back. Gotta put my horse and mule in the shed." The giant wheezed through a laugh. "Don't go nowhere!" Then he walked away.

Mato rolled over so he could see the giant when he returned. As he rolled, he noticed a small hand waving to him from beneath a large, wooden desk. "Who are you?" he asked in a whisper.

A moment later he saw the face of a young female from the clan. She smiled at him as only the hopelessly stupid can.

"Ember?"

She motioned for him to be quiet then

slipped back into the darkness.

The giant returned with a collection of metal screens in his hands. He set them on the floor and arranged them in a box shape, grunting as he did so. After fiddling with one thing and another he pronounced it "ready."

Mato stared at a cage directly in front of him.

"I had me a fightin' dog once, only he weren't worth a damn. I kept him in this here crate between fights, but he didn't last long. He'd bleed a lot in there, but that shouldn't hurt you none."

The giant walked to Mato, picked him up by the cords still binding him, and tossed him inside the cage. He closed the door and secured it with a dainty lock, then stuck the key in a pocket of his grubby overalls.

"If you'll wiggle closer, I'll cut the rope so you can move around in there."

Mato considered pretending he didn't understand, but the prospect of freedom from his bonds proved overwhelming. He scooted close enough to the side of the cage to feel the cold metal against his back.

He couldn't see what the giant used to cut the constricting cords, but he didn't care. His first thought was to get free of them and the vile hunk of cloth in his mouth.

For his part, the giant seemed to find Mato's

struggles comical. He laughed as his diminutive captive shrugged off his bindings and the gag. When he was finally able to stand up and face his captor, Mato placed his hands on his hips and glared.

"You look pretty tough for such a little shit," the giant said. "But I'm way tougher, as you'll soon find out. Yer gonna tell me where your people hid their gold. You savvy 'gold?'"

Mato pretended not to understand, which wasn't the least bit difficult.

The giant took something from his pocket and set it on the floor near the cage, but not close enough for Mato to grab it.

"That's gold. Don't pretend you don't have any. And if not you, then yer chief or yer medicine man, or whatever you call 'em. All you have to do is show me where it is, and I'll let you go."

Mato remained silent having caught the flavor of his remarks if not the precise meaning.

"And I'll bet yer hungry. Well, tough luck. I'm havin' beans and weenies, right outta the can. If there's any left when I'm done, I might give you some." He chuckled. "If you tell me about the gold."

Mato tried to remember some of the things giants said which Tori had warned were "not nice." He wasn't quite sure what that meant at the time, but he wished he could recall something Nate or Cal had said when hurt or angry. Only one came to mind.

"Screw you and the house you rode in on," Mato said, trying to work as much bile into his voice as possible.

The giant giggled. "It's 'horse,' asshole, not 'house.'"

Mato shrugged. Horse, house—he didn't care about the difference. Any insult would do.

When the giant turned away, Mato spared a quick glance at the space beneath the big, wooden desk. There he saw the girl again, this time looking at him as if he'd sprouted antlers.

Mato repeated his curse, updating it as instructed by the giant.

Ember smiled back.

Leonard knew it wouldn't be easy to build a coalition that could protect the little people. Fortunately, he could do the early work online. He searched for chat rooms, discussion groups, and any hints of people talking about the Cloud Peak, even if they made no mention of a primitive tribe living there. He was intent on making connections, ferreting out those who might help, and identifying those who might interfere.

It was during one such search that he came upon a post by someone in Hawaii who complained about having to work on an airship to prepare it for what he described as "a suicidal mission to the Cloud Peak Wilderness." The writer mentioned something about the machine belonging to Puck Productions which operated a fancy resort on one of the islands. Leonard read on but found no other details.

An airship? Seriously? Didn't they all blow up back before World War II? He remembered reading something about a big Zeppelin exploding over New Jersey. His Dad told him, "It served the friggin' Nazis right. They filled the damned thing up with hydrogen 'cause we wouldn't sell Der Führer any helium."

Leonard shook off the memory and questioned the message poster about why he thought the trip would end in disaster. *Surely, they aren't still using hydrogen, are they?*

"We're in Hawaii," came the response, "where it's summer all year long. Why fly a gigantic airship all the way across the ocean to some obscure mountain peak in Wyoming in the dead of winter? It's ridiculous! And no one seems willing or able to answer the big question everyone here is asking: Why, for heaven's sake?"

Why indeed, thought Leonard.

Chapter Eleven

*"If you look at the primitive societies that we know
about, the worst thing that could have happened to you
was to be captured and be turned over to the women."*
—Jeff Lindsay

Smoke couldn't see too much from her hiding place beneath the squarish wooden object that dominated the interior of the giant's hut without risking exposure. At best, all she could see of him were his colossal feet as he shuffled about.

She longed to be able to talk to Mato who was trapped in a cage that would not yield to the knife she carried, nor any of which she knew. There had to be another way. She supposed Mato had some ideas since he claimed to have lived among the giants, but she preferred to solve the problem in her own way. Else, why had she bothered to come?

For his part, Mato seemed content to give her odd looks, quizzical at times and frustrated at others. She had found the younger males among the People to be profoundly simple, while the older ones often confused her with too many concepts, too many unproven beliefs, and too many customs with which she disagreed.

Waiting seemed to be her best option. Surely the giant would have to sleep sometime, but for now he seemed content to stand in front of a great metal contraption that gave off heat. For that, at least, she was grateful.

Soon, she became aware of a new scent, not unpleasant, but unlike the aromas she'd grown up with. He was cooking something, she realized, and he was likely using the room's only heat source to do it.

Slipping quietly out from her dark refuge, but keeping it between herself and the giant, Smoke glanced up to confirm her suspicions. Just as she did so, he turned and reached for something on top of her hiding place.

She ducked back, heart racing, praying she hadn't been seen. At any moment she expected the giant would come thundering around the big wooden object, and she would be doomed. He would add her to whatever he was cooking, and that would be the end of her. But at least it might delay Mato's death for a time. Such sad comfort did little for her.

When the giant didn't come after her, she began to berate herself for having foolish doubts. If she couldn't deal with her situation, there would be no hope for Mato. So, once again, she risked being seen in order to observe the giant.

He remained standing, occasionally drinking from a flat, dark brown container. After each swallow he would shake his head and exhale. He turned slightly and placed the container on top of Smoke's hiding place then belched and busied himself once again with his meal preparations.

Smoke's injured leg had throbbed continually, and now that she was inside, warm and relatively comfortable, she thought about using a pinch of the powder Winter Woman had given her for pain. As she reached inside her carrybag for the pouch containing the powder, she recalled the elder's admonition that she take care and not use too much as it would cause her to sleep. And then she recalled the elder's final caution that if she used too much, she might not wake up at all.

Suddenly, she knew how to deal with the giant!

If she could just distract him long enough, she could dump *all* the powder in his food. Once he'd satisfied his hunger, he'd fall asleep, never to awake—a perfect outcome!

Except she had no way to distract him.

Mato sat in his cage, arms crossed, looking angry. It was the only thing he *could* do. Perhaps, she thought, if he made enough noise, he might divert the giant's attention allowing her to dispense the poison.

But climbing up on the cooking surface would be difficult if not impossible. And besides, how much longer would it be before the giant started eating? And then she recalled he had been drinking something, and that something currently sat on the wooden thing almost directly overhead.

Maybe it could provide just the distraction she needed....

~*~

"Damn it, Mags! You scared the crap outta me takin' off like that." Nate's composure had worn tissue thin owing to feelings of anger, guilt, and finally, relief.

"Sorry," she said, "but I couldn't see any point in fiddlin' around when a potential shelter was available."

"But what if—"

"Some awful critter ate me? Well, you three would still be alive, wouldn't ya?"

"I s'pose, but—"

"Anyway, the cave's empty. So, end of discussion. Now, let's drag our whiney little friend over to the entrance. You and Chuck will have to crawl in first, then turn around, and drag him in after you. I don't expect he'll be able to do much to help."

Maggie was right about Buddy; he spent his

energy moaning and groaning while Nate and Chuck maneuvered him through the opening and into the cave beyond. By the time they got him settled, Maggie had already started a fire. Smoke from the nascent blaze drifted upward and out through an unseen opening.

The four huddled close, waiting for the fire to grow.

Maggie ignored the injured brother and addressed the younger one. "Since we're gonna be stuck here for a while, why don't you tell us why you two came all the way up here."

"Oh, that's easy," the young man said. "We wanted to see if we could spot any Mindians."

Maggie squinted at him.

"Mindian—it's a combination of 'mini' and 'Indian,'" Nate said. "Pretty stupid, if you ask me."

"Where'd you hear it?" she asked.

"Tori told me about it. That and another one that's even more stupid."

"Oh," said Chuck, "you must mean Lilipindians."

Nate just rolled his eyes.

"I don't even want to know where that one came from," Maggie said. "So, anyhow, did you see any little people?"

"Naw. We hadn't even started to really hunt for 'em when Buddy got hurt." He looked over at his brother who studiously ignored everyone else. "When do you suppose the rescue helicopter will arrive?"

"What rescue helicopter?" Nate asked.

Chuck appeared surprised by the question. "That's how they always do it in the movies."

"And on TV," echoed Maggie with a laugh.

"D'ya mean we've gotta *walk* back down? Buddy'll never make it."

"You never know," Maggie said. "Chuckles over there might feel a lot better in the morning. And once he's given the choice between living in here for a while or walking back down to civilization, he might just have a miraculous recovery."

"Fat chance," Buddy said. "And don't call me 'Chuckles.'"

Nate chortled. "I dunno. I kinda like it— Chuck and Chuckles. It's got a nice ring to it."

"Can't we just phone somebody?" Chuck asked. "Seriously, Buddy's ankle is swollen all to hell. He's not gonna be walkin' on it anytime soon."

"Cell phones rarely work up here," Maggie said. "But I've got a radio, and once the weather clears and I can go back outside, I'll put in a call to the ranger station. They might want to use a snowmobile."

"That'd be a bit of a bumpy ride," Nate said.

"But it'd be a whole lot cheaper than paying for a chopper to fly up here."

"We'd have to pay for that?" Buddy asked. He looked shocked.

"Helicopters aren't allowed to land in a wilderness area," Maggie explained. "Unless it's a really serious situation. Life and death, maybe. Otherwise, they have to land near the wilderness boundary. I've got the coordinates for that, but—" she glanced at Buddy "—that's about the best you can hope for since you don't look very close to bein' dead."

"How much would a helicopter ride cost?" Nate asked. "Got any idea?"

Maggie threw another branch on the fire. "Last I heard it was around $1800 an hour."

Nate glanced at Buddy who suddenly looked a great deal worse than he had before.

~*~

Tori grabbed her phone the instant she heard it ring and without looking at the caller's name. "Nate?"

"Sorry to disappoint you. It's just me, Randi."

"Oh."

"Boy, do you sound glum. What's up?"

"Nate's up in the Cloud Peak, and we're in the middle of a snow storm. I'm worried sick about him."

There was a moment's silence before Randi responded. "I'm— Geez. I had no idea. Have you spoken with that ranger friend of yours, Margaret?"

"Maggie? No. In fact, I'm pretty sure she's with Nate. I spoke with Cal, her husband. He's just as worried as I am. What kills me is that there's not a damn thing I can do. Nothing."

"They know what they're doing," Randi said. "I'm sure."

"I hope so. Anyway, what can I do for you?"

"Well, in light of what you just told me, this is going to sound like a pretty odd question, but how would you feel about flying up to the Cloud Peak in our airship?"

"Tonight?"

Randi laughed. "No. Definitely not tonight. Not for a few days. Hopefully, when the weather clears a bit."

"This is all about your deal with Mato and his tribe, isn't it? And about giving them some modern comforts?"

"Right," Randi said. "On both counts. I'll definitely be there, and since you're the one who actually broke the ice with Mato... Well, I figured it would only be right to have you involved. What d'ya say?"

Tori had wondered about the deal that Randi was trying to make for Puck Productions. She wasn't completely on board with it, but she wasn't completely against it either. She worried that Mato's clan would be exploited, but she also felt that they would benefit from many of the things the Puck company could provide. She knew Nate felt much the same way.

"Yes," she said at length. "Yes, I'd like to be there."

"Good. I'm glad to hear it. You and Nate are special to me, and I'm not just saying that. I'd like to think we'll be friends for a long time to come."

Tori felt a twinge of embarrassment. "Can I be honest?"

"Of course."

"When I first met you—"

"In Hawaii?"

"Yeah. I was a little afraid that... Well, you know... Maybe that you and Nate...."

"Please," Randi said, with a smile in her voice. "Nate is a great guy, and if he weren't already married, I might try to build a relationship with him. But he is married. And he's deeply, and I mean *deeply*, in love with you. I would never think of trying to change that. I respect both of you far too much."

"Promise?"

"Absolutely."

Tori felt a bigger wave of relief than she'd expected. "Thank you," she said. "I mean that."

"Don't give it another thought."

"I'll try not to," Tori said.

"Okay then, I'll make sure you're on the passenger list. We'll be flying out of the Worland airfield. I presume you know where that is."

"Yep."

"Good. I'll give you the date and time as soon as I have it. Welcome aboard!"

~*~

Mato stared at Ember crouched on the far side of the giant's desk and wondered what she had in mind. While his captor busied himself heating up a can of beans, the girl quietly snagged a coil of rope from a nearby pile of gear, dragged it to the desk, and climbed up on it. She reached across the desk toward the bottle from which the giant had been drinking.

What is she doing? Has she gone mad?

But she didn't appear to be trying to grab the bottle. Rather, she seemed to want to tip it over; she just couldn't reach it. The look of determination on her face convinced Mato he had to help her, somehow. Ember had committed herself to a course of action, but if he didn't do something, she was sure to be spotted and worse, caught. Just like him.

The giant wrapped a discolored rag around the hot can, picked it up, and began to turn toward his desk. Mato let out a strident yell. The startled giant set the can down on the desk and gave all his attention to his prisoner.

"What the hell are you squawking about?"

Mato kept his focus squarely on the giant and motioned for him to come closer.

The giant made a face, but took two steps away from the desk and stove. "What is it?"

Mato put his hand on his groin and danced in place as if he desperately needed to relieve himself.

"Aw fer cryin' out loud. Go ahead and pee on the floor, ya dumb runt." The giant laughed. "What're you good for? A tablespoon or two? Go on. See if I care."

While the giant was busy laughing at his own profound wit, Mato spared a quick look beyond him and saw Ember use a pencil to knock over the bottle. It landed on some scattered papers and flowed out over the desktop. The girl quickly and silently retreated.

The giant soon straightened, his laughter exhausted. Once again, he turned his attention to his meal, only then noticing his previously bottled beverage spreading across his desk and dripping onto his chair and the floor. He unleashed a burst of expletives and scanned the room as if expecting to find an intruder.

He saw none.

Still cursing, he began sopping up the liquid on his desk with the rag he'd wrapped around the can. When he realized he had more spillage than the rag could handle, he left the cramped office without ever closing the door.

Mato still had no idea what Ember intended to do, but watched, fascinated, as she climbed up on the desk and dumped something from a small pouch into the giant's can of beans. She stirred it with the spoon he'd left in it, then retreated once again to her hiding place under the desk.

"Ember?" he called out in a whisper. "What are you up to?"

She frowned at him. "My name is Smoke!"

"Yes, of course. Smoke." He shook his head. "So, what are you doing?"

"You will see," she whispered back. "The old have little patience."

"*What?*"

"And no imagination."

~*~

"You should let me take a look at that ankle of yours," Maggie said.

Buddy Grogan frowned at her. "Why?"

214

"Because, knucklehead," Nate said, "she's a ranger, and she knows first aid. She deals with hikers all the time."

"It's broke. First aid won't help."

Nate looked at Maggie. "Well, there you have it, a complete diagnosis direct from Doctor Knucklehead himself."

"We might need to pack it in ice," Maggie said, ignoring Nate's remark. "That'll reduce the swelling. It'll probably hurt less."

"Yeah," said Buddy, "and then how will I get my damn shoe back on?"

"Gosh, I can't imagine," said Nate. "Oh, wait. Look at that! It's not a hiking boot; it's a sneaker for God's sake."

Buddy's brother chimed in, "C'mon, man. Let her take a look. What can it hurt?"

Maggie continued, "We need to know if it needs a splint. If it's just a sprain—"

"It's not! Just leave me the hell alone." Buddy crossed his arms and shifted his body enough to face away from her.

"Suit yourself," Maggie said.

The evening passed slowly, and discussion centered mostly on when and how they might be able to return to civilization. Maggie retrieved four Mylar emergency blankets from her backpack and handed them out.

"What's this for?" Buddy asked.

"It'll keep you warm," she explained.

"How? There's nothing to it. It doesn't weigh anything."

"Do your best to wrap up in it; the Mylar will retain almost all your body heat. They used to call these things 'space blankets' because NASA invented them. They work pretty well."

"I'm more concerned about running out of firewood," Nate said, eyeing their dwindling supply.

"I guess a couple of us could go out and look for more when the snow stops falling," offered Chuck, the younger of the two brothers. "Did you know the Eskimos have, like, a thousand different words for snow? We've got, what? Maybe one or two?"

Nate stared at him. "Don't you think that's a bit of a stretch?"

"Only 'cause it's nonsense," Maggie said. "First off, the word 'Eskimo' refers to any of the indigenous people who live in or near the Arctic. That'd be Aleuts, Sami—"

"How do you know all this shit?" Buddy asked, showing a rare bit of interest in something other than himself.

Maggie shrugged. "I get the question every once in a while, especially from winter visitors. So, I looked it up. Anyway, the Sami—who live mostly in Scandinavia and herd reindeer—have quite a few words related to snow and ice. But a thousand? No way."

"I'd take her word for it," Nate said. "She's an authority figure."

Maggie smiled. "Why, thank you, Sherriff."

"You're a *cop?*" Buddy shook his head. "I shoulda known."

"What's that supposed to mean?" Maggie asked.

"Cops are always pushin' people around, acting arrogant. They think their own shit don't stink."

"Geez, Buddy," Chuck said. "Lighten up a little."

"Hey, I'm entitled to have an opinion. It's a free country, and if you ask me—"

"Nobody did," Maggie said.

"So what? It's true! Cops are total ass—"

"How's your ankle, Buddy?" Nate asked.

"Huh?"

"Think you can walk on it? All the way out of the mountains?"

"Are you nuts? Of course not."

"Well then, if you intend to lean on me for that descent, I suggest you keep your opinions to yourself."

"Or what?"

"Or I might just leave you in this cave to rot."

Chuck offered a hurried, "He wouldn't do that!"

Nate shrugged. "There's only one way to find out."

The four fell into an uneasy silence, paired up on opposite sides of the dying fire. Maggie leaned close to Nate and whispered his name to get his attention.

"Hm?"

"We might have a wee little problem," she said, her voice barely audible.

"Yeah, well, that's kinda obvious, isn't it?" He smiled to lighten the snark.

"Sure, but there's something else, and I'm not ready to admit it to our two friends here."

"I can keep a secret," Nate said. "Most days, anyway. What's this new problem?"

"You remember when I got the emergency blankets outta my pack? Well, I took a sec to check the battery on my radio."

"And?"

She pursed her lips. "It's dead as a hammer."

~*~

Leonard turned his rapidly improving social media skills toward learning more about Puck's Paradise Resort. What he found proved curious at first and then disturbing. The property was riddled with cartoonish versions of the tiny island people known as the Menehune.

The artists who worked for Puck Productions capitalized on many of the legends associated with the tiny race and portrayed them as clever, skilled, and in some cases, vengeful. Their efforts resulted in a feature length, animated film called "Warriors and Coconuts" in which the Menehune play a critical role. Though not a box office smash hit, the film attracted enough Puck Productions fans to generate demand for a sequel that was currently in development.

Because the company was well known for keeping a tight lid on employee remarks concerning Puck protocols and politics, Leonard doubted he'd be able to dig up anything of value through scuttlebutt. Social media proved him wrong.

Rummaging around in the same chat room that yielded the hint about the Puck airship flying to Wyoming, Leonard became aware of the Puck company's failure to find suitable candidates to play the roles of Menehune hosts—and pranksters—at the posh new resort on Kauai.

And suddenly Leonard realized what the company had in mind for the little people of the Cloud Peak Wilderness. It would begin with a form of slavery, he imagined, and end in disease and death.

He simply couldn't let such an atrocity happen.

~*~

Smoke had no idea how long it might take for Winter Woman's powder to put the giant down. However long that was, it couldn't happen fast enough to suit her, not that she had any choice.

The giant spent little time cleaning up the spill, and all the while he kept up a steady stream of grunts and words which Smoke assumed were not allowed in polite company. Eventually the brute straightened up, threw the wet rag and the empty bottle into a container already full of cast-off material and stalked to a cabinet at the back of the room.

After briefly rummaging around in it, he growled, "That was my last damn bottle of tequila! Dadgum it, and I need a drink. Hell, I've earned myself a drink."

Smoke had no idea what his words meant, but it was abundantly clear the giant wasn't happy. She prayed he hadn't forgotten about his food, especially after she went to all the trouble to add the special spice.

The big brute turned to Mato and shook a fist at him. "This is all yer fault, ya little shit. I don't know how the hell you did it, but that damn bottle didn't fall over on its own."

Mato responded with a stream of urine Smoke could smell from across the room. It amused her so much she had to cover her mouth with her hands to keep from making any noise.

The giant kicked Mato's cage, then slumped into a chair behind the desk and dug into the beans as if he hadn't eaten in days.

Smoke looked up toward the ceiling and silently thanked the Spirits for their aid.

In no time at all the giant emptied the can and tossed it alongside the rag and the empty bottle. He stood up and resolutely approached the peg on which his coat and hat were hung.

He squinted at his watch, belched or grunted—Smoke wasn't quite sure which—and said, "You just sit tight, my friend. I kin git another bottle if the roads ain't too bad. And when I git back, you and me are gonna have us a little chat. About gold. You can count on that."

He then jammed his hat on his head and hurried out into the weather, securing the door behind him.

Smoke wasn't about to leave her hiding place until she was certain the giant had actually gone away. Where he went didn't matter in the least. She stayed put until Mato called out to her.

"You have done a good job of making him mad," he said. "I hope you are happy."

Smoke slithered out from under the desk and brushed dirt and clots of dust and cobwebs from her clothes. "Oh, I am happy. Very happy. Did you see him eat all his food?"

"It is not something I cared to watch. Why? What did you put in it? The sleeping paste? That only works if it goes in the blood. It is why—"

"I am not stupid," she said. "I know how it works, and I know how to make it. Do you?"

"Of course not," Mato replied. "Only females can make it."

Smoke shook her head. "Only females know how."

Mato had his arms crossed and a look of exasperation plastered on his face. "So, what do you think you have accomplished?"

"So many questions, and yet you do not wait for answers."

"I am waiting now," he said.

"I used a powder given to me by Winter Woman. She said it would ease the pain in my leg. But she also said if I used too much I would go to sleep and never wake up."

Mato nodded. "I have heard of it, but I doubt you know how it is made. Winter Woman keeps that a secret from nearly all the People. She shares her knowledge with Reyna and maybe a few others. You are not old enough, or wise enough, to have the clan leader's trust."

222

"And yet, here I am, alone. While all the rest merely wonder where you are."

"That is unfortunate," Mato said. "But it is something we cannot change. I thank you for trying to help me."

"When we get home—"

"*If* we get home," he said.

"*When* we get home, be sure to ask Stone Fist why he did not try to help."

Mato stared at her in surprise. "He knew I had been trapped?"

"Oh, yes. And he had a good laugh over it, just before he walked away and left you behind."

Chapter Twelve

"Freedom is the oxygen of the soul." —Moshe Dayan

Tori waited all night for a call from Nate, but her phone never rang. It would not have awakened her in any event; she hardly slept. She assumed the sun had come up because the world outside her windows became somewhat visible through the heavy snowfall. She figured Cal would be up soon, if he wasn't already, and called him.

"Cal? Hi, it's Tori. I hope I didn't wake you."

"Nah. I was just fixin' myself a cup of joe."

Tori ignored the image of Cal dumping one spoonful of sugar after another into the blond brew he called coffee. "I still can't reach Nate. I've left messages, but he hasn't called me back. Have you heard anything?"

"Nope, and it's starting to worry me. Maggie and Nate went looking for some yahoos they think are stuck up in the wilderness area. Evidently, they weren't smart enough to get out before the snowstorm hit. The ranger station's been trying to reach Maggie by radio, but she hasn't responded."

Tori's pulse doubled. "You don't think—"

"Right now, I'm not thinkin' much of anything, sweetheart. I keep tellin' myself Maggie is a big girl, and she knows how to take care of herself. And she's partnered up with Nate. If she needed someone to look after her, he'd probably be the best man for the job."

"I know that," Tori said. "It's just— I can't help thinking something terrible has happened. Y'know?"

"All I really know is that thinkin' stuff like that isn't gonna do anyone a darn bit of good. You'd be better off figuring out how we might be able to get up to the Peak and look for 'em."

"It's still snowing like crazy."

"I 'spect it's a heap worse up in the mountains," Cal said.

"That's a happy thought."

"The roads are a mess. And it'll take a while to plow 'em once the snow lets up, and you know the major routes take priority. It'll be a good long while before they get out your way. If you don't have a snowmobile, you aren't likely to go anywhere."

"I do have one," Tori said. "But it's old and slow."

Cal chuckled. "Kinda like me?"

"Oh, stop. You aren't old."

"You must not have seen me the last time Shadow knocked me on my butt."

Tori recalled the incident all too well. "He didn't mean you any harm!"

"I know that, but my ribs didn't. I couldn't lie on my left side for a couple weeks."

"I would've paid for you to see a chiropractor." Tori said.

"You know how I feel about doctors, and anyway I'm fine now. So, tell me about this snowmobile of yours. I had no idea you were a hotshot rider."

"I'm not," Tori said. "Nate calls my ride a 'sledneck.' I mostly just use it to get to my mailbox when the driveway is—"

Cal started laughing at the word "driveway."

"What's so funny?" she asked, already knowing the answer. "It's way better than it was. Nate had somebody come out with one of those mini-bulldozers and grade it. There are still some big old boulders here and there, but at least they've been pushed to the side. The UPS delivery truck still won't drive down all the way, but cars can get in and out a lot better than before."

"Nate told me about that. Said he had to do something, or he'd have to carry his building supplies in with a wheelbarrow."

"True. Anyway, as for the 'snowmo,' I don't use it much. It can be hard to crank. Nate's is newer. You aren't a rider, are you?"

"Darlin', I've ridden pretty much anything and everything out here. Doesn't much matter how many wheels it has, or legs, for that matter."

Tori laughed. "I'm tryin' to picture you in racing gear."

"Don't bother. I'm not that good, but I enjoy riding. Sadly, it wouldn't do us any good in the Cloud Peak. Snowmobiles aren't allowed up there."

"Yeah, I know."

There was an uncomfortably long silence which Tori eventually broke. "What're we gonna do?"

"We're going to wait," Cal said. "You and Shadow are welcome to stay here with me if you want. I can come get you when the snowstorm passes, provided you can make it out to the road. We can chain your snowmobile to the mailbox."

"Thanks, Cal. I'd like that. It can get lonely out here."

"No problem. I've just got one question."

"Shoot."

"How did you train Shadow to ride double on the sledneck?"

~*~

Mato strained to bend the metal bars of his cage but made little progress. The girl, who insisted on being called Smoke, tried to help as well. The bars would not yield. Neither would the lock, despite Smoke's efforts to pull it apart.

Mato poked his finger at the device. "The giant has the piece of metal that will open this. I saw him put it in his clothing."

"He has been gone a long time," Smoke said. "I think he must be dead."

Mato had his doubts. "Or maybe he is just sleeping somewhere else. I do not believe he lives here."

"Why not?"

"Because there is no bed. There is no kitchen. Giants always keep food nearby. They do not have to hunt for it every day."

Smoke seemed impressed. "Does their food not spoil?" She sniffed the air in the room.

"They have boxes which stay cold," Mato said. "The giants call them 'freh-gez.'"

"Freh-gez," Smoke said, testing the new word.

"It means 'keeps things cold.' They have many such words."

"And you know them all?"

Mato snorted. "I know some, but I lived among the giants for only a short time. I learned enough to talk to them. That's all."

"I wish I could talk to them," she said. "I would tell them to go away and leave us alone."

"I would rather learn from them. They have many things the People could use. One of the giants I know will give us some of these things."

Smoke crossed her arms. "I would rather take what I want from them. I do not wish to accept gifts from those who would kill us."

"Not all giants are bad," Mato said. "I believe most are good. They do not want to hurt the People. But very few know we exist. I was on my way to deliver a message from one of them I trust. She wants the elders to come and visit. She promises to share many wondrous things."

The girl appeared unconvinced. "How do you know it is not a trick? How do you know they will not kill all our leaders at once?"

"Because I know them well. And do not forget, Winter Woman and Reyna, among others, have known a giant who showed she could be trusted. She saved Reyna's life."

"I have heard such stories," Smoke said. "But the old ones tell tales of the trickster, too. I do not believe those accounts either."

~*~

"D'ya think it's stopped snowing yet?"

229

Chuck asked.

Nate shrugged. "Hard to say without a window handy. You feel like diggin' one?"

"Cops aren't s'posed to be cute," Buddy said. "And yet here we have a real live stand-up comedian. Must be our lucky day."

Nate tapped the face of his watch. "Goodness gracious; you made it almost a whole hour without saying something to piss me off. Congratulations."

Buddy looked at Maggie. "I'm hungry."

"We need to stretch what we have," she said. "I don't know how long we'll have to stay in here."

Chuck threw off his Mylar blanket. "How 'bout I crawl back out and look around? See if we can start going down."

"Finally," Buddy said, "someone's doing something useful."

"I'll go with you," Nate said, glaring at Chuck's big-mouth brother. "I could use a little fresh air."

He turned to Maggie and asked, "Do I need to collect any snow? How're we doing on drinking water?"

"We're low on that, too. We've got two empty canteens. If you can pack 'em with snow, we'll get a few swallows each out of it when it melts."

Nate handed a canteen to Chuck. "Hang onto this, okay? And follow me."

As they approached the low, narrow passage, Chuck tapped Nate's leg to get his attention. In a low voice, he said, "Don't pay much attention to Buddy. I know he kinda runs his mouth without thinkin' sometimes, but he doesn't mean to be... You know."

"A jerk?"

"Yeah."

"Just between you and me, I'd love to be around when he runs into someone who doesn't take his opinions as kindly as I do. My guess is he'd get laid out flat and pronto. In fact, I'd be surprised to hear it hasn't already happened."

"Not yet, that I know of," Chuck said. "He's a pretty big guy."

Nate grimaced. "He's young; there's plenty of time for him to meet the wrong man. Be sure to get some photos in case I'm not there."

He crawled through the passage with his flashlight illuminating the narrow channel they'd traversed the previous day. When he reached the end, he gingerly felt through the snow that had drifted inside. Beyond that, a wall of snow blocked the passage. Nate stuck a gloved hand into it and felt little resistance. He was able to compress it to both sides and create a channel which he widened still further.

The snow felt light but not quite feathery, and he continued to push and pack it. Eventually he created a tunnel to the outside. Resting on his knees, he stuck his head above the thick white layer into the open. He had hoped bright sunshine would greet him. Instead, the sky remained dark and grey, and the snow fell even harder than it had the day before.

There seemed to be no sounds except the wind and no smells other than those from his own body. Everything was cloaked in a thick layer that should have been white. In the presence of minimal sunlight, the world appeared as a study in grey.

Nate dropped down and wriggled his way back into the cavern.

"How's it look?" Chuck asked.

"Go see for yourself."

The younger man dutifully followed suit only to return a minute or two later with a scowl on his face. "We aren't gettin' outta here today, are we?"

~*~

Stone Fist stared at Reyna. "You are being foolish."

"Because I do not want to be with you? That does not sound foolish to me." Reyna tried to step away from him, but he blocked her path. "Have you nothing better to do than bother me?"

"It is no bother for me. And it makes perfect sense. I am the strongest member of the clan, the best hunter, and the most—"

"Annoying," Reyna said, finishing his sentence. "Leave me alone."

"A joining makes sense," he continued. "You are the most desirable female; I am the most desirable male. We should be together. Our children—"

"Stop! Go away. I already have a mate, and if you keep pestering me, I will have him remove your bones and offer them to the Spirits."

Stone fist only laughed.

"You will not be laughing when Mato returns."

"Now you really are being foolish," he said. "What makes you think Mato will ever return?"

Reyna stared directly at him. "He always does."

Though he longed to tell her Mato had fallen prey to a giant, he kept the information to himself. He could be patient. When Mato failed to return, she would have no choice but to seek the shelter of his arms and the warmth of his firepit.

"You are very close to Winter Woman."

She looked at him quizzically. "So?"

"You think the leadership of the clan will fall to you someday."

"That is her wish, not mine. I do not think it is a good idea. There must be someone better."

"Oh," he assured her. "There is." He stood straighter, the better for her to see his physique. "The People have already begun to move away from her."

"Because of your stupid words at the Elder's fire?"

"Because she leads us to disaster. The giants come in greater numbers than ever before, and she does nothing. The People starve, yet she tells us to stay hidden. 'Hunting can wait until the giants are gone,' she says. But that makes no sense. We need food now."

"I have things to do," Reyna said. "Go away. And take your foolish speeches somewhere else. I have no ears for them."

"You may think differently when I lead the clan," Stone Fist said, his voice low and menacing.

Reyna glared at him. "If that day comes, my child and I will go to Mato, wherever he is."

Stone Fist slowly shook his head from side to side. "Do that, and it will be the last mistake you ever make."

~*~

Leonard put significant effort into recruitment of like-minded people to aid him in defeating the Puck raid on the little ones. Since he began his plans to link his future with that of the

Cloud Peak's primitive tribe, he had ignored most of his university classes. His visits to his advisor's office had become a thing of the past. He no longer cared about his thesis or a graduate degree. He had an entirely new goal: saving the little people.

His Little Lives Matter slogan had attracted only a few dedicated respondents. Unfortunately, none of them lived nearby. The closest were hours away by car, and some lived on the coasts.

As the clock ticked inexorably closer to the day when the great Puck airship would descend on the little people's domain, Leonard grew increasingly fearful that he would have to face the corporate foe single-handed. With images of David and Goliath haunting his thoughts, he pressed harder in his recruiting efforts.

He had no idea how he might divert the airship, or failing that, how he might destroy it without being caught and prosecuted. The fact that he had no assets the Puck legal team might wish to claim gave him little comfort. What mattered, he kept telling himself—the *only* thing that mattered—were the little folk. That Puck Productions would cast them as literal pawns in their diabolical race to accumulate wealth struck him as despicable.

That idea became the basis for his recruiting efforts. He told prospective followers that the massive entertainment company was hiding behind the face of its most famous animated character. And yet, wasn't Puck the very essence of a trickster? Why shouldn't the entire enterprise be suspected of similar treacherous dealings?

Though he couldn't point to anything specific Puck Productions had done that might corroborate his corporate greed theory, he relied on tales of other misdeeds—oil spills, stock manipulation, fraudulent emissions test results, and the failure to protect credit information for millions of Americans, among other transgressions. Why, he asked, should Puck be treated any differently than the other commercial crooks?

Over time, he pulled together a cadre of supporters he called Pilcher's People, for lack of a catchier name. Their level of commitment and their suggestions for dealing with the airship challenge were wide ranging and imaginative. If they had one thing in common, it was their claim to membership in the brotherhood of social justice warriors, though they were tired of being lost in the crowd. They all desired to be big fish in a small but critically important pond.

Rather than choose a method on his own, Leonard promised his gang—all five of them—that he would give them the opportunity to vote on how they would proceed. In exchange, they all promised to do whatever was necessary to join him on the field of battle.

~*~

At the insistence of her boss, the relentless

Timothy Archer, Randi Rhoades reviewed the status reports on all the projects she'd launched in order to fulfill Archer's desire to lure the little people to his ridiculously expensive Hawaiian resort. Projects bearing Archer's imprimatur were routinely pushed to the front of everyone's schedule. Work that would normally have taken years was concluded in months. The same sort of speed boost went into the airship refit, the construction of housing, and the delivery of clothing for Archer's "guests."

Archer himself pulled off the biggest coup by obtaining permission from a senior bureaucrat in the National Parks Service to briefly land *Puck Two* in the Cloud Peak Wilderness, something Randi could never have accomplished.

The airship was currently somewhere over the Pacific Ocean, chugging along at roughly the speed of traffic on an Interstate highway. The housing units would take a bit longer to complete than originally planned. Archer wasn't happy to hear that one-time suppliers could not be coerced into working faster as easily as employees.

Randi tried to sweet talk the makers of the furnishings destined for the Mato-sized buildings but made little headway. Archer solved the problem by offering to pay a bonus for early deliveries. She suspected he also threatened to withhold payment for late ones, not that he'd get away with it. The courts would back the suppliers, but Archer could make it a long and tedious process.

Why stories of such dealings never made it into the press had puzzled her once. Over time she realized just how far Archer's reach extended into the world of media, and not just for entertainment. He knew which buttons to press when it came to news reporting as well. Someone once confided to her over a few too many drinks, that it would be very unwise to "fuck with Puck." She believed it.

According to Timothy Archer, the bottom line had no emotions. Projects were either completed or not; profits were either made or lost; and people were merely a part of the process, as interchangeable as nuts and bolts.

The buildings would soon be on the road, fully furnished. The clothing Randi had ordered from the various Puck retail locations would likewise be delivered on time. Finally, she'd been able to contract two food trucks to provide meals and treats.

All she needed now was a way to convince Mother Nature to quit dumping snow on the entire enterprise.

~*~

Smoke couldn't fathom how Mato remained so calm. If she had been the one locked in a cage, she would likely have driven herself mad trying to escape. The powder she put in the giant's food should have at least put him to sleep. The longer he stayed gone, the more her hopes rose that the powder had killed him. Despite this, they expected the giant to return at any moment.

It required a nearly monumental effort, but with Mato's directions, Smoke managed to open the door on the front of the metal box which kept the room warm. She dutifully loaded wood into it. She wished she had the strength to drag Mato's cage closer to the fire. He told her he was warm enough, but she knew he was lying. Mato called the giant's home a "kah-bin," and he coached her until she could pronounce it with ease. He then insisted she learn still more words.

"Why must I learn the giants' tongue?" she asked.

"Because you may need to ask for their help."

"Bah! Just teach me how to say 'Go away!'"

Mato shook his head. "You are not stupid. Look where we are. We are both trapped. We have no food, and there is little wood left for the fire. When that is gone...."

She didn't need him to finish the thought. Freezing air from outside leaked through the kah-bin walls. It would not take long for them to freeze to death. With that thought in mind, she rummaged through the gear piled around the room.

At long last she found some heavy cloth in which she could wrap herself and stay warm. She shouted about her discovery to Mato who watched her with eyes devoid of hope.

"Look," she said, "there are two of them!"

"And all we have to do is open the cage so I can use one," he said.

She wagged a finger at him, as if admonishing a child. "Do not give up so easily."

He continued to watch as she twisted a corner of the cloth and jammed it through the largest opening in the cage. "Now, pull from the inside as I continue to twist."

"This will take forever," Mato said.

Smoke grinned. "Have you anything else to do?"

They both knew it would be a long, cold night.

~*~

Maggie's efforts to stretch their supplies earned equal amounts of Nate's gratitude and Buddy's disdain. The injured hiker rarely spoke, but when he did, the gist of his remarks were routinely negative. In addition to the pain in his ankle, he was cold, hungry, and bored. Nate refrained from offering to put an end to his suffering by shooting him in the head, but the idea's appeal grew with each of Buddy's complaints

Working from the light of a feeble fire,

Maggie broke out the last of their rations, the final MRE Nate had previously wanted to leave behind. As they neared the end of their third day in the cave, his attitude about the prepackaged meals had changed drastically. Even though the day before it had to be split four ways, the hot, Mexican-style meal had seemed like a dream fulfilled.

The remaining MRE would also have to be shared. When Maggie delivered a portion to Buddy, his response remained true to form. "Where's the meat?"

Nate's patience had disappeared along with their rations and their firewood. "It's a vegetarian meal, dumb ass," he said.

"*Vegetarian?* Are you shitting me?" the injured hiker asked.

Nate aimed the phoniest of smiles at him. "Have you heard the one about beggars and choosers?

"Screw you."

"Your gratitude is overwhelming," Nate said. "But if you really don't want it, we can save it in case we have to spend another day or two in here."

Buddy's scowl seemed overly dramatic, but he tore into the meat-free offering and chewed as if to spite the lawman.

"Thanks for not killing him," Maggie said.

Nate exhaled as if he'd been holding his

breath. "There's still plenty of time."

He took a bite of his own portion of the MRE and chewed. "You're right. It's really not too bad."

"And it's hot. That's worth something," she said. She leaned closer and added, "I've got the chemical heating element from the MRE under my Mylar blanket."

Nate smiled. "Is it helping?"

"Definitely. Give me another minute, and I'll let you use it."

"That's okay. I'm really not all that cold."

"You big liar. You don't need to be all macho with me, Nate. Take the damn thing." She pushed the still hot paper container toward him, and he slipped it under his own thin, reflective blanket.

He thanked her and soon felt the delicious warmth spread. It wasn't much, and it wouldn't last long, but it helped at a time when their situation had gone from grim to desperate. "We're down to one flashlight that still works, no food, and little more than wrappers from the MRE to add to the fire." He glanced at the few remaining embers. "We've gotta get out of here."

Maggie checked her watch. "We should at least wait 'til first light. It's going to be bad enough trudging through deep snow. We sure as hell don't want to do it in the dark."

"I guess you're right," said Nate, his voice resigned. "We don't even know if it's still snowing."

With a knowing nod, she said, "We'll find that out in the morning, too."

"What'll we do with Prince Charming?" Nate asked. "I don't suppose we can leave him behind."

"Probably not. Somebody would miss him."

"Seriously? Who?"

"Okay," she said, then giggled. "We could always go the Donner Party route."

"And eat him?"

"Sure!"

Nate looked again at their dying fire. "How long d'you suppose we'd have to roast him?"

"A good, long while," she said, still smiling. "I've heard people taste like pork."

"Seriously?"

"I dunno, it's what I've heard. I don't recall seeing human on the menu anywhere."

Nate chuckled. "Are you suggesting Buddy's actually human?"

"Of course not," she said. "I don't know what I was thinking."

Nate returned the heating element which had lost a good deal of its warmth. "Take advantage of what's left. It's gonna get a lot colder in here."

"We could snuggle," she said. "That might

help."

"I'm game, as long as we don't mention it to Tori."

Maggie slid close to him, with her back to his front and got settled under the thin sheet of Mylar. "If it keeps us alive, she won't care."

"You sure?" he said as he wrapped an arm around her.

"Oh, hell no."

Chapter Thirteen

"Extinction is the rule. Survival is the exception."
—Carl Sagan

Leonard stared at the people on his screen. Five of the six who had pledged their active and involved support stared back at him from computers in their homes. As a security measure, they had all agreed not to use their last names. Leonard's, of course, was known to all of them, but his was the only surname revealed.

The online meeting had just begun, and the questions from his allies were not surprising.

Paulie, a bald, heavyset accountant from somewhere in Idaho, spoke first. "How the hell are we supposed to keep a blimp from taking off? Shoot it?" Paulie's heavy jowls shook when he spoke. If he hadn't had ears, Leonard thought, his head would have been perfectly round.

"Absolutely not," said Hazel, a retired hair stylist from Cheyenne. "I don't hold with guns. This ain't the Wild West anymore."

It wasn't, mused Leonard, but Hazel appeared old enough to have lived through it.

"It's just a big gas bag, right? Like a birthday balloon, only, you know, much bigger." The comment issued from a heavily whiskered follower who called himself Blue. Leonard wasn't sure where he lived and didn't care since the burly, bearded man swore he'd get himself to Wyoming when the time came, no doubt riding a monster truck or a big Harley. Leonard inquired no further.

"It's actually a dirigible," Leonard said. "Not a blimp. According to what I've read, it has a rigid frame which houses a bunch of temperature-controlled helium cells. Even though each of the cells is quite large, the ship could still fly if one or two were somehow deflated."

"One or two?" Paulie sounded surprised. "We could get 'em all with a decent little .38 automatic. Pop, pop, pop, and it's done. Dead blimp."

"Airship," Leonard said. If they were ever going to present themselves as dedicated professionals—compensation would come later, if at all—then they needed to use the proper terminology.

"Are you deaf?" queried Hazel. "I said no guns!"

Yuvi, a man with olive skin, dark eyes, and a

British accent piped up, "Pardon me, Mum, but are you the guv'nuh now? I thought it was Lennie."

"It is, and I am," Leonard said. "But please don't call me Lennie."

"Why not?" Paulie asked. "I think it's kinda cute."

"Leave him alone, you animal," Hazel said, her eyes aimed overhead. "Gun lovers. God help us."

"Listen, lady," Paulie began. "If you think—"

"Hang on, everyone," Leonard yelped, hoping to de-escalate things before people dropped out of the coalition. "Let's focus on the big picture, okay? On the things that matter. Most importantly, we all agree that no rich corporation has the right to grab someone, no matter what size they are. But," he paused dramatically, "the smallest of people are now facing the greatest risk."

There were muttered words of agreement from all concerned.

"One big question remains," said the last member of the group, a thirty-something female with short-cropped blonde hair, named Annette. She sported a number of tattoos and a surprising collection of piercings, mostly in her ears. "We still don't know how to ground a blimp, or a dirigible, or whatever the hell it is."

"Are they flammable?" Paulie asked. "Maybe

we could firebomb it."

"Oh, that's a lovely idea," opined Hazel, operating in full snark. "Instead of taking a chance on shooting someone inside the blimp, we'll simply burn them all to death. It's brilliant."

"Look, lady," Paulie growled, "you're not the only one standing on moral high ground. This is a mission to *save* lives. But I'm talking about the lives of the little ones, not the asshats trying to enslave them."

"An excellent point," said Yuvi. "Bravo."

"It is a good point," echoed Leonard. "And we need to keep that thought uppermost in mind."

"And yet," muttered Annette, "we still don't know what we're gonna do."

"We could we ram it with a lorry," suggested Yuvi. "A truck of some kind, or better yet, some sort of Earth mover."

"Do we even know where it's gonna land?" Blue asked. "Those things don't need roads, y'know. They just need space. A whole lotta space. They could land way out in the boondocks, places where trucks couldn't go."

"If I may," Yuvi said, "a bit of history might help. I'm sure you've all heard of the Bengal Lancers. There's a very good reason why they were called that."

"'Cause they hunted Bengal tigers?" Paulie asked, unable to hide his sarcasm.

"Because, my friend, they carried lances. Vicious weapons in the hands of skilled warriors. They made quick work of any infantry which stood against them."

Blue made a face. "Yeah, right up until somebody gave the infantry guns."

"Here we go again," muttered Hazel.

Leonard picked up the thread. "Lances. Long poles with sharp points. Like spears, right?"

"Correct," said Yuvi. "Only a good bit longer. If a lancer impaled an infantryman, it made it astonishingly difficult for the poor bugger to retaliate."

"How'd they get the lances outta the guys on the ground?" Paulie asked.

"That's an excellent question." Yuvi twisted his lips. "Alas, I haven't got an answer."

"It doesn't matter," interjected Leonard. "Lances might just do the trick. We can stab the gas bags right through the outer covering. Nobody has to die."

"But," said Hazel, "we'd be standing right there when all the gas comes spewing out. That wouldn't be safe, would it?"

"It's just helium," Blue said. "It might make our voices squeaky for a while, but that's all."

"We'll sound like a squad of rabid chipmunks," Annette said. "That'll strike fear in

249

their hearts."

Leonard let them chatter, and there was considerable discussion of the lance idea, but no one seemed adamantly opposed to it.

"I think our best bet," Leonard said when the conversation had gone on long enough, "is to let the idea percolate. Let's take some time to think about all this. We can meet online again tomorrow and work out the details."

Once again, several people spoke at once, but all Leonard could think about was the name they could adopt. "Leonard's Lancers" had a nice ring to it.

~*~

"We will never get out of here," Smoke said. "I want to go home."

"I do, too," said Mato. "I have things to tell the People."

The girl hesitated for a moment, then said, "You know they all think you are lying."

Mato couldn't help but frown; she'd hit his sore spot. "Do *you* believe that? And if so, tell me why I would make up such stories."

"To impress the People? If not that, then I— I do not know."

"Before the giant trapped me, I was on my way home. I had something in my carrybag to show Winter Woman and the other elders. But now, everything I had is gone."

Smoke had an odd look on her face. "Was it something very thin with bright colors on it?"

"Yes!" Mato said. "Did you see it? Did the giant take it?"

"No," she said. "I have it. I planned to look at it later to see if I could make sense of it."

Mato gripped the metal bars of his cage. "Get it, and I will explain."

He watched as the girl rummaged in her own belongings and extracted the colorful folder Randi had given him. "That's it! Bring it closer."

Smoke unfolded the pamphlet to reveal a full-page view of the fabulous Puck Paradise Resort.

"That is where I was!" Mato exclaimed. "I lived with the giants there. And I discovered there are others, just like us, who live there, too."

"Others? Like the People?"

"Yes! Their language is not the same as ours, but it is very close. I could speak with them."

Smoke eyed him warily. "And this?" she asked, pointing to an image on the back of the printed sheet.

"That is the bah-limp!" Mato said, his despair lifted, if only for a moment. "I have been inside it. I made it fly."

"Oh, Mato," she said. "You are doing it again."

"What?"

"Lying. We are not big enough to make such things move." She tapped the photo with her finger. "It is nearly as big as the mountains around it!"

Mato laughed. "It is big. It is the biggest thing in the world, but I am not lying." He crossed his arms. "I can prove it."

"How?"

"By having the bah-limp brought here so the People can ride in it, too."

"Here?" Smoke looked around, confused.

"Not to this place," Mato said. "To the mountains. To the home of the People."

The girl put her face in her hands and groaned. "Mato," she said without looking up, "we are stuck here. We will never get home."

Suddenly Mato remembered the other thing the redheaded giant had given him. "Did you find anything else in my carrybag?"

"Only some stupid giant tool," she said. "I do not know what they use it for."

"Do you still have it?"

She squinted at him. "Why? Is it dangerous? It looks nothing like the thing that exploded when I picked it up."

"It is called a flip-fon," he said. "It means 'talk thing' in the language of the giants. I can call Nate to come and get us."

"Who is Nate?"

"My friend."

"No one among the People has such a strange name."

"He is a giant."

"But—"

"Get it," he said, his patience gone. "Now!"

Smoke dove back into her bag, brought out the device, and held it next to the cage. It wasn't small enough to pass through the bars.

Exasperated, but unwilling to give up, Mato told Smoke to listen carefully and follow his instructions. He had her open the device, locate a button on the side, and press it. The tiny screen lit up, and the device gave off a loud beep. The noise startled the girl, who dropped it and scampered backwards like a squirrel retreating from a thrown stone.

"It cannot hurt you," Mato told her, though she appeared far from convinced. He smiled as he urged her to pick it up and bring it close to him.

"It will make more sounds," he warned. "It is a tool the giants use to talk to each other across great distances."

"We can shout," Smoke said, "but from in

here, no one will hear us."

"Giants have no such problems. Look closely. Do you see any faces?"

"Yes," she said. "Two. One with a hat, and one with red hair." She looked wistful. "She is beautiful."

"I know. She is also a friend. Now, press the picture of the male giant with your finger and wait until you hear a voice. Ignore the other sounds."

"A voice?" Smoke appeared stricken.

"Yes. That will be Nate. When he answers, hold the phone near the cage so I can talk to him."

Smoke stared down at the device in her hands and marveled at it, but she did as he asked. They heard a ringing sound repeated several times before a voice broke through.

"This is Deputy Sherriff Nathan Sheffield. I'm not available right now, but if you'll leave a detailed message at the beep, I'll get back to you. If this is an emergency, dial nine-one-one."

Shortly after that, the phone gave out a sharp, chirping sound, then went silent. Eventually, it switched to an annoying hum. Mato told Smoke to fold it up again, hoping that would end the noise.

It did.

Nate's instructions had come too fast, and Mato didn't understand them. He did not know how to leave a message and had no clue what a "bee-puh" was or where it might be. At Tori's, probably. Sadly, he wouldn't be going there any time soon. He wouldn't be going anywhere.

"I think we will die here," Smoke said. "We have no food; the fire is almost gone, and the cold slips in through cracks in the walls. We are doomed."

"Be quiet," Mato snapped, more forcefully than he'd intended. "We must try again. Open the talk thing."

"But—"

"Just do it. Push on the face of the redheaded woman."

As before, the talk thing made a ringing noise, but this time when it ended, they heard a woman's voice. Mato recognized it as Randi's.

"Hello?" she said. "Mato? Is that really you? How are you?"

"Mato cold," he said.

"Oh, you poor thing! I'm surprised the phone works way up there in the mountains."

"No mountains. Cabin. Cage."

"What? I don't understand."

"Smoke and Mato. No get out."

There was a brief silence, then Randi's voice returned. "Don't worry. I'll take care of this."

Her voice then went away and was replaced by the annoying hum they heard before.

Not wanting to discourage Smoke, Mato smiled and told her to refold the talk thing. "Everything will be all right," he said. But even if Randi could find them, he doubted she would arrive before they froze to death.

~*~

"Tori? This is Randi. I can't reach Nate. He doesn't answer his phone."

"I know, I know. And it's killing me," Tori said. She looked out a window to check on the weather for what likely would be the millionth time. "Oh, my Lord."

"What is it?" Randi sounded worried.

"The snow stopped. I can see some sunlight and a little slice of blue sky. The storm's over. I've gotta go."

"Wait!" Randi yelped. "Don't hang up. Mato's in trouble."

Tori shook her head and squinted at the phone. "Mato's up in the Cloud Peak with his clan. How do you know he's in trouble?"

"'Cause I just spoke to him a few minutes ago. Remember that flip phone I gave him before he and Nate took off?"

"Yeah. I'm surprised he remembered how to use it."

"Well, I was a little worried about that, too, but we went over it a few times. He's no dummy."

"That's a fact," Tori said. "But what kinda trouble is he in?"

"He said he was trapped. He mentioned a cage, a cabin, and another word I didn't understand."

"That doesn't necessarily mean he's in trouble. Conversations with Mato can be... challenging."

"I'm all too aware of that, but it was his tone that gave him away," Randi said. "Anyway, I know exactly where he is. I installed a program that tracks the location of his cell phone. It's not a very sophisticated phone, but it's good enough to support that little program."

"Okay, so where is he?"

Randi gave her the address. It wasn't far from where Caleb and Maggie Jones lived in the unincorporated town of Charm, population very nearly nothing.

"Can you go find him?" Randi asked. "He said he was cold. He's not very big on adjectives."

"Or sentences longer than three or four words," Tori said, remembering the hours she'd spent laboring to teach him rudimentary English and checking, adding, or correcting entries in the translation list she kept. "I'd go there now, but I'm pretty much snowed in. I'll see if Cal can do something, and if all else fails, I'll call the sheriff's office. I'd rather not get them involved. At least, not yet. Oh, God, how I wish Nate were here!"

"I know you'll do what you can," Randi said. "And please call me when Mato is safe. I'm really worried about the little guy."

"I am too, but he's not the only one I'm worried about. We're pretty sure Nate is stuck somewhere up in the mountains. He and Maggie went looking for some hikers. That was several days ago, and we haven't heard from them since. Maggie has a park-issued radio, but she hasn't responded to calls on that or her cell phone."

"I had no idea. I'm so sorry."

"We haven't given up hope. Between them, Nate and Maggie are pretty darn smart when it comes to the out-of-doors. They're creative, almost in a sneaky sorta way."

"You make that sound like a bad thing," Randi said.

"It's not," Tori assured her. "Okay, let me get busy. I'll buzz you later with an update."

Tori wasted no time dialing Cal and sharing Randi's information.

"That sounds like the place ol' Jed Krantz uses for an office," Cal said. "He claims to be a mountain guide when he's not runnin' some other scam. The place is a real dump. It's a one-room cabin with a crapper out back. I think he keeps a horse or two somewhere out there as well."

"According to Randi, that's where Mato is. She thinks he might be locked up because he used the word 'cage.' Is there any way you can go check on him? It could be a while before I can get the sledneck running."

"He said *cage?* Great. This reminds me of our little trip to New York when we rescued his girlfriend." He let his breath out in a whoosh. "I'll bring bolt cutters and a hack saw," he said. "I'll head over there on my snowmobile. Most of the roads are still impassable. It's gonna be a long while before things get back to normal, whatever that is."

"What about this Krantz guy? What if he's hurt Mato?"

"Then I'll hurt Krantz. He's such a weasel, it won't take much more than a threat, and he'll fold like a cheap tent. But, just in case, I'll recruit a young fella I know. He's a nice kid, but he can look and act tough. His mom runs the restaurant here in Charm."

"Do what you think is best, Cal, but hurry. I'll join you as soon as I can."

~*~

Smoke had wrapped herself in whatever she could find that wouldn't hinder her movement around the room. She used smaller pieces of cloth to fill the spaces between the logs that made up the walls. Her supply of useable material had all but run out.

Between the two of them, they had forced enough of the blanket she found earlier into the cage with Mato. He had taken advantage of it, and could do little else but offer encouragement. She knew, however, that her efforts merely delayed their impending deaths.

She had plugged all of the largest breaks and several of the smaller ones when they heard the ominous sounds that could only come from machines of the giants. Smoke instantly quit her efforts to improve the walls and retreated to her hiding place. From there she looked at Mato, still trapped in the cruel cage, and very likely to die at the hands of whoever entered the building.

"Mato! You in there?" came a voice from outside.

"Yes, Cal!" he yelled back.

Smoke stared at him as if he had suddenly become a demon spirit. "You know that voice?" she whispered at him.

"Yes," he said from within his blanket. "It is the giant called Cal, but his spirit name is 'Kay-lehb.' We are friends. I saved his life, and now he owes me mine. It is only fair."

"And what about me?" she asked, unable to hide the fear in her voice.

"You?" He considered the question, then

said, "He will probably eat you."

Smoke let out a startled scream.

"Hush, girl," Mato said. "I made a joke, and now I see it was a bad one. Giants do it all the time. Forgive me. You will like Cal; he is an honorable giant. You have nothing to fear."

Those words did little to still her rapidly beating heart. Nor did the sounds coming from outside the cabin. The machine noises had stopped but were replaced with the sounds of something heavy hammering the door.

She watched as the heavy wood began to splinter under the assault and marveled at the strength needed to do such a thing. The People had no one strong enough, nor a tool heavy enough, to even attempt it.

Before long, the door gave way, breaking lengthwise down the center of a thick, wooden plank. Huge hands then grabbed the edges and yanked them aside. All the while, Mato huddled in his cage with a smile on his face.

Smoke thought her world would soon end, no matter what Mato said. She remained under the desk, the sound of her beating heart loud in her ears.

Two giants entered the cabin. One was much older than the other and wore a beard that covered his face and the front of his neck. It was the second, much younger giant, however, who captured her attention. Tall and lean, he stood with a massive hammer at his side, and she instinctively knew he had done the worst of the damage to the door.

His hair was much shorter than that of the males among the People, but it framed a face which was simultaneously ruggedly handsome yet sensitive. *If only he were a third as tall!*

She felt her heart shift to a different beat, one she had never before felt.

He pushed his knitted cap to the back of his head and looked around. "You were right, Mr. Jones. This place really is a dump." He pointed to one of the wads of cloth Smoke had stuffed into an opening. "Whoever uses this place is an idiot. He patched the holes with rags. They won't even last 'til the next storm."

Smoke, of course, couldn't understand a word he said and assumed he had been complimentary. She looked over at Mato and proudly tapped her thumb to her chest.

The older giant walked directly to Mato's cage and asked, "What the heck are you doin' in there, son?"

"Oh, my, God," said the younger giant when he got a look at Mato. "I didn't really believe you when you said we had to go rescue a little person. He's... gosh, I don't even know how to describe him. He's—"

"He's my *friend*," Cal said. "His name is Mato, and he's pretty danged smart. That's why I'm so surprised to see him stuck in there."

"You told me he saved your life once. But I can't imagine how."

The older giant shrugged. "I 'spect there'll come a time when I can tell you. But that time hasn't come yet. Now, help me get him outta there."

After a brief examination of the cage, he addressed Mato directly. "This here is Adam Franconi. He helps out in my store from time to time. Adam, say hello to Mato. I don't know if he has a last name. I never asked."

"Howdy, sir," the lad said. "We'll get you outta there as quick as we can." He turned and looked at the demolished door. "Now I kinda wish I hadn't torn up that door so bad. It's gettin' even colder in here."

"Don't give it a thought. We'll take Mato to my place, get him warmed up, and fed. He's tough. He'll be just fine."

The older giant gave the younger one a strange tool with two long handles that operated what appeared to be a sharp, metal beak, like that of a hawk or an eagle. He used it to chew through the device which she and Mato had failed to break. It snapped, he removed the pieces, and set Mato free.

Smoke listened to the conversation without

any idea what they were chatting about. It mattered little. She was content to listen to the younger giant's voice. It had a pleasant quality, and she wanted to hear more of it.

"Look," Mato said, pointing at Smoke's hiding place. "Smoke."

The younger giant didn't understand, and Mato repeated the girl's name twice more before changing it to a meaningless giant word.

"What?" said the giant named Adam. "I don't see any smoke."

Mato stepped close to the desk, knelt, and pointed at her. Smoke told herself to be brave, but she couldn't stop shaking.

The younger giant casually dropped to the floor and looked under the desk. "Well, I'll be dam— Oops, sorry Mr. Jones, I didn't—"

"What's down there?" Cal asked.

"It's a girl," the handsome young giant said. "She's real small, like Mr. Mato. And she's... well sir, she's really, really pretty."

Chapter Fourteen

*"Men just want women they can rescue. And I refuse to
be one of them."* —Koena Mitra

Nate crawled back into the cave after
clearing a new path to the outside. The snowstorm
had relented a great deal, but light, fluffy flakes
continued to fall. He figured it was as good a time
as any to begin their descent. Maggie had been
waiting for his report and gave a resigned nod to
his conclusion.

"How're we going to handle Mr. Happy?" he
asked. "Has he even tried to stand up?"

Maggie frowned. "Are you kidding? He
claims his ankle hurts when he breathes."

"What's his brother saying?"

"He's still covering for him," she said. "I
guess he thinks he's being loyal."

Nate surveyed the narrow passage leading
to the outside. "We dragged him in, so I reckon

we'll be able to drag him back out." He rubbed his jaw with a gloved hand, still wet from his efforts to clear snow from their exit. "If he can't stand up, how will we get him down the mountain? I wish we had a sled."

"We could make one," Maggie said. "Of sorts. We've got the Mylar blankets, and I have some nylon line in my backpack. We could string the rope through the grommets on a blanket and drag him."

"Those blankets don't look very strong," Nate said. "Wouldn't they just tear?"

"I don't know," she responded. "It was just a thought. I've never actually tried it. But maybe we could stack 'em and run the rope through two or three."

It was Nate's turn to frown. "Why not use all four?"

"Because we'll need to keep him wrapped up in one. We'll be generating heat by exercise; he won't."

"Exercise or hard labor?" Nate grunted. "I swear, if that moron complains one time while we're hauling his sorry butt down the mountain, I'll punch his lights out."

Maggie chuckled. "That's prob'ly not a great idea, Sherriff. You know he'd just sue you."

"I'm not worried," Nate said. "I know the world's best defense attorney. Met her in Hawaii. I don't think she's ever lost a case."

"Seriously?"

"I don't actually know her track record, but Princess Shaniqua is, without a doubt—"

"*Princess* Shaniqua?" Maggie cracked up. "There's a killer's name if I ever heard one."

"I wouldn't put killin' past her," Nate said. "When she was in college, a coach tried to recruit her to play on the line for the football team."

"No kidding?"

"That's what I heard. The other guys on the line threatened to quit the team if they let her play. Rumor had it they were afraid she'd show 'em up."

"Oh, my."

"So, yeah, she's a big girl, and she's as sharp as they come. A top trial lawyer."

"Okay then, if you think she can help you get away with it, feel free to lay ol' Buddy out cold. But please do it when I'm not looking. That way I won't have to testify."

They walked a little deeper into the cave where the floor leveled out. Had they slept any closer to the exit, they would have slid down an increasingly steep side slope. They had attempted to survey it with their flashlights when they first arrived, but the drop off ended beyond the beam of their lights.

"All right, gentlemen," Nate said, addressing

the brothers, "it's the moment you've been waiting for. We're leaving."

"It's about damned time," Buddy muttered.

Nate gave him the stink eye. "Listen, champ. Nobody in here would've stopped you if you'd tried to leave earlier. If anything, we'd have helped you pack."

"I still have a broken ankle, genius. How the hell would I walk down the mountain or even leave on my own?"

"Those are really good questions," Nate replied. "We're still workin' on 'em."

Buddy nudged his brother, Chuck. "I guess that means I've earned Deputy Dumbass's undying support."

"I wish you two would both shut up," Maggie said. "I don't need that much snark and whine in my life."

Neither of them responded.

"Now, here's what we're going to do." She explained her idea for turning three layers of Mylar into a surface on which they could drag Buddy out of the cave and down the mountain trail.

"I dunno about this," Buddy said. "If my ankle gets banged on the ground, it's going to hurt like hell."

"Most likely, yes," said Nate. "So, if I were you, I'd hold my foot off the ground. Of course, that would require you to make an effort on your own. But, you're free to do whatever you want. If you're gonna scream, however, try to knock it down a few decibels. We don't want to terrify the wildlife."

"Enough!" snapped Maggie. "Let's get started."

~*~

"Well?" Archer asked.

Randi knew exactly what he wanted to hear; he didn't need to preface his question. "We're mostly on target. *Puck Two* is set to arrive later today, and the delivery trucks with the little houses are somewhere between here and Vegas."

"Glad to hear it," he said. "Any potential problems? I'd hate to see this thing get screwed up when we're so close to the finish line."

"The only issue I can think of is the weather. We could've picked a better time of year to do this."

"Is that a criticism, Ms. Rhoades? I don't recall hearing you mention weather when we did the original planning."

As if *you* did any of the original planning, mused Randi. "I operated under the impression you didn't want to wait."

"Yes, well...."

"And since winter in Hawaii is no big deal, I thought you wanted to forge ahead."

"Whatever. So, how bad is it? Are the roads

open? Can *Puck Two* still land?"

"I don't know about the roads up around Ten Sleep," Randi said, "but *Puck Two's* pilot assured me they could operate in the winter."

"Ten *what?*"

Clearly, Randi thought, Archer had not kept up with project details. "That's where we'll take the little people. We'll pick them up in the mountains and fly them down to a spot near the town of Ten Sleep. We've made arrangements to house them on property owned by trusted contacts. You remember Nathan Sheffield, I'm sure. He ran security at the resort."

"Yes, yes. I remember. Got himself shot, and then that smart ass lawyer of his finagled a big settlement out of us. How could I forget a betrayal like that?"

"He almost died protecting the property," Randi said, struggling to keep her temper under control. "How is that 'betrayal?'"

"I was talking about the lawsuit. We paid for his care. That should've earned us some gratitude."

"I'm sure it did," she said.

Archer exhaled emphatically. "Well, I'm not." He paused briefly before going on. "Are there any decent hotels near Ten Schlep?"

"It's Ten *Sleep*. But I don't know about the accommodations there. I usually stay in Worland. Why?"

270

"Because I'd like to be there to greet the little guys. After all, if they're going to work for me, we ought to get to meet each other."

"You're aware, I'm sure, that only one of them speaks any English," Randi said, trying not to laugh, "and I wouldn't exactly call him fluent."

"Actions speak louder than words. Isn't that what they say?"

"Well, I suppose. But—"

"But nothing. I'll have my secretary set everything up. I may even ride in that insanely expensive blimp we bought."

"It's called an airship, sir," Randi said, trying not to sound too timid.

"I'll call it any damned thing I want!"

~*~

Mato remained wrapped in the cloth he and Smoke had worked through the bars of the cage. Cal and Adam had little trouble extracting it, and Adam had used a knife to slice it in half so Smoke could have some, too.

"If you think it's cold in here, just wait 'til we get on the machines outside," Cal said. "That's the bad news. The good news is we don't have too far to ride."

Mato urged Smoke to wrap herself in the material they offered, and to his surprise she didn't resist when Adam snugged it around her. She

271

smiled her thanks at him.

"I aim to please," he said, smiling back.

They left Krantz's cabin and approached two large machines the likes of which Mato had never seen before. He looked up at Cal in confusion.

"They're snowmobiles," he said. "You're going to ride with me." He swung his leg over the back of the device the way Mato had seen giants mount horses. There was no way he could duplicate the feat without a running start and a snow-free path.

"C'mon over here," Cal said. "I'll pick you up. You're gonna ride in front of me since you don't take up much room. Besides, you'll get some protection from the windshield, and you won't have to hang on as tight. I won't let you fall off."

Mato followed his instructions, and Cal lifted him up and settled him gently in place.

"Mato, what's happening?" Smoke asked, far less enthusiastic about the snowmobiles than she'd been about Adam wrapping her up for travel.

"Go with the younger one," he said. "Ride with him."

"Are they taking us *home?*" she asked, her voice anxious. "Did you tell them where the People live? They must never find out!"

"What are you two yackin' about?" Cal asked.

"Where we go?" Mato responded from his cloth cocoon.

"To my house," Cal said. "Tori will be there sooner or later. After that, we'll head up into the mountains. But first I aim to make sure you two are warm and have some food. How's that sound?"

Mato couldn't keep up with Cal's rapid-fire response, but he made out a few encouraging words. Two stood out: "Tori" and "food." He'd been around Cal enough to know he could be trusted.

"They will take care of us," Mato assured Smoke, "and another giant friend is coming. You will like her."

Smoke remained dubious. "Is she the one with red hair?"

"No. But with female giants, one never knows. They do many odd things with their hair and clothing." He gave her a resigned shrug. "Such things are mysteries."

Adam climbed on his machine and motioned for Smoke to join him.

"Go now, get on," Mato said. "I am hungry."

"And I am worried!"

Mato laughed. "After the way you looked at him?" He tilted his head toward Adam. "You are wasting time." He patted Cal's leg and said, "We go now."

A moment later he heard the engine of the

second machine and knew instinctively that Smoke and Adam were right behind them. The ride was cold and noisy, but fairly comfortable, and true to Cal's word, it didn't last very long. Mato kept his head covered to stay warm and peeked out, turtle-style, when they came to a halt. The machine's loud noises stopped as did the vibrations it made.

Mato expected to see one of the buildings giants typically lived in. Instead, they had stopped beside a vehicle all but covered in snow. Mato glanced at Smoke whose face reflected terror. She seemed to be struggling with the cloth in which she was swaddled.

He called out to her, "What is it? What are you afraid of?"

"The bad giant! He brought us here in that..." She pointed to the truck. "That *thing*."

"Just stay where you are," Cal said before addressing Mato. "Please tell your friend not to worry. I just want to see if there's anyone inside. We won't be here long."

Mato did as he asked, and Smoke appeared to relax. She slowly eased back into Adam's chest, and he wrapped his arms gently around her.

Cal got off his machine and left Mato sitting on it. He walked to the truck, wiped snow from the windshield, and peered inside. "It's Krantz," he said. "He's not looking so good."

"Is he alive?" Adam asked.

"I hope he's just sleeping." Cal banged on the windshield and then on the roof of cab. "But he's not moving." Cal stepped to the door and struggled to open it.

Adam started to dismount. "Can I help?"

"No," Cal said. "Stay there. I've got this."

Eventually he got the door open and leaned inside. Moments later he withdrew shaking his head.

"Is he—" Adam began.

"Frozen solid," Cal said. "God only knows how long he's been out here, the poor bugger."

Mato gleaned the essentials from their brief conversation and again called to Smoke. "The bad giant is dead."

"Good," she responded.

Cal pulled a flip-fon from his pocket. It looked similar to the one Mato had gotten from Randi. Cal used it to talk to someone, then slipped it back into his clothing.

"I'll call the animal control folks when we get to the house," Cal said. "Someone needs to check on his horses. He sure won't be feeding 'em."

Mato was pleased when they left the truck and the dead man behind. He felt no hint of remorse; Smoke's poison had obviously worked. The man's death could have been much worse, and would have been had it been left up to the little warrior.

The four of them resumed their journey, and only a short while later they halted in front of a house Mato had not visited before. Whenever he, and sometimes Reyna, had met with giants previously, it had been at Tori's cabin, somewhere in Hawaii, or on the road to a place where giants intended one of them harm. Cal's home, he assumed, would be safe.

Both he and Smoke were ushered quickly inside. A fireplace held a roaring blaze, and Cal set cushions on the floor in front of it for his two small guests. He then provided something hot to drink. The containers he served it in were a bit large but manageable, and the frothy, brown beverage was new to both Mato and Smoke. Tiny bits of something sweet and white floated in the thick, steaming liquid. They had an odd, soft texture but a pleasing taste.

Smoke licked a thin line of the creamy beverage from her upper lip. "What *is* this stuff?"

"The giants call it 'chauk-laht,'" he said. "But wait until you taste the stuff they call 'bay-kahn.'"

~*~

Despite having a cadre of followers he hoped he could count on, Leonard Pilcher continued to spend his time scouring social media sites for anything related to Puck Productions, little people, the Cloud Peak Wilderness, and either Mindians or Lilipindians, though he

276

despised both terms. He ran through the usual chatter, ignoring sarcastic remarks and the inevitable arguments between people he neither knew nor cared about.

He failed to find any recruits for the Lancers, but he did stumble across an anonymous and supposedly humorous post by someone who had to be connected to one of the top executives at the entertainment complex named after Puck, a character from Shakespeare's "A Midsummer Night's Dream." The aforenamed character, in cartoon style, appeared at the heart of the company's all-too-familiar logo.

Leonard frowned immediately upon finding the post, but grew increasingly pleased as he read through it. "How," the writer wondered, "could someone who's supposed to be brilliant, not think to check the name of the ultimate destination for the company's airship?" The address the writer had on file listed a place called Ten *Sleep*, not Ten *Sheep*.

Leonard knew precisely where that little town was and eagerly passed the information on to the Lancers.

"So, what'll we do with just a town name?" asked Paulie at their next online conference.

"Have you forgotten how big the bloody thing is?" asked Yuvi. "If we catch it at the airfield in Worland, we should be able to keep it in sight."

"It's going into the mountains first, isn't it?"

Hazel asked.

"Yes," said Leonard, "but it'll come out of the mountains and head toward Ten Sleep. We should be able to follow it to any location in the general area. C'mon! This is fantastic news."

They all agreed, and then began arguing about who would supply the lances, how they would pay for them, and most importantly, how they would go about using them on the blimp.

"It's not a blimp!" Leonard snapped.

Blue summed up the feelings of the others in one word, "Whatever."

~*~

Nate longed for earplugs. As expected, Buddy howled like a punctured goat as they dragged him through the narrow opening that led to the outside world.

"Can't you see I'm in pain?" he asked when Nate and Chuck finally had him outside.

"I can't see it," Nate said, "but I can sure as hell hear it."

Maggie had been the first to go through the tunnel-like opening. She swatted Nate on the shoulder and told him to hush. Then, to the others, she said, "Let's take this slow until we see how the Mylar holds up. Nate, you and Chuck can each drag a corner, that'll allow Buddy to slide along on top of the snow in the middle."

"I'm cold," Buddy said.

Maggie gave Nate a look that dared him to say anything. When he remained quiet, Maggie said, "So are we."

Maggie's suggestion that they move slowly proved unnecessary. The best they could do amounted to a crawl. The nylon line Nate and Chuck were pulling bit into their flesh despite the gloves they wore. Additional padding helped, but only temporarily, and both men had to stop regularly to catch their breath in the thin air and rub their palms to restore circulation.

"If we could find a stick to tie the line to, it'd make things easier," Nate said.

Reaching over her shoulder, Maggie patted her backpack. "I've got a lightweight hatchet in here. We can trim and shape a tree limb as soon as we get back down to where the trees grow."

They pressed on. The snow continued to fall, but the wind had died down significantly. Visibility remained limited.

Maggie spelled Chuck for awhile and then did the same for Nate. Buddy remained inexplicably quiet, and Nate wondered if he'd died or merely fallen asleep. He didn't care enough to check.

After two hours, all three were exhausted. The snow reached mid-thigh on Nate and higher on Maggie and Chuck. Wading through it while dragging Chuck's helpless brother further drained their energy.

"Won't the rangers send someone up to look for us?" Chuck asked. "Maybe it'd be better if we made some kind of sign in the snow and waited for a helicopter to fly over."

"Of course, they'll send out search parties, but the Cloud Peak covers a lot of ground," Maggie said. "And we didn't have a specific place in mind when we left to find you and your brother. Who knows how long it'll take for them to reach us?"

"We need to at least make our way into the trees," Nate said. "This rope is killing our hands."

Buddy raised his head to look at the others. "You know what I think?"

"Nobody gives a shit what you think," Chuck muttered.

"Well, if—"

Chuck threw a snowball that splattered against the side of Buddy's head. "Just. Shut. Up."

Nate gave Chuck a toothy grin but said nothing, and Maggie pointed downhill. "Let's keep moving."

~*~

After a frustrating half hour spent trying to start Sledneck, Tori finally triumphed over the cantankerous machine. Thoroughly chilled and anxious to get to Cal's house, she clambered onto the machine and was halfway down her driveway when she remembered the package for Mato she'd left near the front door.

She'd held it for a good long while and simply forgot to give it to him when he came and spoke with Randi. Though late, the timing now was much better. The two, child-size snowsuits she'd purchased for Mato and Reyna would come in handy in the weather they now labored in. He'd be happy to have it, and hopefully even happier to have a gift for his mate.

Tori secured the package, got back on her snowmobile, and headed straight for Cal's place. Since the road to her house hadn't been plowed, and since no one else had traveled it, she took that route and churned along at a good clip.

She remained worried about both Mato and Nate, and hadn't heard from Cal since her call to him. She couldn't get to his house fast enough. Free of other traffic, she wound Sledneck's motor well past the point she normally chose when simply retrieving her mail. This time, the journey mattered.

Though it was her first ride since the previous winter, she felt comfortable with the controls. Sledneck handled reasonably well once it agreed to operate. She patted the gas tank. "Just don't let me down, y'hear?"

She slid to a stop in Cal's front yard and parked between two other snowmobiles already there. With her helmet in one hand and the package for Mato in the other, she made her way to the front door and tapped it lightly with a booted foot.

"Come in, come in!" said Cal.

His cheery voice instantly relieved her of a portion of her anxiety.

"Come meet a couple new faces."

Tori assumed he meant the Franconi boy who took care of Cal's store when he and Maggie were in Hawaii. Tori had no idea who the other face belonged to. She strolled into the house, eager to find out.

Mato sat in front of a comfy fire alongside a girl who appeared to be in her teens and for whom the word "petite" didn't begin to do justice.

"Hey, Mato," she said. "Who's your friend? And what happened to Reyna?"

"Reyna with baby." He waved his hand at the girl. "This Smoke."

The child clearly wasn't comfortable in the midst of people who were so much bigger. Tori wished she could ease Smoke's fears. She felt embarrassed for not bringing her word list, a limited, hand-compiled dictionary she and Mato had worked on, and she silently cursed herself for not practicing some of the words he taught her.

She did remember one greeting, however, though she wasn't entirely sure what it meant.

Throwing caution into potentially hurricane force winds, she offered it up with a smile.

Smoke's head snapped back in surprise, and she immediately responded with a lengthy string of verbiage, none of which made a lick of sense to Tori.

Mato tapped the girl on the arm and said a few words which quickly dampened her enthusiasm.

"What did you tell her?" Tori asked.

"Mato say giant speak only giant." With that, he returned to the remains of a ham and cheese sandwich in his hands. The girl did the same, pausing only long enough to take a sip of her hot chocolate.

"This is Adam," Cal said, finally introducing the last of his guests. Like the little people, Adam, too, made short work of a sandwich. The white bread spoke of Cal's limited expertise as a chef.

"Mr. Jones told me about you," Adam said. "You're an author." He wiped his right hand on his shirt and extended it toward Tori.

"I am," she said. "I write novels, although lately I haven't accomplished much."

"I've never met a real, live author before."

She grinned. "Then I guess this is your lucky day. Do you like to write?"

"No, ma'am," he said. "I do real work."

Tori's laughter came out in a snort.

Adam looked suddenly anguished. "I didn't— I mean... The kinda work I do is, you know, regular. Boring." He turned to look at Cal. "Can I have another sandwich? I can't talk as much if I'm eating, and so I won't embarrass myself as much."

"Don't give it a thought," Tori said. "Sometimes it's hard for me to think of writing as real work."

"You want anything to eat?" Cal said. "I got enough stuff to make sandwiches for the whole Third Army."

"No thanks," she said. "I'm eager to start looking for Nate and Mags."

Cal nodded. "Me, too. We'll need to drop Mato and Smoke off while we're up there, assuming he'll tell us where we need to go. I just wish I had something else they could wear. I could feel Mato shivering during the trip over here."

"Oh!' Tori said, suddenly remembering— for the second time—the package she'd brought for Mato. She glanced at Smoke and tried to remember how tall Reyna was, then decided it didn't matter. The snowsuits wouldn't be a perfect fit anyway, but they'd be way better than nothing.

Chapter Fifteen

"Preservation of one's own culture does not require contempt or disrespect for other cultures."
—Cesar Chavez

Smoke had never experienced food and drink like that which the giant named Cal gave her. She had been suspicious at first, and watched Mato sample everything. But, since Adam and Cal both consumed the same things, and since Mato showed no ill effects, she tried it, too.

"How do you like giant food?" Mato asked as they watched the three huge humans prepare to ride once more on their noisy machines.

"It is wonderful. Do they eat this well every day?"

Mato chuckled knowingly. "They call this 'snak,' something to make them more hungry."

"*More?* But I am full now! I cannot eat another bite."

"You forget; giants have big stomachs. I have seen a giant so fat he could not walk."

Smoke took a sharp breath. "Impossible! Where did you see this?"

"On a machine the giants call 'tee-vee.' It is quite amazing."

"Those who are too fat to move live in the tee-vee?" No matter how hard she tried, she simply could not make sense of it. The look on her face must have conveyed her confusion, for Mato interrupted the giants and asked Cal to show Smoke the device.

"Sure thing," Cal said. He picked up a short stick of some sort, pointed it at a large, flat, dark surface, and somehow brought it to life. People appeared, though dressed like giants. And they not only talked, *they moved*.

It took several moments for Smoke to overcome her initial surprise. "Can I touch it?"

"Of course," Mato said. "You see the giants in it, and sometimes they have weapons, but the tee-vee machine is harmless."

She tried to peek behind the arm-thick slab but found only wall. "How did they squeeze the giants in there?"

Mato held his hands out to his sides, palms up. "I do not know. They have a word for such things—things the People would call magic. They call it 'tek-na-lo-gee.' But do not ask me what that means."

"Show me the fat ones." Smoke peered closely at the moving images, trying to see who or what might be behind them. "Where are they?"

"They live in different places inside the tee-vee which are called 'pro-groms.' It is very hard to explain. Some pro-groms are real and some are not. The ones where giants die are not real."

"But the one with the fat giant who cannot walk—that one is real?"

"Yes. Tori said so."

"And she does not lie?"

Mato took some time before answering the question. "I know some things she says are true and some others do not seem possible. But, most giant words have more than one meaning. That makes talking to them very hard."

Smoke worried that thinking about such things any further would make her head hurt. Instead, she returned to the subject of giant food. "If snak is not enough for them, what else would they want?"

"They eat many things. I cannot name them all, but there is very little that I do not like. I asked Cal if he had any of the wonderful round food. They call it pee-something. It is flat and looks strange, but it is so good. Eating it will make you smile."

"Mato," said the giant called Tori, holding up a bundle for them to see. "I brought gifts for you and Reyna, but it would make more sense for you and Smoke to use them."

Smoke heard her name in giant speak; Mato suggested it when they struggled to say her real name. She did not understand why they could not use the People's words; they made so much more sense.

Tori handed the package to Mato who quickly opened it to reveal giant-style clothing but in sizes that would fit them.

"They're snowsuits," Tori said. "I hope they're okay. I got them online, it's just about the only place that has camo in kid sizes."

Smoke ignored her words since she couldn't understand them anyway and focused on the clothing. It felt thick and soft, and the seams were so precise and tiny it must have taken several seasons to stitch together.

"Put them on," urged Tori who helped Mato wriggle into his outfit. She brought something for his feet and hands as well.

"Oh, thank God," the giant woman exclaimed. "It fits!" She turned toward Smoke and held out the remaining collection of clothes. "It's your turn now."

Smoke took the items from Tori and handed them to Adam. He seemed reluctant to accept them, but she smiled at him and made a gesture of helplessness.

Adam smiled back and went to work. In no time at all he had her dressed. The new clothes, which she wore over her deerskin shirt and leggings, felt warm and comfortable. And the fasteners were amazing. They made a funny noise when pulled up or down, but when sealed were almost invisible. There were no drawstrings and no knots. Smoke marveled at the giants' ingenuity.

She got Mato's attention and asked, "Did Tori make these?"

He shook his head, no, started to explain, and then stopped. "You would not understand."

"It's time to get moving," Cal said. He faced Tori and asked, "Can your machine keep up?"

"I hope so."

Adam had attached something to the back of his machine and, when finished, he called to Cal. "The freight sled is locked on. Should we put Smoke and Mato in it?" The look on his face was decidedly dubious.

Cal gave him a quick headshake, no. "It's bound to be rough where we're headed. I'd hate to see 'em tossed around. They'd get hurt."

"That's what I was thinking, too," Adam said, now smiling. "They can ride like they did before."

Tori waved her arms, shooing Mato and Smoke from the house. "Okay guys, it's time. Let's go, go, go!"

~*~

The rest stops not only grew more frequent, they lasted longer. Maggie did her best to spell the two men, but because of her smaller size, the depth of the snow worked against her more than it did against Nate and Chuck. Buddy occasionally offered his comments which garnered only frowns and snarls from the three people laboring on his behalf.

"I'm gonna kill 'im," Nate breathed during a particularly long halt. "Assuming we don't all freeze to death first."

Maggie giggled.

"What?"

"I was gonna tell you to just chill."

Nate pursed his lips, acknowledging he'd lost his ability to find humor in anything.

"C'mon, Nate," she said with a gentle poke to his ribs. "Lighten up."

"For you," he said, with a reluctant smile, "I'll try."

Once more they began the slog down the mountain. What would have been a fairly easy descent on snow skis was the exact opposite on foot. They had previously taken pains to keep Buddy's makeshift sled from bouncing too much, but his attitude convinced them they needn't bother. They couldn't move quickly enough to do anything but drag him slowly over the rough spots anyway.

"At this rate," Nate said to Maggie after negotiating a difficult section of terrain, "we won't make it down today."

"We're almost at the tree line," she said. "We'll get some wood and make the adjustments we talked about. We'll be able to go faster."

Nate knew happy talk when he heard it; he also knew better than to sabotage optimism with reality. And besides, he thought, maybe she's right.

They trudged on.

~*~

Knowing he had little time to prepare, Leonard focused on finding appropriate tools for the conflict ahead. He began by exploring the Internet for javelins, the sort used in field sports, hoping he could find something inexpensive.

The modern variety ranged in price from ridiculous to bizarre.

"It's just a silly, pointed stick," he muttered to himself. "Why would something like that cost so much?"

He read about balance, high-tech materials, and the preferences of world-class athletes, all of which resulted in ever higher prices.

Switching tactics, he searched for ancient weapons and found an abundance of hand-cast spearheads of various styles based on the historical period in which they were used. Just how a novice might attach one to a wooden shaft was rarely mentioned.

Panic had begun to set in when he latched on to the idea of using closet poles. Readily available in lengths up to eight feet, the poles were light enough to carry and offered the perfect solution, provided he could figure out how to either sharpen one like a gigantic pencil, or add a needle-like metal point.

He found the answer when visiting a building supply company to purchase the half-dozen poles the Lancers needed. A helpful salesperson directed him to an aisle which featured, among other things, foot-long, steel spikes suitable for securing railroad ties. And, though they already came with a pointy end, that could be easily enhanced using the grinder in his father's garage. If it worked to sharpen knives, it would serve admirably in sharpening the spikes.

Though he wasn't quite sure of the best way to attach a spike to the end of a pole, if all else failed he could use duct tape. The Lancers needed something that worked, not something that looked pretty.

Leonard found everything he needed in the building supply store. That afternoon he began assembling the tools his team would use to free the little ones from bondage.

~*~

A full stomach and warm clothing invigorated Mato. When Tori urged him along with Smoke to get back on the snow riding machines, he had but one question. This he put to Tori as they headed toward the front door of Caleb Jones' house: "We go home now?"

"Yes," she said. "As quick as we can. Then Cal, Adam, and I will go look for Nate and Maggie."

"Nate smart," Mato said. "Maggie smarter. They live."

Tori exhaled mightily. "I hope you're right."

He patted her on the leg as he walked by. "Mato always right."

If he had looked up at her instead of pretending everything would work out well, his false bluster would have collapsed. Though he hadn't had a vision about the two giants, he had a bad feeling about them. The People knew how to survive in snowy terrain. Severe weather lasted much longer where they lived, and he'd spent his life learning what he needed to know to stay alive. Nate and Maggie, like all the giants he knew, depended on their tek-na-lo-gee for everything.

But, since there seemed little he might offer in order to help, Mato turned his attention back to the People for whom he had an urgent message. There might still be time to win them over to his plan for a flight in the bah-limp. He hoped Smoke's brief encounter with good giants would make her an ally in his efforts. He wanted to discuss it with her, but Tori's demand that they leave put an end to the idea.

He found it amusing that when seated on the snow riding machine, the girl so readily nestled up against Adam who stood more than three times her height. It wasn't the first time he'd seen someone smitten. He'd experienced it himself with Reyna though her pregnancy had dampened his ardor somewhat. Hopefully, it would return to full force when their child grew a bit older.

"C'mon, Mato!" Cal said, struggling to be heard over the roar of three snow riding machines.

Mato allowed himself to be hauled up onto a familiar spot in front of Caleb, his legs dangling to either side of the machine. He settled back against the giant and prepared for another exhilarating ride, though this time he'd be a great deal warmer thanks to the clothing Tori had given him. He wondered if Smoke would mind the additional padding between her and Adam, then decided it would not be in his best interests to mention it—to anyone.

The three machines, with Adam in the lead, raced through the relatively flat areas below the mountains then slowed when the terrain changed and became decidedly uphill.

"I'm glad you chose this entrance," Cal said when they came to a halt. "There aren't any rangers here."

"I knew they wouldn't be happy if they

294

thought we were headed to the Cloud Peak," Adam said.

Mato followed the conversation as well as he could. A quick glance at Smoke convinced him she couldn't have cared less what was being discussed. She was content to look up at her driver.

"What're we waiting for?" Tori asked. "We've got a long way to go before we're done."

With that, all three machines rumbled louder and took off. Mato hung on as best he could, though he trusted Cal to keep him from falling.

The landscape whistled by as they drove headlong into the mountains. Mato had never covered this sort of ground so fast. The drivers completely ignored wildlife and anything else they encountered. Eventually they broke through the tree line, and Adam signaled a halt.

Caleb shifted Mato further toward the front of his machine, up against what he called a windshield. "Okay. You're the boss now. Where do we go from here?"

Mato stood up on the machine and looked over the top of the windshield. It took him a few moments to get oriented, then he sighted a familiar peak and pointed at it. "We go there," he said.

Cal sighted along his arm and raised both hands above his head. "Follow me," he yelled as Mato scrambled to regain his seat. Having barely settled back against Cal, the snow riding machine rumbled to life and raced toward the peak Mato had pointed to.

He gave a quick glance toward Smoke to be sure she was still safe. Though her face remained in shadow, the way she pressed herself close to the young giant told Mato all he needed to know. She was as safe as she might ever be. He chose not to think about what might happen if she were left alone with him.

They forged on, occasionally stopping to let Mato direct their travel. Cal commented from time to time about how much trouble they would be in if the park rangers found out they had driven their snow machines into the Cloud Peak. Mato had no idea what he was talking about. The rangers had nothing to do with the People, and the mountains belonged to them, after all. He had no interest in what the rangers thought or did. Maggie was the only exception, because she was a comrade.

Eventually they reached the edge of a plateau familiar to both Mato and Smoke. The entrance to the People's domain sat a short distance away, but there were enough rocks and boulders to make hiding their tracks fairly easy. Mato and Smoke dismounted, thanked their hosts, and waited for them to leave. Even though all three giants could be considered friends, they couldn't be trusted with the knowledge of where and how the People accessed their underground home.

Mato put his arm around his young companion as they watched the giants speed away downhill.

"I miss him already," Smoke said.

Mato gave her an understanding smile. "You will live."

~*~

Since Adam seemed to have a better handle on the various routes into and out of the wilderness area, Cal and Tori let him resume the lead. They had previously discussed the location of the ranger station from which Nate and Maggie departed, but they couldn't be sure where, exactly, the two went. The park visitors they went to rescue could have gone anywhere.

"Based on what Mags told me," Cal said, "they were looking for little people."

Tori felt a moment of exasperation. "Yes, I agree. But where would they *go to look?*"

Adam slapped his forehead. "Of course— *Mindians!*"

Cal squinted at him. "What're you talkin' about?"

"The two little ones. Smoke and Mato," he said. "They're Mindians."

Tori felt compelled to explain it to Cal. "Some bonehead on the Internet came up with that Mindian nonsense. It's supposed to stand for mini-Indian. Me? I think it's dumb."

"I think it's cool," Adam said. "And I got to

meet 'em. I can't wait to tell people."

"Yeah, about that," Cal said, "it might be better to wait awhile. We'll explain later. For now, I suggest we find the shortest route between where we dropped off Mato and Smoke, and the ranger station. I'm guessing they'll be somewhere in between."

"Okay then. I got this. Follow me." Adam revved the engine of his machine and took off. The freight sled behind his vehicle bounced on the uneven snow but didn't slow him down.

Thus far, Sledneck had worked well enough for Tori to keep up, and she prayed it would continue for the length of the mission. Unfortunately, the engine began to make coughing noises, and she wondered how long it would be before it gave up a mechanical lung.

"You okay back there?" Cal yelled when he noticed she had dropped behind. His voice barely broke above the sound of the snowmobile engines. He and Adam turned around and raced back to her.

"I think I've pushed my ride a little too hard," she said.

Adam waved the comment off. "Then we'll just slow down."

"No! Definitely not." Tori crossed her arms and shook her head. "Y'all go on. I can follow your tracks. The sooner somebody finds Nate and Maggie, the better."

"And what happens if ol' Sledneck there craps out?" Cal asked.

"Then y'all will have to come back up here and get me, too."

"But—" Cal began.

"But nothing. I've only been out here a few hours. Nate and Maggie have been stuck up here for days. I'm warm and well fed; I can survive for a while."

Adam dismounted and raised the seat on his machine. He reached inside and extracted a package which contained a flare gun which he handed to Tori. "Just in case," he said.

Tori stared down at the gun-like device and the four rounds that looked very much like the shells she used in her 12-gauge shotgun. "I've never used one of these."

"Just point it straight up and pull the trigger," Adam said. "Hopefully, you won't need it, and if not, I'd really like to have it back. They're kinda expensive."

Tori looked at his snazzy snowmobile and concluded the young man had means. She doubted Cal paid him all that well to mind his store. "Based on that machine, you don't look like you're hurting."

He chuckled. "I wish it was mine. Dad let me use it to help find Mrs. Jones and Deputy Sheffield."

"Well then, you'd best get back to doing

that. Don't worry about me. I'll catch up."

She watched the two of them depart, and as they crested a hill and dropped out of sight, she heard a wolf howl. That was all the encouragement she needed to tear open the packaged flare gun and load it.

~*~

Smoke followed Mato into the cavern, happy to be home. Word of her arrival spread quickly through the other youngsters in the clan, and they gathered to greet her near the central fire.

Though her leg still ached, the rides she and Mato had been given by the giants had been both electrifying and revitalizing; Adam's presence made it even better. How many times had she wished he was one of the People instead of being a giant?

Quickly surrounded by her young companions, she laughed to see how excited they were. Their questions came rapid-fire:

"Where have you been?"

"Were you hurt?"

"What are you wearing?"

"Tell us everything!"

The voices of her friends swelled, and several older members of the clan joined in with questions of their own.

Smoke looked for Mato, then recalled that

he intended to speak with the elders. He said the topics were vital to everyone, and she assumed he would address the clan once the elders understood the issues. Meanwhile, she was free to rejoin her friends and regale them with her most recent adventure.

Mato had asked her not to mention Stone Fist's betrayal, an issue he would take up either with the council of elders or with the arrogant warrior personally.

"Will you kill him?" she had asked.

Mato responded with a shrug. "Probably not, but the elders may have other ideas."

Skipping over the details about Stone Fist, Smoke gave her listeners a brief account of her discovery of Mato's plight and her efforts to free him. She described the cold, forbidding cabin, the cage, and their rescue by the giants Adam and Cal.

Her comments about the younger giant, which included an appraisal of his good looks, his great strength, and his gentle manner, had the other females grinning. The young males were universally unimpressed.

"He is a giant," one exclaimed. "You make him sound like one of us."

Smoke laughed at him. "None of you are like Adam."

"You have spent too much time with Mato," said another. "We all know his words are false."

Smoke sneered at the boy who had defamed Mato. "I have spent enough time with him to know he speaks the truth! He knows the giants' tongue. He understands their magic. He has many friends among them, and if we are smart, we will listen to him. He has never lied to me."

One of Smoke's closest friends approached her, speaking in a soft voice. "Few of us are brave enough to do what you have done."

Since her encounter with the three giants in Cal's home, Smoke had given thought to her previous efforts to torment and/or steal from the giants who came near the People's home. What had once been a source of pride had now become a source of shame.

"Most giants do not wish us harm," she told them.

"If that is true," asked an older male, "then why was Mato trapped? Why was he put in a cage?"

"Some giants *are* evil," she said, "but not all of them." She scanned the tight crowd gathered around her. "We are all different. Some of you are fast, and some are not. Some hunt well, others cannot hunt at all. Some of us are brave, like Mato, and others—" She caught herself before saying anything about Stone Fist. "Others are not."

"So," continued the older male, "you think Mato speaks the truth when he says the giants have a huge flying machine?"

"Have we not seen them in the sky with our own eyes?"

"Yes, but—"

"I have ridden on one of their snow machines," Smoke said. "It was loud and scary, but even so, it was wonderful! We raced through the drifts, swift as a hawk and shifty as a hare. I have been inside one of their homes; I have eaten their food, and look—look at this!" She pointed to her snowsuit, unzipping it to reveal her regular garments underneath. "This was a *gift*. It kept me warm during our return. Mato has one like it."

"Kindness from giants? It must be a trick," said another doubter who was also much older than Smoke's friends. "I would never trust them."

"Then do not waste my time with your foolish questions," she snapped. "You believe only what you have been told; you know nothing about giants."

The younger members of the gathering crowded closer, and several reached out to touch Smoke's new clothing. They marveled, as she had, at the fine workmanship. Several asked to try it on, and Smoke readily agreed to let them.

"There's more," she said. "Giant food is better than anything I have ever tasted. I ate my fill, every bite delicious. And what they gave us was not their best!"

The parent of a friend burst out with, "Ah

ha! You see? They are not as generous as you say. Where do they hunt?"

Another asked, "And why can we not hunt there, too?"

"I do not know," she admitted. "But I believe the giants would tell us if we ask. I know Adam will."

"Little Smoke has a big lover," one of the boys remarked, drawing snickers from his friends.

Smoke glared at him, but offered no denial. "Listen," she said. "The old ones think they know best, but they have not been near the giants. They have not seen the giants' magic. I have. I want everyone to see it."

"How?" asked a girl.

"When?" asked another.

"Will you lead us?" asked a third.

"Yes! But we must stick together, act together. We must listen to Mato, for he has a message that could change all our lives for the better. I fear the elders will not listen; their fear drives them. I am not afraid. And you must not be afraid either."

"Fear is not always bad," said a voice from the back. "I fear bears."

Several others chimed in. "Badgers!"

"Wolves!"

"How do we know the giants can be trusted?" asked a young hunter. "Just because one of them turned your head? Why would he care about us?"

Smoke looked at the young people still gathered around her. Most looked weary and drawn; they had not eaten well, and life in the cavern, while safe, had never been pleasant. "We will be smart. When we follow Mato, we will carry our darts, our blowtubes, and our sleeping paste. If there is treachery, we will be ready."

That brought a great many smiles and nods. Smoke knew the next time she went among the giants she would not go alone.

Chapter Sixteen

"Technology... is a queer thing. It brings you great gifts with one hand, and it stabs you in the back with the other." —Carrie Snow

During what Nate thought must have been their one hundredth rest stop, he dug his cell phone out of his pocket only to remember that the battery was dead.

It's as useless as Buddy.

While in the cave, the headlamp and flashlights Maggie brought along eventually failed, and they had switched to using the lights built into their cell phones.

He addressed the others, "Do any of you have any juice left in your cell phone?"

"I do," said Buddy.

Nate wasn't surprised. "Do you have any service yet?"

"Nah. I checked a little while ago."

Nate figured the weather had cleared enough to allow for helicopter flights, but they had yet to see one.

"We should keep moving," Buddy said.

Nate did his best to control his temper. His efforts did not go unnoticed. Maggie put her hand on his arm and gave her head a tiny shake. It was enough. Nate aimed his thoughts at something else.

"I'm not takin' another step until we find a stick or a branch or something we can use with this rope," he said. "My hands can't take much more."

"Wait a sec," said Chuck. "Do you guys hear something?"

Nate and Maggie peeled off their knitted caps and cupped their ears with their hands.

"It sounds like a motorcycle," Nate said.

Maggie broke out in a smile. "Or a snowmobile. But why would it be coming *downhill?*"

"Who cares? We just need to make sure they find us." Nate started waving his arms over his head. Maggie and Chuck quickly joined him. All three shouted to get the riders' attention.

Their spirits improved as the roar of the snowmobile engines grew louder.

"It's about damned time," Buddy muttered as two big snow riding machines cruised to a halt a few feet away.

Cal dismounted and ran to Maggie, plucking her straight out of the snow and hugging her for all he was worth. The weary female ranger responded just as enthusiastically.

Smiling at the reunited couple, Adam approached Nate and introduced himself. "Mr. Jones has told me a lot about you," the young man said. "I'm pleased to finally meet you."

"You couldn't have picked a better time to show up," Nate said. "We're dyin' to get out of these mountains."

"I'm a little worried about your wife, though," Adam said.

Nate felt a sudden jolt of anxiety himself. "Why? What happened? Did she come with you?"

"Yes sir."

"On that crappy old snowmobile of hers?"

"She said you called it 'Sledneck.'"

Nate clamped his jaws together in frustration.

Adam continued, "Miz Sheffield said it was makin' some noise, and she didn't want to push it any harder. She told us to keep going and get you folks. She'll just follow our tracks."

"And if that stupid sled of hers has quit working?" Nate asked.

"We can ride three on a machine if we have to," Adam replied.

Nate did a quick headcount. "That would work. You, Tori, and I can ride yours. Cal, Maggie, and Chuck can ride on Cal's."

"What about me?" Buddy said, sitting upright for the first time since they left the cave. He pointed to the freight sled attached to Adam's rig. "I'm not riding in that damn thing."

"Well, if you can't even stand up, how do you expect to get on a sled?" Chuck stepped closer to his brother, his arms at his sides.

"I just need a little help. Gimme a hand." Buddy reached out and grasped Chuck's arm then rose to his feet, grimacing. "It's not too bad."

Nate stared at him. "You can stand?"

"Whoa," Buddy said. "Nothin' gets by you, genius."

Maggie nudged Nate's arm and whispered, "Don't forget what I said about waiting 'til I'm outta sight before you smack him."

"Ya know what, Mags? I'm gonna let you sort this out. Adam and I are going back to see if Tori's okay. If her machine is still running, Chuck can ride with me. There's no way Tori's machine will carry her and someone else."

"We'll just wait here for a while," Maggie said. She glanced at the horizon. "We've still got some daylight left."

Nate borrowed Cal's machine and Adam climbed on his own. "You ready?" Adam asked.

"Hit it!" Nate said.

With that, Adam did a tight turn that nearly dumped the lawman, then gunned the motor and raced straight back the way he and Cal had come.

Lacking a helmet and goggles, Nate squinted into the wind hoping to catch sight of his wife. The ride was anything but smooth as Adam focused on speed over comfort, and Nate wouldn't have wanted it any other way.

They crossed back above the tree line, their route veering only when necessary. Even so, Nate was impatient, if not a little desperate, to reach her.

And yet, Tori remained out of sight.

~*~

Stone Fist hated winter, and he hated it even more because Winter Woman and her spineless elders had not allowed the People to properly prepare. There had been little or no hunting for days, and everyone was hungry. The first big snowfall of the year lay fresh on the ground, and yet their supply of dried meat was almost gone.

The giants were responsible, too, of course. Had they not flocked to the mountains in greater numbers than ever before, the People would have had more time to ready themselves. They could have gathered more fish and game, to say nothing of firewood, great piles of which they would need for the long, cold days and nights to come.

Aside from being hungry, Stone Fist found himself bored. He contemplated paying another visit to Reyna, Mato's mate, but she had turned him away too many times already. He would wait until she grew tired of Mato's absence. The memory of seeing him swinging, head down, as the result of a giant's simple snare made him smile. It served the liar right.

"Stone Fist! I would speak with you."

He sat up at the sound of Winter Woman's scratchy voice. "Go away. I am busy."

"The elders would also speak with you."

"Why?" he asked. "What do they want?"

Winter Woman stepped out from the shadows and stood looking down at him. She had a fixed expression on her face which he could not read. "Mato has returned, and he has much to say. He asked that you be allowed to sit with the elders and listen."

He returned? How can that be?

Stone Fist sat up. "I— I have no desire to listen to a liar."

"He has something important to discuss, and it involves you," she said.

He could not have seen me! He could not know that I left him and walked away. "What lie is he spreading about me?"

Winter Woman's expression still hadn't changed. "I do not know what he will say. He asked only that we allow you and the girl, Ember, to join us. She, too, has something to say."

"You mean the little thief who calls herself Smoke?" He frowned. "She's a fitting companion for someone who cannot tell the truth."

"We will know soon enough," Winter Woman said. "Join us at the council fire when the sun lingers one fist above the high peak."

"And if I choose not to come?"

"Then you will prove yourself as foolish as you are vain."

Winter Woman walked away before he could think of an appropriate response.

The idea of attending the council meeting bothered him. Normally, he would have been flattered by such an invitation, but since his argument with Winter Woman, he had become more interested in taking her place than answering to her.

And then there was Smoke. What did she have to offer, more toys stolen from the giants? She had been gone for days, but no one missed her. No one of any importance, anyway.

Stone Fist was not used to worrying. He began to think it would be better to face Mato privately. With that in mind, he decided he would bring his sharpest blades.

~*~

Sledneck died shortly after the engine noise from her companions' snowmobiles faded in the distance. Tori assumed Cal and Adam wouldn't have been able to hear the wolf, but she certainly had.

Holding the flare pistol with both hands, Tori scanned the horizon. She fully subscribed to the philosophy of live and let live, but she had no intention of surrendering her life and that of her unborn child so that some wild carnivore could have a nice meal.

Let 'em eat moose!

False bravado, she figured, was better than no bravado at all. If the wolf came 'round, she would be ready, and a good scorching from a flare would likely be something the critter would never forget, assuming it survived.

But wolves travel in packs.

And I'll only have five shots.

And what if I need one to signal Nate?

She heard a second howl and turned sharply ninety degrees to see if she could spot the source. The first wolf responded from somewhere behind her. At least, she hoped it was the first one and not a third.

Climbing back aboard Sledneck, she tried to

313

get the ancient beast started. It rewarded her with sputtering sounds, a whirr, a clank, and silence. Further tries generated nothing but frustration.

She heard another howl, but couldn't tell if it was new or if the first two wolves were comparing notes, or more likely, recipes.

I could start walking. The snow shouldn't be too deep if I stay in the snowmobile tracks. The wolves would have to run through snow up to their chests. They couldn't possibly keep—

Another howl derailed her ruminations.

She squeezed her eyes shut for just a moment, then opened them. *Concentrate!*

The wolves wouldn't be able to keep up with me until... Until they reached the snowmobile tracks, too, and I would've only made them easier to run in.

Damn it, Nate! Why'd you have to volunteer for every rescue job that comes along? How 'bout rescuing me? How 'bout....

The wolves were no longer howling. Tori did a careful, 360-degree scan but saw nothing.

Thank God. They've gone.

She turned and faced downhill, her plan to walk away given new life. If she moved quickly and stuck to the tracks already in the snow, she told herself she could make good time.

And, just in case, I can always use the flare

gun. "Time to go," she said.

Which is when she heard a very low, very ominous growl.

~*~

Leonard had learned a valuable lesson about social media: while it provided cheap entertainment and/or an easy way to stay in touch with friends and family for the masses, for the clever few, it could be a powerful tool for data mining and could be manipulated for social or political gain. Leonard felt comfortable with his humanitarian niche. His followers, though small in number, were stridently vocal in their support, altruists all.

The Lancers had agreed to meet in person as soon as they had a specific date, time, and location with which to work. Once again, social media provided the information, though the informant had no idea she had chummed the Internet waters with a banquet for Leonard's social justice sharks. The same Puck functionary who found Archer's "Ten Sheep" remark hysterical served up the tidbit about the airship's estimated time of arrival.

"It's on in two days," Leonard informed his cadre via a live Internet chat. "Can you all meet me in Ten Sleep?"

"Why?" asked Blue. "You said it would land first in Worland. If it's as big as you say, we can follow it wherever it goes. If we start in Ten Sleep, there's no telling how long it'll take to get there."

For the sake of the team, Leonard concurred and said he would look for a suitable location near the Worland airfield from which they could begin their surveillance. With every tick of the clock, Leonard's enthusiasm grew. His level of trepidation had also grown, but the mere fact that he had comrades in arms balanced his emotions. It wasn't easy being a hero.

But someone had to do it.

~*~

Smoke had never attended a council meeting. The gatherings were meant for elders and those whose input they sought. Winter Woman and the others who led the People considered her a child, therefore she had never been invited.

It must be Mato's doing. He will confront Stone Fist, and my words will have meaning.

Being summoned to a council could be either a great honor or a grave threat. Punishments were more often distributed than rewards.

I have nothing to fear. I did what was right! Mato knows that, and he will tell them.

She also recognized that everyone but Reyna believed Mato to be a liar. Smoke had said as much herself, and not just to her friends. Stone Fist was sure to bring that up and bring it up often.

She straightened her shoulders and walked to the cavern entrance in order to see the horizon. It was nearly time.

Stone Fist is the one who should be afraid.

"Are you ready?"

Smoke turned to face a smiling Mato, still wearing the clothes the giant called Tori gave him. He held the colorful, folded sheet of the skin the giants called "pay-purr" in his hand.

"Yes," she said. "I am ready."

"Where are the things Tori gave you to wear?"

She swallowed. "I let someone else wear them. I did not know—"

Mato smiled and held up both hands, palms out. "Do not worry. Almost everyone saw us when we returned. They saw yours, and I still have mine." He did a slow turn as if to show the outfit off and then pointed in the general direction of the central firepit. "We should go now."

"What do you think Stone Fist will say when I tell the elders what I saw?"

"He will say you lie." Mato showed no concern over the statement.

"But—"

He put his finger to his lip in the universal gesture for silence, then bent close and whispered, "He has my knife. Reyna saw it hanging from his

317

neck on the cord she made for me."

The implication would be too great to ignore. If Stone Fist had the knife, there was only one way he could have gotten it. Mato would never have given it away. Not only was it a great source of pride and a token of his friendship with an important giant, it was also an incredibly useful tool.

"There will be many questions," Mato cautioned her. "Be truthful, but do not waste words." He patted her on the shoulder. "You are as brave as any warrior I know. I would gladly have you at my side in times of trouble."

She blinked back a tear. "You honor me."

"No," said Mato. "I now see you for who you really are."

~*~

Randi found it terribly frustrating that she couldn't reach any of her contacts in Wyoming by phone. None of them answered. She assumed all of them were out in the mountains where cell phone service didn't exist.

She needed them to know the timetable. The special cottages were on the way, and *Puck Two* had an arrival date scheduled in Worland in two days. The clothing she'd ordered had been assembled in Los Angeles and was loaded on a truck that would follow the ones carrying the cottages. A food truck hired in Cheyanne had been given directions to Tori's cabin with instructions to be ready to feed a small army. She had not told them how small, or for that matter, how many. Randi still had no idea if Mato's entire tribe would accompany him or just a few. She was determined, however, to feed, clothe, and house as many as possible.

Archer remained cagey about whether or not he would attend the summit with the little people. In one meeting he claimed to have set aside time for it, while in another he said his schedule wouldn't allow it. Randi had reached the point where she didn't give a damn what he wanted to do as long as he made a commitment of *some* kind.

Yanking chains is part of his management style. God knows he does it often enough; calls it part of his "Puck mystique." I think it's his Puck mistake.

Ranting wouldn't change anything, but it made her feel a little better. She called Captain Bradley who would pilot *Puck Two* to Wyoming and confirmed she would be flying with them when they left Los Angeles. Much to the man's dismay, she advised that Tim Archer might also be on the flight.

"Do you know what he likes to drink?" he asked.

"Why? Are you thinking of poisoning him?" The idea had crossed her mind on multiple occasions. When Bradley didn't respond right away, she worried he might think she was serious.

"I'm joking," she added. "Sorta."

"Right. So, I take it you two don't get along all that well."

"What? No. Don't be silly. We're like… I dunno. A husband and wife, maybe. You know, in divorce court."

"Gotcha. Listen, I'm just trying to make the man comfortable, y'know? I don't want to get between you and him. But I'm guessing you've spent a lot of time around him. So, surely you know what he likes to drink."

Randi thought about it for a moment, then recalled a whiskey she'd heard about which she found completely revolting.

"I know just the thing, if you can find it," she said. "He likes Gilpin single malt whiskey, straight up."

He pulled a ballpoint pen from his pocket and jotted "Gilpin's" on his palm. "Got it. Thanks!"

"No problem. See you soon," she said and ended the call. She wondered if he'd feel differently when he discovered that Gilpin's not-so-secret ingredient was urine donated by diabetics. It was purified with the sugar extracted and used to speed up the fermentation process.

"Cheers!" Randi said, holding a phantom highball glass aloft. "Bottoms up, you old reprobate!"

~*~

Mato had always considered Stone Fist just another member of the clan, who like everyone else, struggled to eat and stay alive. It never occurred to him that the warrior might leave him, presumably to die. The People had high ethical standards based almost entirely on the need for unity. One wasn't required to love all those with whom he lived, but the survival of the group required everyone to pull together in difficult times. No one was exempt.

The People took this issue more seriously than any other, and betrayals like that of Stone Fist were met harshly. Unless proven false, Smoke's accusation would result in the elder's forcing him to choose between two unspeakably difficult options: banishment or death.

The elders had already encircled the council fire when Mato and Smoke arrived. Stone Fist strode in among them as the final member of the gathering.

Winter Woman stood and addressed the three younger ones. "We have heard something from someone we trust that brings us no joy."

Stone Fist crossed his arms, looked to the side, and exhaled noisily through his nose. "There has been no joy here for many days. What has changed?"

The clan's leader turned angry eyes at him. "You will not speak again until invited."

"Who—"

He stopped speaking the moment a spear tip dug into the base of his spine. A quick look over his shoulder verified the presence of a warrior twice Stone Fist's age who held the weapon at his back. Though much older, the aging warrior still had enough strength to drive the spear deep. Stone Fist closed his mouth.

Winter Woman then turned to Smoke and asked her to recount what went on during her recent absence from the People's campfires.

Smoke's voice quavered slightly when she began, so Mato smiled at her, hoping to raise the girl's spirits. It seemed to work, as her words tumbled out louder and faster as she recalled the time she spent with Mato in the cabin of the giant who had captured him.

She then spoke almost reverently about being rescued by three other giants who fed them, gave them clothing, and returned them to the People's land.

"How is it that a giant captured Mato in the first place?" one elder asked.

"He used a snare," she said.

"I saw something the giants call a 'guhn,'" Mato said. "When I bent down to get it, the giant set off the trap. I hit my head on the ground and did not wake up for some time."

Mato cast a quick glance at Stone Fist who, though he tried to look brave and confident, betrayed himself with occasional furtive glances as if seeking an avenue of escape.

"Tell me, Ember... I mean, Smoke. Why did you not help Mato when he was first captured?" Winter Woman asked. "You saw him dangling and helpless."

"I could not reach him in time," the girl said. "That is why I followed behind, hoping to free him when I could."

Stone Fist seemed to be calming down, Mato thought. He did not appear nearly as nervous as he had before.

Winter Woman continued, "And you saw no one else who might have freed him?"

Smoke swallowed, turned toward Stone Fist, and pointed at him. "I saw him, but he did nothing to help. He laughed at Mato."

The accused warrior twisted to one side and with a quick backhand, knocked the spear aside. "She lies!" His voice came harsh and flat.

"He took something from around Mato's neck," Smoke added. "I could not tell what it was."

"It was my knife," Mato said. "He wears it around his own neck now."

"They are both lying," Stone Fist growled while casting hard looks at each of the assembled elders. "I can prove it."

"How?" asked Winter Woman.

"Give me a moment," he said, "and I will bring proof that these two lie. They cannot be trusted."

Winter Woman motioned for the elder with the spear to go with him. Stone Fist's eyes narrowed as he grudgingly agreed to the directive.

"Do not waste our time!" admonished Winter Woman.

Stone Fist left without saying more.

Smoke reached out to Mato, visibly upset. "He will just run away."

"Probably," he replied. "But what else can he do? If the elders do not face him when they pass judgment, he may avoid punishment. At least for a while."

Nate would have preferred to go faster, but he followed Adam's cautious lead as they headed up the mountain. The tracks in the snow were helpful, but they did not ensure an unimpeded route. Adam often had to slow down to negotiate a drop made with little difficulty when approached from the opposite direction. Nate appreciated that, but at the same time, he hated the resulting delays.

He knew it would be dark before they collected everyone and returned to the base of the mountains. They would be lucky to have everyone settled on snowmobiles before Mother Nature turned out the lights.

I wonder if there'll be a full moon tonight. That'd sure help. Next time, I'll be sure to check before I trundle out here into no-man's land.

Adam stopped and signaled for Nate to come alongside, presumably for a quick chat.

"What's up?"

"I think I saw a flare."

Nate ground his teeth in frustration; he had no desire to mount a search for someone else, at least not before he connected with Tori. "We've gotta keep going."

"Yeah, yeah, you're right. It's just—"

"What?"

"I gave Mrs. Sheffield a flare gun, and you guys said the two hikers with Mr. Jones were the only ones still up here."

"*Tori* shot the flare?"

"Yes, sir. I believe so."

"Then what're we doing sitting here, yackin' about it?" Nate gunned the engine of his machine and sped forward.

"Easy!" shouted Adam, his voice barely audible. "And watch out for boulders!"

Chapter Seventeen

"One thing I learned long ago as a prosecutor is that it's tough to get people to obey a law if there is no penalty for breaking it." —Roy Barnes

Tori whirled around to face the beast that growled at her, the flare gun held in both hands, her arms extended.

Her breaths came so slow she worried she might pass out before she got a shot at her attacker. Stealing her nerves as best she could, she looked for the snarling animal she knew would soon be upon her. By crouching down and staying close to Sledneck, she reduced the creature's avenues of attack.

Bring it you hairy sonovabitch! You might get me, but you're gonna pay.

She waited, her breath finally returning to normal, while her pulse punched a rapid and steady beat in her temples.

But the attack didn't come.

326

Instead, she heard new howling, at a distance. It might have come from two animals, but she guessed there were more.

Aw, c'mon! How many of you does it take? I'm all by myself here!

But the closest animal, whose eyes and snarl had all but paralyzed her, *wasn't* coming for her.

It's running away!

Flooded with relief, Tori stood up to watch the carnivores plow through the snow, leaping and growling, their attention drawn to something else.

Tori stood up on Sledneck to get a better view and spotted a very small Indian trying to make his way through the deep snow.

Mato?

Oh, dear God, don't let it be Mato! What's he doing out in the open? Can't he see the—

When wolves appeared on either side of the little warrior, Tori fired the flare gun. It didn't have as much recoil as she thought it might, and she quickly reloaded.

The first flare had dropped toward the ground and buried itself in the snow. She could hear a faint hiss but saw little else. The noise of the pistol going off, however, had been enough to startle the wolves and allow the little Indian to make tracks toward a large, snow-covered boulder.

Tori aimed higher the second time, and got off a flare which sailed high over the heads of the Indian and the wolves. She followed that with a scream, hoping to scare the animals away, then reloaded once more and attempted to charge them.

Trudging uphill through heavy snow proved extremely difficult, and Tori watched in agony as the wolves ignored her and went after the Indian who had been unable to scale the rock.

The wolves, four in all, tore into the little warrior whose cries echoed in the still air.

And as suddenly as they started, they stopped.

All Tori could hear were the wolves growling at each other as they destroyed their prey, tearing chunks of raw meat from the carcass and carrying them away.

When Tori fired the flare gun again, this time from much closer, the animals scattered. All they left behind was a gruesome smear that once had been her friend.

Stunned, Tori dropped to her knees and wept.

~*~

When neither Stone Fist nor the elder who went with him returned, the remaining elders grew concerned. Winter Woman dispatched two more clan members to look for the missing pair.

328

One returned a short while later to report that Stone Fist was gone, but not before he had beaten the elder who accompanied him.

"Is he badly hurt?" she asked.

The elder looked grave. "If the Spirits grant it, he will live."

Smoke tugged on Mato's arm. "Should we not go after Stone Fist?" She couldn't understand why Mato seemed content to do nothing.

"I must tend to my family," he said. "I have been away too long. But I would ask a favor of you."

"What?"

"Go to the high opening. Do you know the one I mean?"

"The one the hunters use? Yes. From there one can see a great distance in many directions, but it is terribly cold."

"Then get the clothing Tori gave you, or wear mine," Mato said. "Go to the opening and look for Stone Fist. Let me know if you see him."

"And that is all?"

"For now," he said.

Smoke squinted at him, unable to ignore a building sense of suspicion. "What are you thinking?"

The seer did not respond for several moments. "When we were trapped in the giant's cabin, I had a vision." His lips twisted briefly before he continued. "It was not a happy one."

~*~

Nate and Adam roared up the mountainside one behind the other, intent on locating Tori. When they spotted her snowmobile, they raced toward it only to discover Tori wasn't there.

Nate saw her footprints in the snow and quickly spotted her huddled form at the end of the trail she'd made. He dismounted and raced along the same path to reach her, called her name as he stumbled forward, then dropped to his knees and wrapped his arms around her. "What happened? Are you all right?"

"Oh, God, Nate," she cried, adding still more tears to those already on her cheeks.

"What is it?"

"It's Mato. The wolves got him." She pointed a trembling hand to a spot in the distance.

"Stay here," he said and signaled for Adam to remain with her. "I'll go look."

"Be careful," she said. "The bastards are still out there somewhere."

"Trust me. I'll be *very* careful." Nate pulled out his sidearm, chambered a round, and proceeded on foot. It wasn't difficult to find the place where the carnage occurred. Bloodstains marked the snow in vivid splashes of red. Bits of flesh and bone littered the ground, but not enough to make identification possible.

As he surveyed the dreadful site, he noticed a cord of some sort lying atop the snow beside the worst of the blood spatter and gore. He reached down, picked it up, and recognized the jackknife attached to it. He had given it to Mato not long after they first met.

He carried it back to Tori and Adam, unable to keep his own tears in check.

"It *was* Mato," he said, shaking his head. He had no desire to relate what he had seen up close, nor did they ask him to.

"After all this... After all he's done for us... For his people," Tori said, gasping as she spoke. "It's just not fair."

"I'm really sorry about this," Adam said. "He seemed like a pretty neat guy."

Nate sniffed and palmed a tear from his cheek. "He had a chance to make a huge difference in the lives of his people, but now...."

Adam looked puzzled. "I don't understand."

Tori briefly described the plans for the airship and the cottages. "The people who run the Puck Resort in Hawaii hoped to talk some of Mato's people into working for them."

"Do they even speak English?" Adam asked. "I mean, I got the impression Mato spoke a little, but that girl, Smoke, didn't seem to understand a word."

"Mato was the only one who could translate, and to be honest, his English wasn't all that hot. But without him, there's no hope at all." Tori put her hand on Nate's shoulder and levered herself upright. "The whole job thing seemed pretty farfetched to me, but his people having the chance to live in modern homes, eat good food, and get medical care... That's the part that interested me. And I think it's what motivated Mato, too."

Nate got to his feet. "As much as I hate to say it, there's nothing we can do about him now." He looked up at the sky and the rapidly fading light. "We need to get moving. I have no interest in spending another night up here in the mountains."

"What'll we do about Miz Sheffield's ride?" Adam asked when they returned to their vehicles.

"Leave it for now. It's not like anyone's going to wander by and steal it," Nate said. He gave Tori a squint. "I can't believe you actually rode this piece of junk all the way up here."

Tori patted the machine. "Don't be cruel. He meant well."

Nate resisted the urge to roll his eyes toward the sky then pointed at the snowmobile he'd borrowed from Cal. "You're riding with me, babe. Hop on."

~*~

Mato sat beside Reyna in a space they'd set

aside for themselves when Reyna became pregnant. That had been quite a while back, and their son was now old enough to toddle around on his own. Reyna never let him wander far.

"Are you back to stay this time?" she asked.

He knew the question would be coming, and he'd rehearsed several answers, though he knew none of them would please her. "The bah-limp is coming," he said, "and we—"

Reyna stood and turned away. "You must stop this," she said. "You think the giants are our friends, but we know they are not."

"What about Tori and Nate? What about Cal and Maggie? Did they not help us when we needed it?"

"Yes, they did, but we survived because of our own efforts. Giants are impossible to understand. Their language is crazy, and they cannot survive without all their stupid tools."

Mato felt a sense of defeat crawling inexorably into his mind. He couldn't let it get a foothold. "Please listen to me," he said. "Try to understand. There is—"

"Mato! Come quick!"

Smoke's squeal startled both Mato and Reyna. Their young child began to cry.

Reyna gave the girl a harsh stare. "You have frightened my son."

Mato ignored Reyna and focused on Smoke. "What is it?"

"Stone Fist. He is..." She swallowed. "He is dead!"

"How?" Reyna asked before Mato could.

"Wolves," she said. "He had no chance."

Mato nodded, thinking perhaps it was just as well. Death delivered by a wolf would be quick if nothing else. "What would you have me do?"

"Your giant friend, the one who gave us these—" she tapped her snowsuit "—she is out there, too."

"Facing *wolves?*"

"Not now, but she looks hurt. She is curled up in the snow."

Tori? Hurt by wolves?

He had no choice. "I must go, Reyna. But I will be back."

Mato's mate simply shook her head. "Do what you must. My life will go on, but do not expect to find a place by my fire when you return."

The warrior ignored her comment and raced through the cavern to reach the nearest opening to the outside. Smoke trailed after him.

"Do you want me to come with you?" she cried.

"Yes," said Mato. "No." He brushed his hand

through the air. "Fetch Winter Woman! Tell her I need a healer. Join us when you can."

Mato hurried past members of the clan, young and old, who stared at him as he ran. Their thoughts meant nothing to him. Reaching Tori was the only thing that mattered. The vision he'd had featured wolves.

And a great deal of blood.

It did not reveal the victim.

He left the cavern and immediately searched the area downhill for signs of Tori. Smoke had watched from a higher elevation and could therefore see farther. But Mato knew in which direction Tori, Nate, and Cal had gone after they dropped him off. He went that way as quickly as he could, often sliding down the steeper parts.

In the distance he spotted three snow riding machines and his giant friends. He called to them, but since they didn't look his way, he assumed they couldn't hear him above the noise of their rides.

He slowed his mad dash down the mountain when he saw Tori standing, though at that distance he couldn't see any blood.

While waving his arms above his head, he called out to them again. They still didn't respond and instead got back on two of their machines. The third they left behind.

Why am I running? Tori looks fine.

And yet, he kept going, kept shouting, and kept waving his arms.

The two machines began to move. Tori, seated behind Nate, turned to look behind and finally saw Mato. She tapped Nate on the shoulder, and he turned the machine back uphill.

Mato collapsed in the snow.

Tori jumped off the sled when it came to a stop and dropped down beside him. "Are you hurt? I thought you were dead! The wolves—"

Mato shook his head. "They got another. He... He deserved it."

Nate looked surprised. "Whoever it was, he must've really pissed *someone* off."

Mato wasn't sure what that meant, but he didn't care. It was enough to know Tori had escaped injury.

"We can't stay," Nate said. "It's getting dark."

Mato looked directly at Tori. "Bah-limp still come?"

"Yes," she said.

"When?"

Tori shrugged. "Soon."

Mato took a deep breath, then exhaled. He still had time to convince Winter Woman and the elders that they could ride in the huge flying machine. And more importantly, he could regain his credibility.

"We really have to go now," Nate said, his tone insistent.

Mato touched Tori's leg. "Bah-limp bring food?"

"Food? For who?"

"The People."

"How many?" she asked.

"All of them!"

"I— Uh… Okay."

"Bring round food." Mato made a big circle with his arms.

Tori laughed. "You mean pizza?"

"Yes," said Mato. "Peet-zah!"

~*~

The longer Nate and Adam were gone, the more worried Maggie became. Cal tried to be a calming influence, but Buddy, the injured hiker, countered with enough negatives to nullify Cal's efforts.

"It'll be dark soon," Buddy said. "We need to get outta here."

Maggie pointed downhill. "Go for it."

"*Walk?* Right. That's not happening." He looked at Cal. "Why can't we ride three on your machine?"

337

"It can handle two, but three? I dunno. Maggie and Chuck aren't that big, so I suppose we could squeeze three on, but it'd be hairy."

Buddy sneered down at the snow. "What if we hooked the Mylar sheets to the snowmobile? I'll bet Chuck could hang on."

Chuck remained silent, but his clenched jaws spoke volumes.

"We'll keep waiting," Maggie said. "Nate and Adam know what they're doing. And it's not dark yet by a long shot."

Buddy shook his head. "We're gonna die out here if we wait too long."

"You heard the lady," Cal said. "We wait."

"Listen, old timer, I—"

Chuck's snowball landed squarely on Buddy's forehead, cutting off his words and leaving him even more sullen and angry. He took a wobbly step toward his brother then grabbed the seat of Cal's snowmobile for support. "You'll pay for that, asshole."

"Pipe down," Maggie said. "I think I hear them."

All four remained motionless, straining to hear the distant sound of rescue.

Maggie felt like clapping her hands and cheering. "It's definitely coming from uphill."

"Took 'em long enough," groused Buddy.

The two machines and three riders pulled to a stop, and encountered a brief hail of questions. "We'll explain everything after we get out of here," Nate said. "Some of it is... Well, unpleasant."

"That works for me," Maggie said. "Okay then, everyone, mount up."

Already standing beside Cal's machine, Buddy found himself on the wrong side of it, unable to swing his good leg over the seat while standing on his bad one. "Gonna need a little help here."

Cal ignored him as he got on and waved for Maggie to join him.

Chuck ambled toward Adam's snowmobile while Buddy looked about in consternation. "Where am I gonna ride?"

Adam nodded toward the freight sled. "You can sit there. Hop on."

"Oh, hell no," Buddy said. "There's no friggin' way I'm riding in that damned thing. One of you is gonna have to get off. I don't have to put up with this kinda sh—"

Chuck closed his brother's mouth with an uppercut that snapped Buddy's head back and sent him reeling into the snow.

It took a few moments for Buddy to open his eyes, and he appeared none too sure of where he was or how he got there. The pain in his jaw eventually kicked in, and he began to rub it.

"Now drag your sorry ass onto that sled," Chuck said, standing over him, "or I swear, I'll punch you again. Only next time I won't hold anything back."

Buddy raised one arm toward his brother. "I— I need help."

"Tough shit. It's about time you pulled your own weight. Now crawl over and climb on the sled, or we'll leave without you."

"No! You can't—"

"Wanna bet?" Chuck turned and stepped back to Adam's sled. He mounted quickly and tapped his driver on the shoulder. "Let's go."

Adam clearly looked uncomfortable. "What about him?"

Chuck swiveled his head toward his brother. "You coming, or not?"

Rather than answer, Buddy crept to the freight sled on his hands and knees then rolled over the edge into it, grunting and groaning all the way.

Maggie watched in silence and wondered how she could thank the younger brother without appearing to endorse violence. Nate and Cal, however, just smiled.

Once settled in the sled, Buddy opened his mouth to say something, but Maggie couldn't hear it over the roar of the three snowmobiles.

~*~

Randi had left messages for everyone in Wyoming she could think of, including Mato. But despite her great hopes, none of them responded, and there were still things to do.

Finally, her phone rang, and she grabbed it as if the device might somehow sneak away. "H'lo?"

"It's Tori. You rang?"

"Yes! I hadn't heard from anyone and... Geez. Is everyone okay?"

"Yep. Nate's even home for a change. Imagine that."

"Sounds like you've been busy," Randi said, hoping to keep things light.

"We only seem to have two speeds around here: dead stop or run like hell." She exhaled into the phone. "Seems like whenever we're in one, I wanna be in the other."

Randi still hadn't figured out quite how to read Nate's wife, but she couldn't waste any more time worrying about it. "I wanted to give you an update. We've got two trucks set to arrive very soon at your place. They'll unload the three cottages, unpack the stuff inside, make sure the plumbing works, and set up the generator that'll power them."

"Makes me glad Nate had some work done on the driveway. It can get pretty nasty in this weather," Tori said. "What's on the second truck?"

"Clothes, boots, and mittens. Not exactly high fashion stuff, but it'll keep our little friends warm. I hope they like the cartoon characters printed on 'em."

"It'll be something new for them," Tori said. "They've never seen cartoons."

"That's the kind of thing I still can't wrap my head around."

Tori snorted. "Those poor people are going to need a heck of a lot more than new clothes before they can show up for work somewhere. At the very least, someone's going to have to teach them to speak English."

"Well, can't Mato—"

"Ah, yes. Mato. We thought he'd been killed up in the Cloud Peak yesterday."

"You're not serious!" Randi said, shocked.

"I'm very serious. There are wolves up there, and it turns out they like to eat little people."

"My God! I had no idea. That's—"

"There's a reason it's called a wilderness," Tori said.

"I know, I know. It's just—"

"I'm worried about the little guys, Randi. It scares me to think some corporate big wig like Tim Archer will turn their world upside-down, and later, when he gets tired of them, will drop them like a bad sit-com."

"He wouldn't do that."

Tori's laugh held little humor. "You obviously have more faith in him than I do. That's why we're calling in Nate's attorney to handle any contracts Puck wants to make with Mato and his people."

Randi couldn't help but smile. "I know the woman you're talking about. Princess Shaniqua, right? She scalped Archer once already—on Nate's behalf, as I'm sure you know. My dear boss won't be pleased to hear she's coming back a second time. But just between you and me, I think it's great. Somebody needs to put him in his place from time to time without having to worry about getting fired."

They chatted on about things that needed to be done before the airship swooped into the mountains to pick up Mato and his tribe. Randi checked the items off her list until she reached the end of it. "I think that's everything."

"Nope," Tori said. "There's one other thing, a request from Mato. Because there have been so many people tromping around up in the Peak looking for the little people, they've stayed in hiding. That means they couldn't adequately prepare for the winter."

"It's not like winter snuck up on them."

"True, but people did."

"So, what're you saying?"

"In short, they're cold and hungry. At the very least, they need food. Mato asked me to tell you to have the airship bring in pizzas."

"You're kidding."

"Nope. He was quite specific."

"How many?"

"I haven't got a clue," Tori said. "In fact, I asked him that same question."

Randi hoped she would finally get an idea of how many little people there were. "What'd he say?"

"He said you needed to bring enough for all of them."

"Oy."

"If it were me," Tori said, "I'd round up fifty or so, for starters. If memory serves, Mato ate about a third of one the night you brought them to the cabin."

"I'll make it sixty," Randi said. "Just in case."

"You can always go back for more."

"How many pizza places are there in Ten Sleep?"

"Only one I can think of," Tori said. "You'd best do your shopping in Worland. And pray the Warriors aren't playing football that same day. I'm told high school football is a pretty big deal over there. The fans get real hungry."

~*~

Leonard resisted the temptation to have another cup of coffee. Even though he had nothing else to do but wait, he knew the caffeine he'd already consumed would keep him wired all day. He had to appear calm; he had to be the sort of take-charge guy he'd never been. He knew he was desperately out of his element.

The pile of carefully folded sugar wrappers and empty creamers sprawled like flotsam on his table. He'd had breakfast, waited a few hours, then had lunch. His team had yet to arrive, though they were due any time.

He kept staring out the window, craning his neck to see the horizon. The Puck dirigible would arrive at some point. The Internet provided the date but not the time.

"Hey, Lennie!"

Paulie's voice boomed, and Leonard felt the blush creeping up his face. He waved the big, bald accountant over to his table. "I prefer Leonard, okay?"

"Yeah, whatever." Paulie absorbed himself in the café's menu. "You eat already?"

"I did."

"Anything good here?"

If he were truthful, he'd explain that anxiety kept him from even thinking about the taste of his food. Eating had simply become something to kill time.

Paulie ordered the house special. "I don't know what all's in it, but it comes with fries and a shake. How bad can that be?"

By the time Paulie had demolished his lunch, two more members of the team trundled in: Yuvi, the dark-complected man with a British accent and Annette, the only one close to his age. Her short, dark hair plus an acre of tattoos and an avalanche of ear piercings gave her the look of a carnival refugee. That hardly mattered to Leonard, as long as she played the part she had promised to fulfill.

"Where's the blimp?" Paulie asked. "Shouldn't it be here by now?"

"I can't say," Leonard replied. "We'll just have to wait."

"Do they have a bar?" Yuvi asked. "I could do with a pint."

Leonard shrugged. "You'll have to ask. I don't drink. Much." He peered out the front window of the restaurant, hoping to see Blue and Hazel. He was curious to see if Blue actually arrived on a Harley. He was shocked to see him climb out from a VW bug though dressed like a Hell's Angel.

As Blue sauntered toward the table, an older woman who had been sitting at the counter stood and followed him. Leonard didn't recognize her at first, then realized it was Hazel decked out in matching white ski pants and parka. She had dyed her gray hair which now appeared a fluffy pink and reminded him of cotton candy.

God help me. I've recruited a menagerie.

They discussed their upcoming mission, and Leonard's role continued to be the peacekeeper. He seated Hazel and Paulie across from each other so they wouldn't come to blows. The mission was too important.

To accomplish their attack, they decided to limit themselves to two vehicles, one of which was Paulie's pickup truck since it was the only one big enough to carry the lances Leonard had strapped to the roof of his mother's car. He had no intention of doing anything which might scratch the finish on it and was only too happy to give the weapons to Paulie.

The group ran out of things to chatter about roughly an hour before *Puck Two* appeared in the distance. Several diners spotted the enormous aircraft, and their excited remarks drew the group's interest.

"Finally," said Blue. "Let's go now and get it over with."

"Don't be stupid," Hazel said. "Attacking that thing here in Worland will only draw the police. We need to take care of business *away* from town. Besides, isn't that what we already agreed to?"

Leonard pulled them back in line. "We wait," he said. "It shouldn't be on the ground long. When it takes off, we can follow it. If you're going to be a driver on this mission, make sure you've got plenty of gas. We won't be able to stop later. If you need it, get it now."

"Good thinking," Paulie said and ordered a burger, fries, and another shake, to go.

Chapter Eighteen

"Real freedom lies in wildness, not in civilization."
—Charles Lindbergh

"You still believe the bah-limp will come?" Smoke asked Mato yet again. And yet again, Mato said, "Yes."

"It looks huge in the picture on the folded skin," she said. "Is it really so big? How can it fly? A rock cannot fly. Even a small one."

"It can if you throw it," Mato said.

"The bah-limp must be magic."

Mato turned his head in her direction. They had been sitting in the high opening for two days. Smoke was not the only one who had lost patience. "They do not call it magic. You should know that by now. It is just a tool. A mighty tool, yes, but just a tool."

"Did Winter Woman agree to go near it?"

"She and the elders are still considering it.

They have not given me an answer. But, no matter. I will go. You should come, too."

"I will," she cried. "I will!"

"Good."

Smoke eased back against a cold, stone wall. "There are others who will follow as well. The young. They trust me. And they will trust you once they know you did not lie."

"They will believe what they wish, just like the elders," Mato said, and then grinned at her. "The bah-limp will bring food for everyone, no matter what they believe."

"Food for *everyone?*" She stared at him in surprise. "Have you told Winter Woman about this?"

"I have. And all the other elders, too. I showed them the folded skin with the bright pictures. But they were more interested in something else I told them; the bah-limp would take them to the sacred cave I found."

"Many say you lied about that, too," Smoke said, then quickly added, "but not me!"

Mato chuckled. "It is under Tori's home. You will see it soon. I promise."

"Will Adam be there?"

"That I do not know. We will see."

~*~

350

Tori watched quietly as *Puck Two* descended on the Worland airfield. Though she had seen its massive predecessor in Hawaii, she still had trouble grasping just how much bigger the newer contraption was. She'd given the whole idea of such aircraft very little thought before then. Now, confronted with an aerodynamically designed and radically updated version of the old, German Zeppelin, she realized what marvelous technological leaps its creators had made.

Her recent visit to the Cloud Peak Wilderness, and her proximity to Mato's homeland, gave her confidence that the gigantic flying machine would actually be able to touch down as planned. It was almost certain, however, to scare the bejeezus out of the little people. Mato would more than have his hands full convincing them to hop aboard for a ride.

She would have preferred that Nate come with her, but he needed to stay behind and make sure everything at the cabin was ready for their guests. Though they both had reservations about the entire enterprise, they would do their best for Mato and his clan.

Tori absently rubbed her tummy. There was a little Sheffield in there, and Nate had been elated to hear the news. "Why didn't you tell me sooner?" he'd asked.

"Probably 'cause you were busy trying to stay alive," she'd told him.

"Now I'm even more glad I succeeded."

"Yeah, me, too," she said.

After that they spent some time catching up, non-verbally. The memory made her smile. Their child wasn't due for seven months or so, plenty of time for all the snow to melt. With any luck, she'd have a house with a nursery by then. She opted not to bring the topic up for discussion until they'd finished dealing with Mato and the Puck proposal.

The next step would take place in the Worland airport.

She didn't wait long before the passengers she expected showed up. Randi, the statuesque redhead, greeted her with a huge smile and then introduced her to Timothy Archer, the Puck Productions CEO. They were accompanied by Capt. Bradley, the senior pilot, who trailed behind them looking more like a chauffeur than an airline captain.

Before Tori could initiate a conversation with Archer, Bradley got his attention. "I had hoped to present you with a gift from the flight deck," he said. "Unfortunately, we couldn't locate a bottle of the right stuff here in the States."

"What're you talking about?" Archer asked, his manner jovial. "I had some good single malt on the way in."

"Of course," Bradley said. "But we were

hoping to find you a bottle of Gilpin's. I understand that's your fav—"

"*Gilpin's?*"

"Yes, sir. We heard you really—"

"I've heard of the stuff. You know it's made from piss, right?"

Bradley's face took on the pallor of freshly laundered bedsheets. "I— Uh...."

Archer patted him on the shoulder. "Let me know if you ever get your hands on some. There are a couple jerks I'd love to give it to."

"Of course. I'll— Uhm..." He shot Randi an evil look. "I'll see what I can do."

"Good man," Archer said, and with one hand on the back of each of his female companions, he escorted them away.

Tori separated herself from Archer and sidled closer to Randi. "Did you have any luck with the pizza order?"

"I split it between four places and called them just before we left LA. They promised to have twenty pies each, delivered here when we landed. I had bottled water loaded before we left. It's in the four-ounce size." She chuckled. "I didn't know they came that small."

"*Eighty* pizzas?" Archer said. "Why so many? And why not just appetizers? We don't have to feed the whole tribe, do we?"

"Actually," Tori said, "that's exactly what we've been asked to do."

Archer frowned. "By whom?"

"By the guy who's going to make or break this deal," Randi said. "His name is Mato. He's the little fellow you saw in the security video from the resort."

"And what makes him so special? I'd rather talk to the chief. Is that him?"

Tori stepped in to respond. "No, sir. That would be a lady named Winter Woman. She leads the clan."

"A woman? Well, I suppose I can see how that might happen. I'll bet she wields a mean tomahawk."

Archer laughed, while Tori took pains to keep from slapping him. "There's a good reason we'll be working through Mato."

"Why's that?"

"He's the only one who speaks any English. But I have to warn you—"

"You obviously don't know who I am," Archer said, dismissing her with a shake of his head. "I know how to wheel and deal, and if I do say so myself, I'm damned good at it."

"I guess we'll find out, won't we?" Tori said.

Randi briefly intervened. "I'm going to check on the pizza. I'll see you back aboard the airship as soon as everything's loaded."

"I think I need a drink," Tori said, then remembered she was pregnant.

Archer began looking for a bar. "My treat."

Tori shook her head. "Some other time, maybe. The airport doesn't have enough traffic to support a lounge or a restaurant."

Archer compressed his lips. "That's a shame."

"Yeah," Tori said, trying not to sound relieved. "A real bummer."

~*~

"Is *that* it?" Smoke asked, staring at an odd shape floating in the distant sky.

Mato crawled forward to join her in the high opening. "Yes."

"It is not very big," she said.

"Wait until it comes closer." For the first time in a long, long while he believed his hopes would finally be realized. "I must tell Winter Woman and the elders."

She looked at him, wide-eyed. "I should tell my friends. We must... prepare."

Suddenly suspicious, Mato asked, "What do you mean, 'prepare?'"

"Several of them have told me they fear the giants will trick us. If what you say is true, and the bah-limp brings us a gift of food, some have said they will not eat it."

Mato pursed his lips. "These giants are my friends. They would not hurt us."

"Just the same, only a few are brave enough to come with me. We will be on the lookout for deceit."

"Suit yourself," Mato said, looking deep into her eyes. "But do nothing unless you tell me first. Do you understand?"

She nodded.

"Good. And make sure your friends do the same. Otherwise, they will not join us when we fly to Tori's home."

Mato doubted it would take the bah-limp long to reach the high pasture just below the peaks where the People lived. He wanted all the elders to see it as it approached, and he wanted them to experience the same awe he felt when he first saw the immense flying machine.

When he reached Winter Woman, she was tending to the needs of an infant and tried to put him off.

"The bah-limp comes," he said.

"I am busy."

"I see that. But all of us depend on you, not just this child."

"The child comes first."

"No," said Mato. "The *People* come first. Or would you have them led by someone else? Someone like Stone Fist?"

Winter Woman sighed and handed the child back to its mother. "Stone Fist is gone. You see what his ambition got him. Do you wish to take his place?"

"I wish the People to have something to eat!" Though tempted to shout, Mato kept his voice level. "I want them to live in peace with the giants, and I want them to live without fear." He paused, trying to read the woman's mind by studying her face and manner. "Or are you so afraid of the giants that you'd rather see us starve than meet with them?"

"Only fools have no fear," she said.

"Only fools let their fear ruin their lives."

Winter Woman glared at him, but he could see that he'd forced her to think, and not just of herself.

"We will go together," Mato said. "All the elders will come, too."

"If there is treachery—"

"There will be no treachery. We—" He paused, thinking of Smoke's band of followers. Though young and unproven, they had courage, and according to the bold teen, they were prepared. "If something bad happens, we will be ready. A plan is in place."

"I hope that is true," she said. "For all our sakes."

~*~

Cal smiled at his young friend. "You're really an amazing guy, ya know that?"

Adam slipped into "aw shucks" mode. "It wasn't a big deal. The engine on Miz Sheffield's snowmobile just had a clogged fuel line. Fixin' it was pretty easy."

"Just the same," Cal said, "you knew what to do. I've been riding these things for a long time, but I wouldn't even have known what to look for, let alone how to fix it. Anyway, I'm glad you were available."

"It was nothing, really."

Cal sensed there was more to it than simple neighborliness. He recalled how much more observant of their surroundings the lad had been on their second trip. Adam had suggested retrieving Tori's snowmobile shortly after their return with Maggie, Nate, and the hikers.

"You were looking for that girl, weren't you? *Smoke?*"

Slightly embarrassed at first, Adam's face slowly gave up a grin. "Yeah. Guess I'm pretty pathetic, huh? It's just... She's so... y'know, little."

"And cute as a button."

"Yeah." He stuck his hands in the pockets of

his coveralls. "I'm just bein' stupid; I know. There's no way I'll ever see her again. And even if I did, I couldn't talk to her."

"But you know what you'd say if you could?"

He shook his head. "Actually, no. Not really."

"Young love," Cal said. "Ain't nothin' like it." He felt sorry for the kid. "Y'know, there might be a chance you could catch up with her somewhere else."

"Really? Where?"

"I'm not supposed to tell anyone about this, but seein' as how you were really there for us...."

The look of hope and anticipation on Adam's face gave Cal all the permission he needed. Maggie might fuss at him, but he'd get over it. "Why don't you ride Tori's sled over to her place? I'll give you the directions. She'll be happy to have it back, I'm sure. She or Nate can bring you home again later."

Adam's positive expression faded. "Aw c'mon. You really think Smoke'll be *there?*"

"Maggie's gonna skin me alive for tellin' you this—and I could be completely wrong about your little miss Smoke—but here's the deal: Puck Productions, the company that makes all those dumb cartoon movies, is flying a blimp out here. They plan to pick up some of the little people and take them to Tori's place. They've got housing built for them and everything."

"But why? What's the point?"

"The guy that runs Puck—I forget his name—anyway, he thinks he can hire a bunch of 'em to work for him in Hawaii."

"Smoke's going to *Hawaii?*"

"Maybe. Hell, I dunno. But if so, this might be your last chance to see her." Cal jotted Tori's phone number and directions to her cabin on a slip of paper and handed it to him.

"Thanks, Mr. Jones," Adam said. "I'm outta here."

~*~

Randi realized she'd been holding her breath and let it out slowly as *Puck Two* settled into the snow in a shallow valley spread out among the mountain tops. The landing seemed almost surreal until Tim Archer got to his feet and announced, "Well, kids, it's time to go play cowboys and Indians!"

Too bad drowning you in a tub of Gilpin's isn't an option. "Is there a chance," she asked him, "that you might dial back your enthusiasm for conquest, and be both cordial and diplomatic?"

"I'll be the perfect gentleman, as always."

Tori, who had been sitting next to Randi, spoke up. "Okay then, why don't you climb into your parka and get ready to meet our guests?"

"Aren't you two going to join me?"

"Of course," said Randi. "But first I need to touch base with Captain Bradley and see that the pizzas are set out."

"Fine. Just… don't dally."

She glanced at him, noting his expression. *Is he actually apprehensive? He looks odd.* "Are you feeling all right, sir?"

"Oh—my God—you called me 'sir.'"

"Consider it a weak moment."

"I'm okay, really. I think maybe the altitude's getting to me."

"Why don't you stay here and rest?" Tori suggested. "You'll be better able to connect with our guests when they arrive. Okay?"

Archer agreed, and the two women walked far enough away to exchange a few private words. "You know," Randi said, "it'll probably go better if just you and I meet Winter Woman."

"Kind of a girl-to-girl thing?"

"Yeah. Archer can be overbearing, especially when he thinks he's being charming. If it's just us, it might put her more at ease."

Happy to leave Archer behind, Randi touched base with Bradley, who still hadn't forgiven her for the Gilpin's incident. He explained that he would stay at the helm and monitor the ship and the weather. "How long will we need to stay here?" he asked.

"Not long, I imagine," she replied. "It all depends on how Mato's people react. Hopefully, the food will help."

Once the pizzas and bottled water had been piled just inside the door of the ship, Randi and Tori prepared for Mato and an entourage of little people. Part of that preparation called for a pair of snowblowers that crewmembers offloaded, cranked up, and used to clear a path from the airship's exit to a spot about halfway up the hillside as directed by Tori. There they stopped and waited for additional instructions.

Randi and Tori waited with them, happy to be free of Archer.

Mato appeared as if by magic and began working his way down toward them.

"He's no fool," Tori said. "He knows we're trying to clear a path and make it easier for them." She waved to him, and he waved back.

Randi expected to see the tribal leaders making their way along with him. Instead, a gaggle of much younger little people trailed behind, creating a well-tramped trail from the peak toward the mid-point where she waited.

Dismissing the snowblowers, Randi signaled for the pizzas and water to be brought out. These were loaded on lightweight toboggans and dragged to the midpoint, arriving about the same time as Mato and his team of youngsters.

She welcomed him with a smile and gestured toward the flat-bottomed sleds.

"The pizzas taste better when they're hot," added Tori. "Try one." She opened the nearest box and offered it for his inspection. She also showed him how to open a water bottle.

He looked at the pizza, then signaled to a young female behind him and said something neither woman could understand. Mato then lifted a slice of the pizza, took a bite, and chewed. He ate as if famished. The girl joined him.

"That's Smoke," Tori whispered.

Randi nodded. "I thought she looked a little young to be Winter Woman."

Once Smoke and Mato had demolished most of the slices they'd dug into, the other teens surged forward and helped themselves.

"Yikes," said Randi. "It's a feeding frenzy."

Tori's expression changed to one of dismay.

"What is it?"

"I witnessed a *real* feeding frenzy," Tori said. "It was awful. I just… I'd rather not think about it."

Mato waited for his young accomplices to finish eating then sent them to the toboggans and had them start dragging them up the hill. It appeared to be slow going.

"Can we help?" Randi asked. "We have people standing by."

Mato waved her off. "They come back. More peet-zah in bah-limp?"

She shook her head, no. "But we have other things to eat."

"Good."

They waited quietly once the sled pullers slipped out of sight. Randi tried to imagine what would occur once Mato's clan dove into the goodies just delivered. She didn't have to wait long before little people reappeared.

The tiny teens who pulled the toboggans up the hill raced out into the open, and they quickly figured out the best way to use the sleds. They piled on and whooshed downhill, zipping by Mato and the two women. Several riders yelled as they cruised by.

Mato laughed. "They say, 'How stop?'"

Randi relaxed when the sleds hit less steep terrain where the riders dug their heels in the drifts and slowed to a stop. Laughing and jostling each other, they looked just like any other kids she had ever seen playing in the snow. Only much smaller.

"Winter Woman comes," Mato said, causing Randi and Tori to gaze back uphill.

A severe-looking female of Mato's size stepped carefully along the path created by the younger members of her clan. Following close behind were several more clan members all of whom appeared to be at or near her advanced age.

"She certainly looks like a boss, doesn't she," commented Tori.

Randi bowed to them when they drew near. "Welcome," she said.

~*~

"Well, where the hell is it?" Pauli asked. "There's too many clouds."

"Clouds are about the only thing big enough to hide a blimp," said Blue.

Leonard had long since given up on trying to make them call the dirigible an airship. "It doesn't matter," he said. "Sooner or later, it's going to fly somewhere near Ten Sleep."

Paulie's stomach rumbled. "I'm tired of drivin' around for no reason. I need to get out and stretch my legs."

"Then let's do it in Ten Sleep," Blue said. "Not out here in the middle of the boonies."

"That makes sense," Leonard said. "I'll call Hazel and let her know."

They drove into the little town, and Paulie parked in a space right in front of the first bar they came to.

Hazel pulled in beside them. "What's the deal?" she asked as she, Annette, and Yuvi climbed out of her car. "I thought we were chasing the blimp."

Paulie fixed her with a glare. "Do you see any damned blimps around here?"

"Don't use that kind of language with me," she warned.

"Or what? You'll whack me with yer purse?"

Leonard herded them all toward the tavern, but Paulie stopped and pulled one of the homemade lances from the back of his truck.

"Are these things really gonna work?" He swept the pole around and checked it at his side, then made thrusting motions with it as if the airship were parked in front of him. "What if the blimp thingy sits real high off the ground?"

"I've seen photos of it," Leonard assured him. "We'll be able to reach it."

Yuvi spoke up. "Have you given any thought to how we'll escape detection by the authorities? I'd rather not get arrested if possible."

Leonard had worried about the same thing but hadn't hit upon any fool-proof plans. "I figure we'll sneak in a little after dusk; park somewhere out of sight, and advance on foot. We puncture the daylights out of the airship and then run back to our cars."

Blue snickered. "I can't wait to see Paulie and Hazel hightailin' it away from the crime scene."

"The only crime," Hazel said, "is what those monsters with the blimp are planning. This is a rescue mission, not a crime spree."

Paulie scratched his jaw. "I still think we oughta just shoot the damned thing."

Leonard ordered drinks all around knowing full well he didn't have enough cash to pay for them.

~*~

Smoke clenched the fingers on both hands to keep anyone from seeing how they trembled. Though she followed the two female giants and all the elders as they walked toward the gigantic bah-limp, she still felt she held a position of honor. The other members of her team shuffled along behind her, whispering and crowding close together.

She stopped walking long enough to deliver a harsh whisper. "Show no fear. The giants will respect that."

None of them responded, though they all looked to be on the verge of panic. A few held their dart blowers in their hands. Smoke pointed at them. "Keep them hidden!"

They did as they were told which added an additional touch of pride to her status as a leader. "Come," she said. "Soon we will fly."

She had discussed the possibility with them on several occasions, most recently when Mato agreed to let them serve as guards. Most were openly fearful of the prospect, but she countered each of their arguments with assurances she barely believed in herself.

A leader must lead.

As the elders ahead of her crossed the threshold into the bah-limp, she heard them exclaim at the wonders they beheld there. Their excitement quickly spread among the younger members of the party. When Smoke entered the bah-limp, she too was stunned by the opulence of their surroundings.

She could never have dreamed what the interior of the flying machine looked like; it was simply beyond her imagination. The walls slanted outward and what she thought were great rectangular holes turned out to be something solid and yet transparent. The floor had a covering that was both soft and pleasant. The design reminded her of reeds near a stream.

The giants, including a stout male with gray hair, stood at the far end of the space and gestured for their visitors to sit on the other objects in the room—huge, padded surfaces from which one could see out through the holes, and on which one could lounge in complete comfort, assuming the giants intended them no harm.

Once the younger ones settled themselves near the back of the open space, the elders and the giants took seats around a flat surface which Mato called a "tay-bol." He looked extremely busy. The giants would say something to him, and then he would say something to Winter Woman. She would respond, and he would then address the giants.

It appeared very tiring, and she was happy not to be involved.

The female giant with beautiful red hair stood and made an announcement which Mato translated for the People onboard. "Be ready," he told them. "The bah-limp will soon fly. There will be some noise, but you are safe."

He stepped close to one of the holes and tapped it with his hand. "This is called 'win-doe,'" he said. "Stay seated and watch. We will soon join the birds."

Moments later the bah-limp did make the noises he predicted, though Smoke wasn't frightened by them. That came when the immense machine began to float up into the air.

Fighting to keep her fear in check, she looked behind to see if the door remained open in case she wanted to get out. A female giant she hadn't seen before stepped out and smiled at her.

The message was clear: there would be no escape.

Chapter Nineteen

"You can't call it an adventure unless it's tinged with danger. The greatest danger in life, though, is not taking the adventure at all." —Brian Blessed

Leonard knew his own limit for adult beverages, but he had no idea how much Paulie and Blue could consume without getting blotto. Yuvi held himself to a beer while Hazel and Annette sipped wine. "We should go outside," he said to the team. "We can't see anything in here."

"Why don't you go?" Paulie asked. "You ain't drinkin' anyway. It's cold outside, and there's no need for all of us to freeze."

"I'll go with you," Hazel said, pushing her half-empty wine glass to the center of the table and casting a disapproving eye at Paulie. "I could really use some fresh air."

The two stepped outside together and were immediately struck by the sudden drop in temperature. Leonard shivered. "Looks like Paulie was right about the cold."

"That would be a first," she said.

They stood silently in the frigid air, scanning the sky for the airship. Just when Leonard was about to announce it was time for a shift change, the massive flying machine drifted into view.

He pointed. "There it is!"

"Time to roust the boozers," Hazel said. "I hope they're still capable of fulfilling their promises."

"Lives are at stake. They won't let us down."

Hazel appeared dubious. "I'm going to my car to warm it up. I'll let you drag out the troops, such as they are."

Within a very few minutes, all six members of Leonard's Lancers were on the move.

Though he tried not to think about her, Adam's thoughts continually drifted back to the dimpled face of Smoke. He just couldn't *not* think about her. The fact that they came from different worlds meant little, but the fact she was so incredibly small *did* mean something. It meant they had no future. They weren't members of different species; they were extremes of the same one—like a whippet and a wolfhound.

All that aside, he felt something for her he'd

never experienced before. Maybe it was puppy love. Maybe not. He'd never been in love before, so how would he know? Falling for her wasn't just stupid, it was crazy. Utterly, undeniably, whole-heartedly insane.

He knew all that. And he just didn't care. He wanted to see her again. And if she somehow ended up in Hawaii, then maybe he'd get an extra job or two and earn enough money to go after her. Hawaii sounded pretty cool, especially when the snow was two or three feet deep here at home.

Rather than attempt to find his way to the Sheffield's cabin going overland, Adam followed the directions he'd been given, riding beside the roads or on snow the plows left piled on either side of them. That made the going slow but gave him plenty of time to think.

And worry.

~*~

Nate tried to keep his mind on the Puck project, but his thoughts kept drifting toward his future—as a dad. He found the idea both exhilarating and frightening. He'd never had much to do with kids, and had absolutely zero experience with infants. The sum total of his baby knowledge consisted of the absolute belief that they were incredibly loud, astonishingly messy, and as a group had a world-class level of bad timing.

What mattered, he repeatedly told himself,

was Tori's reaction. She had seemed reserved when she shared the news with him, as if she expected him to be disappointed. And he wasn't. At all!

I'm gonna be a dad!

The thought paraded through his mind like one of those idiotic melodies that latch onto a smidgeon of one's brain and never let go.

Shadow ambled over to him, sat down, and rested his enormous head in Nate's lap. He absently rubbed the sweet spot behind the dog's ears. Shadow responded with a satisfied groan.

If only it would be this easy with kids.

He let his gaze wander toward the horizon. The Puck airship would be visible soon, assuming it wasn't too far behind schedule. Tori had called him from Worland as soon as they got underway, but an estimate of how long it would take to feed Mato's clan and then convince the leaders to go for a ride was anyone's guess. Fortunately, Mato had made it clear he wanted the flight—and the visit to Tori's cabin—to occur no matter what.

As far as he could tell, everything was ready: the little cabins, the clothing, even the food truck.

It shouldn't be long now.

~*~

Despite Mato's assurances that the bah-limp flight would be pleasant, and that there was no need to be worried, he could tell Smoke was on edge when the giant airship lifted off the ground. He said as much to Randi who signaled to yet another giant at the back of the aircraft. Randi called her an "air hostess," which made no sense to him at all, though when it came to giant words, that was often the case. The air hostess disappeared briefly, then returned pushing a cart.

Though he had only been working as the interpreter for a short while, he found the effort tiring and excused himself to see what was in the cart. He made his way down the aisle, smiling and nodding at Smoke's companions, all of whom looked as if they were in the presence of the worst sorts of demons.

He could smell what the air hostess had in the cart long before he reached her. There were two smells, and either would have made him smile. Together, they were even better.

"Snak," he said when he finally reached Smoke.

The look of relief on her face had an effect on the others, too.

"It is just food," she told them. "The giants call it 'snak,' and you will like it. But do not eat too much. Snak means more and better food is coming."

Mato didn't bother to correct her; that would come with experience. And an experience like the one she was about to have—freshly baked cookies and hot chocolate—would set her mind at ease.

Though he doubted any of the giants noticed, most of Smoke's companions carried concealed blowtubes. Their darts were threaded in thin strips of leather attached to their clothing where they'd be handy if needed. Mato made it clear to several of them that the only threat they'd face on the airship would be his wrath if they acted without his permission.

From there, the flight was uneventful, at least for the younger travelers. Mato helped himself to a cookie and cocoa, then walked slowly back to the elders. Once there, he looked from Winter Woman to Randi, the two primary negotiators. He tried not to look at the older male giant who had been waiting for them when they boarded the bah-limp. He smiled often, but Mato sensed he did so to conceal something else. He wished he knew what that might be.

Randi sensed they were making progress in the talks. The problem—and it was a huge one— was knowing for sure how their ideas were understood by Winter Woman after their journey through Mato's head.

Very early on, Archer picked up on the fact that Mato's grasp of English was less than stellar. Any question or statement which relied on idiomatic English would almost certainly be found confusing. Archer discovered this when he asked Mato to tell Winter Woman what the whole point of the airship visit was.

"Point?" Mato asked.

"Yes, the point."

"Bah-limp no have point. Is smooth, round."

Archer's manner quickly soured. "The reason. The *why!* The purpose, for cryin' out loud."

Mato squinted at him. "You cry for bah-limp?"

After that, Archer left the discussion completely up to Randi. She could tell he forced his smiles, and after a while he opted for a pair of single malts rather than attempt to keep up with the conversation. The air hostess quietly and efficiently saw to his needs.

Randi wanted to make sure all her guests, and especially the elders, had time to see the Big Horn mountains from the air. Their excitement helped boost her spirits. Archer, meanwhile, seemed intent on deflating such feelings. Eventually, she ordered a single malt for herself.

Fortunately, she was able to lean on Tori who brought along a notebook that contained a hand-written collection of words in both English and whatever language Mato's people spoke. Their words had been rendered phonetically which proved to be very helpful. Sadly, Tori couldn't be completely sure she had captured the translations exactly.

By the time *Puck Two* began its descent toward a large open area on Tori's property, everyone—big and small—wanted to give the talks a rest. Randi prayed the goodwill they would harvest from the gifts of food, clothing, and temporary shelter would go a long way.

Archer made it clear he didn't think they would.

~*~

Adam figured the county road leading to the Sheffield cabin would be unplowed since it was so little used. To his surprise, there were deep tracks in it. He was even more surprised to find a car and a pickup truck parked near the Sheffield's mailbox. The vehicles' engines were running, presumably to keep the occupants warm.

Concerned there might be a problem, Adam knocked on the window of the truck. "You okay in there?"

A bald man with heavy jowls rolled the window down and responded, "Yeah. We're fine. What d'you want?"

"Nothing," Adam replied. "I just... Never mind."

He glanced in the back of the truck and saw several long poles with sharp metal points attached. Concerned, he knocked on the window again. "If there's anything you need, I can let 'em know at the house. I'm headed that way now."

"No," said the man. "We're good."

"I hope you won't mind me askin', but what are those poles for?"

The heavy driver frowned. "What? Oh, those. We're uhm... We're here to provide some entertainment. It's a surprise."

A bearded man sitting beside him leaned toward Adam and said, "We're pole dancers."

Unfamiliar with the term, and unwilling to admit it, Adam merely smiled. "Oh. Right. Okay then, I'll let the Sheffields know you're here."

"No, don't!" said the heavyset driver. "Like I said. It's supposed to be a surprise. Please don't spoil it."

"You saw the blimp, right?" asked the bearded man, still leaning toward the window.

Adam nodded at the shape in the distance as it slowly dropped toward the ground. "With all those lights, it's pretty hard to miss."

"Right. Well, the Puck company hired us to come here."

"And dance?"

"Yeah."

Adam responded with a shrug. "Then I guess I'll see you later."

He revved Sledneck and proceeded down

the drive. It would be dark soon, and he looked forward to getting someplace warm. The blimp looked amazing, and he hoped he might get to peek inside. He'd find out soon enough.

Pole dancers? He shook his head, then smiled. *Of course! Those sharp points are to keep the poles stuck in the ground.*

That seemed to make sense even though he'd never seen a really fat dancer.

Nate got a call from Tori to let him know they would arrive shortly.

"So I noticed. Tell the pilot not to land on any buildings, okay?" Standing on the deck outside the cabin, Nate grinned up at the enormous airship, its lights glowing from one end to the other.

"See you soon, sweetheart," she said and rang off.

Nate made sure Shadow was safely parked in the house. It made no sense to let him run loose with so many strangers about to visit. The sounds from *Puck Two's* engines drowned out everything else, including the dog's whines. It didn't take long for Nate to miss the silence that normally cloaked the cabin in winter.

As the gigantic craft settled into the snow, Nate made his way toward it with the snowblower he'd been instructed to have standing by. Tori had volunteered him to clear a path from the airship to the cabin and the cottages. Most of those routes he had already cleared. The last one depended entirely on where *Puck Two* landed.

When the airship stopped moving, and its engines fell silent, Nate worked the snowblower toward the side of the ship where he'd been advised the main access was located. The door was already open when he got there.

Tori waved, urging him to join the crowd inside the aircraft. "Hurry," she said, "it's cold out there!"

He maneuvered the snowblower out of the way and hurried toward the open door. Tori stopped him with a hug and a kiss then directed him toward the front of the luxurious passenger compartment.

Tim Archer occupied a central seat looking less than happy. As Nate got settled, Archer extracted a cigar from a case he carried in his suitcoat. While he prepared to snip the end off before lighting it, the air hostess stopped him.

"I'm sorry, sir" she said, "but government regulations prohibit smoking in here. You'll have to do that outside."

Archer gave her a look that would, under ordinary circumstances, have pealed paint. "You'd think, as the owner of this thing, that we might be able to stretch the rules a bit."

"I'm afraid that's not up to me," she said, offering a sympathetic smile.

"Oh, what the hell," he grumbled as he stood and walked toward the exit. "Get my coat," he told the hostess on his way to the exit. "I'll smoke the damned thing outside."

"What's he so happy about?" Nate asked Randi when Archer was safely out of earshot.

"He's a little upset about the discussions we're having. Seems the level of translation doesn't meet his needs."

"He's a *little* upset?" Nate chuckled.

Tori joined him. "I think he honestly believed Mato's people would be falling over each other in their race to come work for him." She sat down and leaned into him. "I'm glad you're here. We needed a man around who isn't completely full of himself."

"And you think that's *me?*"

She patted his cheek. "You're as close as we could hope for on such short notice."

~*~

Once she consumed the last of her snak, Smoke relaxed, as did those who followed her. Their happy chatter blended with the conversations of the elders and the giants, all of whom she strove to ignore.

As she looked out the large and

381

mysteriously see-through panel beside her seat, she spotted a figure whose features were unmistakable. She would recognize the young giant, Adam, anywhere. The sight of him made her gasp, and she put her hands on the clear panel which stood between them.

She wanted to call out to him, knowing he'd recognize her voice. If she was lucky, he'd be pleased that she had mastered his name, something she'd practiced often and which was one of the very few words in the giants' tongue that she knew. Mato assured her she had it right.

Not wanting to draw attention to herself, she tapped on the clear surface in hopes of getting his attention, but he didn't even look up. He appeared to be walking from one end of the bahlimp to the other.

Does he not know how to get in? I thought all giants knew such things.

She looked toward Mato. If she could signal him, he might be able to help her, but he never even glanced her way; there was too much going on around him.

Looking back outside she saw more giants.

Did he not come alone? And why were the others carrying long poles? What were they up to?

Questions careened through her mind as she watched one of the newly arrived giants swing his great stick and hit Adam in the back of his head.

Her breath caught as she watched him crumple into the snow.

The giant who hit him seemed to be having an argument with another of his kind. Smoke didn't care what or who the quarrel was about, she wanted only to go to Adam. Pulling her blowtube from inside her jacket, Smoke slipped a dart into place as she raced toward the exit door.

The air hostess smiled and offered her more snak, but Smoke brushed past her and grasped the latch which secured the door. It wouldn't move.

Frantic, she turned to the hostess and pantomimed her desire to get out.

"Out?" the woman asked.

Smoke stamped her feet, and screamed, no longer concerned about what anyone thought of her. "Out! Out! Out!"

The hostess seemed dismayed but finally gave in and opened the door. Smoke raced out into the cold.

~*~

Mato's head hurt. He'd been doing his best to turn the giants' words into those of the People, but it seemed like the harder he tried, the more difficult the task became. All too often, the giants' words made no sense. It felt like trying to interpret a demon which could only babble nonsense.

A commotion from the area where Smoke

and her little cadre were seated offered a respite. Most of the girl's companions had left their seats and crowded near the open doorway. The air hostess attempted to shoo them aside, but they wouldn't leave. Mato assumed Smoke would take control and order them to spread out, but she was nowhere to be seen.

Suddenly worried about her, Mato broke free of the giants around him and hurried toward the exit, pushing elders and young warriors aside as he went. "Where is Smoke?" he yelled.

"Outside," they yelled back.

"Why?" he asked, but none of them seemed to know.

Mato cornered one of Smoke's followers and demanded that he surrender his blowtube and darts. If Smoke felt compelled to rush out into the darkness so suddenly, Mato knew better than to chase after her unarmed.

With weapon in hand, Mato punched through the gaggle of youngsters and burst out of the bah-limp.

Once outside, the cold air greeted him with a vengeance. Clenching his teeth, he centered himself and scanned for enemies. There were several. All of them were armed with stout poles, easily thrice his height. A sharp metal spike protruded from the ends and offered a grisly finish to anyone bold enough to try and get close.

They didn't seem interested in him, however. They had found a different target: the man who had tried, and failed, to give Mato orders during the never-ending talks. Something long and brown protruded from his clenched teeth, the end of which smoldered. He was surrounded by giants with poles.

A short distance away Mato spied Smoke tending to a downed giant who looked like Adam, though it was hard to tell with much of his face covered by snow. Smoke appealed to him, but for the moment there was nothing he could do for her.

"Is he alive?"

"Yes," she said, her tears unchecked. "But he does not move."

"Come," he said. "We must hurry."

"I saw who hurt him," she said, her voice little more than a growl. "He was arguing with a female giant. They stopped when the fat man from the bah-limp shouted at them."

"And now," Mato said, "the fat man from the bah-limp is in trouble."

"I do not care!" Smoke shouted.

He knew dragging the girl along would achieve nothing. "Just stay here then," he grumbled.

Voices reached him from the bah-limp's door. "Wait! Mato!"

He spun about to see who called and watched as a half dozen of Smoke's followers scrambled out of the airship and came racing toward him.

"Follow me!" he cried, and resumed his charge toward the fat giant with a pole, praying as he struggled through the snow that the gang of untested youth behind him would, indeed, follow him.

~*~

Leonard and Hazel stood back from the others who had followed Paulie's lead. Flustered at having lost control of his team, and angered by Paulie's unprovoked attack on the young man standing beside the airship, Leonard could do little but sputter his protests.

"This is insane," Hazel told him. "I didn't sign up to commit any violence. *Do something!*"

"Like what?"

She pointed at the four lancers surrounding the man with the cigar. "That," she said. "You know who that is, don't you?"

Leonard shook his head. "I've no idea."

"It's Timothy Archer, head honcho of the Puck company. Do you think for one moment he's going to ignore or forget anyone involved here tonight? He'll sue us all for everything we have, which won't amount to much after we pay our legal fees and go to prison."

Leonard took a tentative step toward the four people menacing the Puck CEO. "Let him go," he said, his voice registering a notch above timid.

When no one seemed to have heard him, he said it again, much louder.

"Why?" asked Blue. "He's the one enslaving the little people. We're just— *Ow!*"

The heavily whiskered lancer slapped at his neck, his face scrunched with concern. Moments later, he slumped to the snow-laden ground, unconscious.

"What the hell happened to him?" Paulie yelled, pulling his lance away from Archer and looking for some explanation.

Archer took advantage of the distraction and screamed for help.

"Forget him. Git the damn blimp!" Paulie angled his pole upward and prepared to stab the fabric covering.

His two companions, Annette and Yuvi, moved to follow suit, but they seemed far less sure of themselves, their attention split between Blue lying in the snow and Paulie screaming at them.

Leonard chose that moment to hustle forward and join the obese accountant. Hazel trailed behind.

~*~

Smoke had been gently patting Adam's face

and repeating his name over and over. She had been able to turn his head just enough that his nose wasn't buried in snow. When he blinked and looked at her face inches from his own, he didn't seem to recognize her.

His mind is gone. He doesn't know me!

Her concern for Adam quickly morphed into anger at the giant who hurt him. As Adam slowly reached a hand toward his head, she stood and knocked the snow from her blowtube. She could barely see the fat giant behind the others.

Mato stood among them somewhere, and her young companions had taken up positions behind him, launching their darts at any giant who moved. Only one, however, had gone down.

The reason seemed obvious; the giants' clothing was too thick. The darts couldn't penetrate deeply enough. Smoke cried out as she joined the fray. Her dart ready, she called out to her companions, "Aim for faces!"

Almost as quickly as she said it, darts flew higher. Many missed their targets, but several landed where they would work. Within moments four more giants lay motionless in the snow. Only two remained, both male, and both overweight.

There was no question in Smoke's mind which of the two giants was the most dangerous. As she prepared to launch a dart in his direction, both of them turned toward her. Her companions, including Mato, had exhausted their darts and looked at each other in dismay.

The giant who hurt Adam dropped his pole and reached for something inside his coat which he withdrew in a leisurely fashion. Smoke recognized the device as similar to the one she had tried to steal; the same one which caused the wound in her leg.

He held it in both hands and pointed it at her companions. He shouted something she couldn't understand, though she assumed it was a threat. Mato looked fearful; the others didn't recognize the danger they were in. But Mato did, and he screamed at them to run and hide.

Smoke was in their way, but they didn't slow down or stop. Instead, they poured on by, some colliding with her in the process and knocking her down.

When she regained her feet, the giant faced her alone, a look of ugly intent on his pudgy face. Smoke raised the blowtube to her lips and realized it had been damaged by her fall. She held it at her side, bent and useless.

The giant pointed his weapon, the opening at the end dark, wide, and foreboding. His face twisted into a smirk as he aimed it straight at her and repeated what he'd said before, "Stupid ingrate!"

Though she couldn't understand him, Smoke knew his words would be the last she would ever hear.

Chapter Twenty

"It's more fun to arrive at a conclusion than to justify it." —Malcolm Forbes

"What's going on out there?" Tori asked, doubting anyone could actually give her an answer. She tugged on Nate's sleeve. "Shouldn't we go see for ourselves?"

His face reflected concern. "Everything seems to be happening toward the front of the ship, by the flight deck. We can't see much of anything from here."

She stood and grabbed his hand. "Well then, Sherriff, let's go check it out."

He gazed down at her stomach, suddenly unsure of himself. "Uhm... Considering that you're—"

"If you'd rather wait here, that's fine," she said. "I'm goin' outside." With that, she hurried toward the exit.

"I'll grab our coats," Nate yelled after her.

She gave him a thumbs up and kept going.

The outside air hit her face like an ice-cold slap, and she realized how stupid she'd been not to grab a jacket before she rushed headlong into the winter weather. Fortunately, Nate caught up with her and helped her into the heavy coat she'd worn to the airfield in Worland.

She thanked him, then added, "Yes, I'm pregnant, but I'm not an invalid."

"Right. Got it. I'm sorry."

She kissed him. "Apology accepted."

"Sheffield! Where the hell have you been?"

The voice belonged to Tim Archer who approached them looking as angry as anyone Tori had ever seen.

"Well, we—"

"Those maniacs tried to kill me!" Archer stood nose-to-nose with Nate and stabbed his index finger in Nate's chest with each word. "What the hell kind of security guard do you think you are?"

Tori forced herself between them, twisting Archer's index finger sideways in the process. His surprised whine gave her a measure of gratification. "He's a sheriff, not one of your rent-a-cops, and you have no right to yell at him."

"But—"

"Or me. Now why don't you close your

mouth and take your stinky cigar-breath back inside the blimp?"

"It's an airship."

Tori drew back her hand, ready to slap him when Nate corralled her in his arms. "I think he got the message, darlin'."

Archer ambled away scowling, and Tori and Nate continued on their way.

"Oh, Lord," Tori said, coming to a stop and pointing ahead. "That's Smoke, isn't it? And that looks like—"

"Adam." Nate pulled her along. "C'mon."

The number of people lying motionless in the snow came as a huge shock. Most were clustered near a heavyset man who appeared to be the only one to suffer any blood loss. An older woman nearby, dressed in a white ski jacket and matching pants, struggled to get to her feet. If she hadn't moved, she would have blended in with the snow.

"Holy Mother of God," Tori muttered, staring at her. "What happened?"

The woman pointed a shaky finger at the fat, prostrate man. "*That idiot* happened. The moron brought a gun. I thought he was going to shoot that tiny girl, but I spiked him before he could do it." Her lips turned up in a satisfied smile as she brandished a pole. "Oh, you should've heard him squeal. You'd have thought I'd cut the pig's leg off."

Nate moved closer to the downed man, walked around his body, and stopped when he located the handgun which he unloaded and slipped in his belt.

"And so, what?" Tori asked. "He passed out from the pain?"

"Nah," said the woman. "When he bent over to look at his leg, the little gal he tried to shoot ran up and stuck something in his hand. He had just enough time to grunt at her before he went down completely." She paused, apparently deep in thought. "Did she kill him? If so, it was self-defense. I'll swear to it in court."

Nate looked suspicious. "How come you didn't get knocked out like all the others?"

"Oh, that." She chuckled. "When I saw them go down, I knew whatever it was that got them was bound to get me, too. So, I pretended it already had, and I dropped like the rest. And it's a good thing I did, too."

Tori stepped away. "I'm going to go check on Smoke and Adam. The boy doesn't look so good. Will you please call an ambulance?"

"I'll take care of it, and I'll get someone from the Sheriff's office to collect these yahoos when they wake up."

"Great idea," she said. "Join me when you can."

Nate already had his cell phone out. "And Tori? See if you can find Mato. I'd love to get his take on all this."

After alerting the authorities, Nate knelt down to examine the hands of the big man in the snow. He extracted something from one of them and stood up, smiling. "I thought so." He flicked the object away, into the night.

"Wasn't that evidence?" asked the woman in white.

"Of what?" Nate shrugged. "It looked like something got stuck in his hand. A thorn, maybe. I dunno. I'm just a dumb rent-a-cop."

~*~

The following morning, Randi arranged for someone to pick up Archer and take him to the airfield in Worland where a corporate jet whisked him back to California. She was as happy to see him go as he was to leave—truly a win-win.

Despite the insanity of the previous evening, she had high hopes for the success of her mission. Archer's massive ego may have suffered, but he'd survive, especially if she pulled off the negotiations with Mato's people.

Once the troublemakers had been carted away, things went smoothly. The food truck was a hit, though Randi and the airship crew, including a balky Captain Bradley, had to deliver the meals. Randi had specified finger foods, assuming eating

394

utensils might prove to be a challenge for her guests. Winter Woman and the elders seemed pleased with the fare, and after they'd consumed surprising portions of a rich dessert, were presented with the clothing from the Puck retailers. That, too, went over well, especially with the younger members of the group.

The evening's finale featured a tour of the three downsized cottages. Randi had worried about how that might be done since only little people could go inside. Fortunately, Mato took the lead, demonstrating light switches, turning on faucets, explaining toilets, and operating television sets, among other things. Randi and Tori had to kneel in the snow and look through the windows to see how the elders reacted.

Being dumped into the 21st century from somewhere in the Paleolithic era was bound to result in some serious shocks for those being dumped. The ride in the airship, however, had served to soften the impact of the technical revelations the little people experienced. Randi could only imagine the sorts of conversations they were having over the pictures on the TV screens and the sounds coming from hidden speakers.

Mato appeared to be the star of the show and acted as if all the miraculous things he introduced were old hat, no big deal at all. Randi could tell, however, that they were in fact, *huge* deals. The younger members of the group seemed more ready and able to adapt to the marvels. They were quick to watch the screens and listen to the music, their excitement clearly evident.

When bedtime finally rolled around, Mato explained there was plenty of room for everyone, and they could choose to sleep in the cottages or onboard the airship. There was no shortage of pillows and blankets. The thing that may have surprised Randi the most was how early they all went to bed. She could only guess about how long they might stay there.

Randi's ongoing talks with Mato and the elders would soon resume, but she needed a break. Tori and Nate provided it.

"I can't believe they didn't lock up anyone other than that big guy," Randi said. She and Tori were sitting with Nate in front of the fireplace in the cabin. "They were all out to do some damage."

"True, but they didn't get much done." Nate sipped coffee and looked pleased with himself. "The big one was the only real threat."

"But the others—"

"They thought they were helping Mato's people," Nate said. "I can understand that. Under different circumstances, I might've wanted to do something, too."

"But trying to wreck Puck's airship? What good would that have done?" Tori asked. "I mean, it was just a means of transportation."

"Which, as you'll recall," Randi said, "one of

them referred to as a 'slave ship.'"

Nate yawned. "Yep. He's the one who organized the attack. A college kid. I met him not long ago in the ranger's office at the park. I'm hoping the prosecutor will offer him a year's worth of community service. He can work it off right here, cooking, cleaning, and helping with all our little guests." He sat up and looked around. "Where's Shadow?"

"He went with Mato," Tori said.

"Where?"

She pointed to the fireplace, and Nate nodded. Randi looked from one to the other hoping for some sort of explanation. "They went to the *fireplace?* What's that supposed to mean?"

Tori laughed. "When I first met Mato—and it seems like such a long time ago—he was searching for a cavern his people had used many, many years ago. Apparently, the tribe originally settled here but moved away when pioneers arrived; they somehow lost track of where the cavern was. Mato figured it out."

Randi still didn't get it. "And?"

"Well, it turns out one of my ancestors stumbled onto it. He also befriended one of the little people. Oh, and he built this cabin." Tori gestured to their surroundings. "Anyway, he hid the entrance to the cave, disguised it. There's an access underneath the cabin. And if there's no fire in the fireplace, there's a way to get to it from in here, too."

"And Mato went down there? Why? I thought we'd be chatting up Winter Woman all day."

"Mato insisted on showing the elders what he discovered. I've no idea how long they'll be down there." She shivered. "I'm not a big fan of caves, and that one is a dog to get in and out of."

Randi remained puzzled. "Do you think the elders are up to crawling down a hole in the ground?"

"They're small enough to walk," Tori said.

"And it's not so steep that they're liable to fall," added Nate. "I've been down there, too. It's quite remarkable, but I can't say I'm keen on going back."

"So, I guess we just wait," Randi said with a smile. "I kinda like that idea."

One week had gone by since the airship took Winter Woman and most of the elders back to the Cloud Peak with the leftover clothing and several cases of uncooked foodstuff. Mato assured Randi that Winter Woman would know what to do with it. The younger members of the clan remained, occupying the three cottages provided by Puck Productions. The food truck had returned to Cheyenne, and Randi had moved into temporary quarters in a Worland hotel.

Nate stood on the cabin's deck and looked out at the scene—a gorgeous valley lay to the east, the cottages stood a short distance from the cabin to the south, and the partially completed house that Tori wanted him to build occupied a wooded spot to the north.

Tori joined him and delivered a steaming cup of coffee. "I hope you're not planning to stay out here very long."

"Nope. Just tryin' to get a handle on everything."

"That's a tall order."

He turned and kissed her on the lips. "Did you ever think you'd end up getting a job out of all this?"

"Never. It just sorta happened."

"I know," said Nate, "but it's logical. You were the best possible choice to teach Mato's people how to speak English."

"And I've got a year to do it."

"Once Archer realized how much the little people needed to learn before they could begin to function in jobs, he left it up to Randi to get it done. I think a one-year deadline is realistic."

Tori pressed her lips together and shivered. "I hope I'm up to the challenge."

"Mato's going to help, isn't he?"

"He's already started. I think he likes being in charge, but I think Smoke's going to be a handful."

"She'll be fine, for a while at least. Especially since she knows Adam's going to help me work on the house. I never knew his dad was a retired contractor. The three of us ought to be able to manage once the weather gets better."

"You're sure you don't mind not being a lawman?"

"For now. I can always go back to it."

She leaned back against him. "And I promise not to give you a hard time about it."

"Fair enough," he said.

They stood quietly looking out at the valley until Nate broke the silence. "You think Winter Woman and the others will ever leave the Cloud Peak?"

"I don't know, but Mato says they want to be closer to the cavern. The younger ones like the comforts of modern living, so I doubt they'll want to go back. Archer is only interested in hiring them anyway. I worry about what's going to happen to the rest of the clan."

"I spoke to Trent Cowart yesterday. I forgot to tell you."

"He's the BIA guy, right?"

"Correct. The Bureau of Indian Affairs is

definitely interested in the health and welfare of the tribe. They're sending an expert out to look into what can be done. I guess Cowart got a lot of heat during the Mindian nonsense."

"You really think bureaucrats are the answer?"

"I guess we'll find out. If nothing else, I'm hoping they'll convert the temporary plumbing and electrical functions for the cottages into something permanent." He turned her around and aimed her at the cabin. "Let's go back inside."

While warming up, Nate noticed a large, unsealed manila envelope laying on their table. "What's that?"

Tori smiled. "It's the weirdest thing. After Mato took the elders on a tour of the cavern, he asked me for paper and pens. He then sat down and started drawing."

"Drawing what?"

"That's the crazy part. He said he saw things on the walls down there that he'd overlooked before and couldn't explain." She shrugged. "Better flashlights must've made a big difference."

Nate scratched his head. "Okay, so what did he draw?"

"Take a look." She handed him the envelope.

He shook the contents out on the table. Three sheets of typing paper each bore a drawing. Nate examined the first one. "*A palm tree?*"

"Sure looks like it to me," Tori said. "I asked him if he remembered the ones we saw in Hawaii, but he said one just like this was on a cave wall. Look at the next sheet."

Nate flipped to the next drawing. "A boat?"

"And not just any boat. It's like the old ones the Polynesians sailed. I looked it up online." She pointed to the artwork. "It's the last sketch that blew me away."

Nate slipped the third drawing out from beneath the others. He recognized it even though the rendering was done without color. "It's one of those— What d'ya call 'em? Huma-huma-things."

"I can't pronounce the Hawaiian name for them," Tori said. "It's a yard-long tongue-twister. But according to the website I referenced, it's also called a reef triggerfish, and get this, it's the official state fish of Hawaii."

"And Mato saw it in the cave, too?"

"So he says."

Nate whistled, set the drawings aside, and smiled at her. "I know you've been struggling to find another book to write. This might just be the story you're looking for."

~End~

About the author:

Josh Langston writes books which amuse, anger, enlighten, and entertain. He regularly mines history for background material that's little known but reliably fascinating. His plots are complex, interconnected, and layered with humor and suspense; his characters are rarely predictable, and even his bad guys tend to be both engaging and diabolical.

When not writing, Josh can be found teaching and/or mentoring new writers. His students rely heavily on his four humorous textbooks. He currently has well over a dozen fiction titles on the market along with an historical fantasy trilogy set in the 1st century BC which he co-authored with his great Canadian friend, Barbara Galler-Smith.

Josh is happy to visit with book clubs online, or locally, where possible. Readers may connect with him through his website: **www.JoshLangston.com**.

And now, turn the page for a preview of Josh's
WWII, paranormal, action-adventure, romance:

Oh, Bits!

Oh, Bits!

Chapter One
Perfidy, Peril, and Predilections

"You can't be serious," Angelica said. "The *mayor* did that? *Our* mayor?"

"Seems so," came the muffled reply. Digby Doolan rarely raised his voice, which made his foghorn-in-the-distance growls even harder to understand. The shocking value of Digby's revelations made the inconvenience easy to overlook. How he sounded didn't matter so long as what he offered remained juicy.

Angelica Rohrbach scratched a concluding line on her notepad. It was nearly full, just like the other eight such notebooks she kept locked in a strongbox in the root cellar, the closest thing she

1

had to a bomb shelter in a time of war. Though it was unlikely any German or Japanese bombers would ever reach Georgia, it never hurt to take precautions. She took similar care in recording the dates and times of each notebook entry. Later, when she wrote up her column for the Atlanta *Clarion*, she would enhance the details and obscure their source. No one ever knew where she got her information, and she aimed to keep it that way.

"What do I owe you?" she asked.

Digby shuffled his feet and fiddled with his cap, mannerisms Angelica had learned to accept along with the cemetery caretaker's odor and his dirt-stained attire. Not that she ever let him in the house; just being in his presence provided all the nerve-jangling she could handle.

"Hun'erd?"

Angelica recognized the inflated first offer and shook her head. "Don't be silly."

"It's about the dadgum mayor," Digby grumbled. "That's worth more than usual."

"It would be if we could prove it. That a man like him would spend time with a—" She paused. "A *streetwalker*, doesn't surprise me. How's fifty dollars sound?"

"Pretty danged chintzy. The information's worth a helluva lot more. Now that I think on it, I reckon it's worth more like *two* hun'erd."

Angelica pursed her lips. "There's no doubt my readers will be delighted to learn that His Honor provided a hussy with a furnished apartment. I, for one, would like to know how he paid for it, and whether or not he used tax money. But in any case, I need proof before I can print any of it."

Digby stopped shuffling and pushed his short-brimmed cap to the back of his head. A shock of unkempt gray hair slumped forward and covered his weathered forehead. "You've started with rumor before. You kin do it again."

"I suppose," she said, trying to reconcile accepting his opening bid with her native frugality. "Let me get my purse." She slipped away and took a grateful breath of air not tainted by the gravedigger's aroma. She found her pocketbook and dug out half of what she needed then hurriedly returned to the back door. "I'll have to go to the bank to get the rest," she said, pushing the money into his outstretched hands. "There'll be fifty more tomorrow; I promise."

"There's only fifty here now," he said. "I told ya two hun'erd."

"Now see here, Digger, we've been doing business for—"

"A long time," he said. "And if you'd like to continue doing bidness, you'll pay what I ask."

"But—"

"A hun'erd an' a half. Tomorrow. Bring it by at lunchtime. I'll be in the shed."

"But—"

"See ya then," he growled over his shoulder as he sauntered away. "Don't be late."

~*~

Still fuming, Digby clambered into his ancient Ford truck and nursed the rusting relic to life. As a cloud of thick exhaust fumes rolled over the Rohrbach residence, he shifted into first gear and eased his foot off the clutch. Had he been a younger, more impetuous man, he might have tried to spin the tires and spew gravel across Angelica's neatly raked driveway. He knew, however, that such an effort would likely have caused the engine to seize and possibly cough up one of its four dinky pistons. As crappy as the truck was, it was the only vehicle the owners of the cemetery provided for him. If he tore it up, they'd take forever to replace it.

And in the meantime, he'd still have to haul his tools around to care for the old graves when he wasn't digging new ones. They called it landscaping. He wasn't sure what the hell it was. Grass-cutting and flower planting, sure, but the worst of it was hauling off deadfall from the acre upon acre of hardwoods that shaded the place and made digging graves so damned difficult.

Even worse, the owners were too cheap to hire additional labor. If they had more than one burial in a day, they'd give him a little extra cash to hire "independent contractors." These were usually winos and/or other down and outs who'd work for the pittance he had to offer. Granted, at fifty cents an hour, it was twice the minimum wage, but who wanted to earn it digging holes big enough and deep enough for caskets?

Thanks to Hitler, Mussolini, and the Emperor of Japan, able-bodied men were scarce, and those willing to dig graves in the summer heat of Atlanta were rarer still. Rather than pocket some of the cash for his trouble, Digby often had to pay double to avoid killing himself with the extra labor.

Years before, when still a young man, Digby entertained thoughts of getting a desk job of some kind, but he'd seen what that did to people, turned 'em into pasty-faced weaklings who spoke like they were always in church. He knew better. He'd gotten the word. Lots of words, actually. Many of which he'd shared with a local paper's gossip columnist. No, he thought. Make that a local paper's *cheapskate* gossip columnist.

He had a good mind to cut her off entirely. No more scoops, at least for a while. It'd serve her right. If she had nothing interesting to write about for a few months, maybe she'd realize how valuable his information was and actually pay him for what it was worth.

That was somewhat problematical, however, because he needed the extra cash she provided in order to pay for a few of the finer things in life which weren't possible on his caretaker's salary.

Impasse. He'd heard Angelica use the term. It meant you and somebody else were going head-to-head, and neither party was willing to back off. He'd avoided locking horns with her for ages on account of her being female and him being single. She'd been married once, way back, and got a house out of the deal. He'd always hoped the two of them might get along better, but it never happened. She always seemed glad to see him, but once she heard what he had to say, she grew standoffish and acted as if he had some dread disease. Measles maybe, or the clap. It pissed him off, but he always got over it. *Before.* Their meeting that day, however, hit him the wrong way, and harder than ever.

She wouldn't get away with it this time. Nope. This time he'd keep his tips to himself until she came around to the fact that she couldn't cheat him anymore.

If only he had the option of selling the information somewhere else, but the city of Atlanta, and *The Atlanta Clarion* in particular, could only support one gossip monger.

What the town really needed was a newspaper with an alternative gossip columnist.

~*~

Stormy Green sat in her 1928 Willys

Whippet coupe with her forehead pressed against the steering wheel. Though the car could squeeze more miles out of a gallon of gas than most other vehicles, it couldn't do so forever. Her little two-door had wheezed its last and shuddered to a stop *almost* off the road. Close enough, she hoped, that people would think she'd just done a lousy parking job. She had one gas ration coupon left and no idea how to get the fuel or where to go once she had it.

She straightened, and with a puff of determined breath, fluffed the bangs covering her forehead. The time had come. No sense putting it off any longer. But then she glanced at her legs, bare from mid-thigh down, she still couldn't make herself comfortable in the outfit her former roommate, Lorraine, had sewn for her.

"It's called a romper, and it's all the rage," Lorraine said. "As slim as you are, you'll look spectacular, and not just at the beach." She handed Stormy a page ripped from a Hollywood fan magazine. It featured three starlets in matching rompers, all styled to look like sailor suits.

"They're cute," Stormy admitted. "And would be great for a long trip in a hot car. But go out in public dressed like that? I dunno."

"When did you turn into Mrs. Grundy?" Lorraine handed her a cream-colored romper with green trim. "Try this on. I made one for each of us, only yours is about five sizes smaller."

Stormy smiled at her plump friend. "You're

too good to me."

The exchange had occurred three short weeks earlier and now the cream-colored jumper was the only clean piece of clothing she owned. It couldn't be helped; she'd have to wear it for her interview.

The editorial offices of *The Atlanta Clarion* stood half way down the block. While not exactly a prestigious publication, it had a respectable circulation for a small city's second daily. Stormy hoped her credentials as the assistant editor of her college paper would be enough to wrangle a job. Though less than optimistic, based on failed attempts with five other newspapers in as many towns, Stormy tried to ignore her ridiculous outfit and focus her thoughts in a positive fashion.

Failure meant going hungry, sleeping in her car, or worse—going home, hat in hand, to an avalanche of I-told-you-sos from her family. She wasn't above working any reasonable job to survive, but she'd always dreamed of becoming a journalist, and she wasn't about to give up on the idea. At least, not yet.

After a last check of her hair and make-up in the Whippet's minuscule rearview mirror, Stormy slipped out from behind the wheel, grabbed her portfolio from the passenger seat, and aimed her steps toward the future. Or what she hoped might be her future.

~*~

Angelica Rohrbach realized she'd made a mistake in bargaining with Digby for his information, but she'd become accustomed to the practice. And he never seemed to mind. It was a game, that's all. If he couldn't see it, that wasn't her problem.

At least, it hadn't been before that day. Now the old reprobate seemed determined to not only set his prices high, but to stick with them, too. It wasn't fair. How was she supposed to keep up with the vagaries of an old man's mind?

Maybe it was time for her to teach him a lesson. She had already heard everything he had to share about the mayor. Now it was up to her to find some way to confirm it. Maybe it would be best if she held off paying him another nickel until she had some solid proof about the mayor's shenanigans. On the other hand, Digby had never been wrong before. He might have gotten a detail or two confused, and sometimes the reality didn't measure up to its potential, but he never gave her bad information.

The phone rang as she ruminated on her plan to put Digby Doolan back in his place.

"This is Angelica," she said.

"Your column was due an hour ago, Angie. What am I supposed to do, make something up for ya?"

She found her editor's voice nearly as grating as Digby's, though for different reasons.

Though Nathan Sparks ran *The Clarion* like the ringmaster of a circus, his vocal range was much higher than Digby's. It was also significantly more nasal and came accompanied by a good deal of wheezing and coughing, no doubt the product of his three-pack-a-day habit. Angelica maintained the same odor-isolating distance from both men.

"Well?" Nathan said, his voice rising an octave over the course of a single syllable.

"I'm workin' on it, but I've got some things to nail down, first."

"So, I should just leave a blank space where your words are supposed to go? Readers will love that."

"Of course not. I just need you to be a little patient."

"There's no such thing as patience in the news business. You've been around long enough to know that."

"Obviously."

"Then why do you drive me to utter distraction every week? You know what your deadline is. Why must I call you every time to remind you of it?"

"But you *don't* have to do that!"

Nathan's response was part cough and part wheeze. Angelica wondered if he was having another heart attack. "You okay?" she asked.

"Hell no, I'm not okay!" he roared back. "I've got a paper to put out, and all I have to go on your page is a furniture ad and fifteen column inches of empty space."

"Calm down. I'll come up with something. I always do."

He exhaled heavily.

"Seriously," she added. "All I need is a couple hours more."

"Oh, no problem. I'll tell the gang in the press room to sit back and relax 'cause Angie needs a couple extra hours. They'll love hearing that. It means they'll get overtime. It means my whole damned budget goes up in flames. It means everyone else on staff will wonder why they have to get their shit in on time when you don't. It means—"

"Okay, okay. I get it," she said. "Just use my back-up column. I'll keep working on the juicy new stuff I've got, and next week you'll be all smiles. I promise." She couldn't actually remember seeing him smile.

"I used your back-up column the last time you missed your deadline, remember?"

"Oh." She actually *didn't* remember, but she didn't dare tell him that. "You know I don't just make this stuff up. It takes time and effort to get to the truth."

"You're a regular Horace Greeley."

"Now you're just bein' mean."

"Angie, I swear, the only reason I put up with your crap is because it usually pans out, and sometimes I can get an actual news story from it. I don't suppose that'll happen this time."

She chuckled. "When I said 'all smiles' before, I meant it. This new story could be huge. Gigantic!"

"I'm getting too old for this," he muttered.

"I'm serious!"

"And I don't really give a shit," he said. "Get me something in an hour. That's all the time I can spare. Your usual five hundred words of inspired innuendo will do."

He was *definitely* being mean. She'd have to make it a rumor and be careful not to identify the subject of Digby's revelation. Digby, of course, would remain anonymous as usual. No way she'd ever give up her source.

"So, you'll do it? You won't let me down?"

"I swear! You won't regret it."

He grunted. "I already regret it."

Angelica raced to hang up before he could.

~*~

Digby Doolan liked the tool shed. He thought of it as his office, even though it more closely resembled a metal-roofed barn. He had

12

walled off a section for his personal use and installed a folding cot with a thin but useable mattress, a cupboard for his beer and snacks, and a radio so he could keep tabs on his favorite teams. College sports ruled the south, and he could usually find a game if he tried hard enough. One could be a fan without ever having been a student, and that description fit Digby perfectly.

Sports and coffins, he mused. He never seemed to run out of either.

The most valuable thing in the shed, however, was neither a tool nor a domestic convenience. That designation belonged to an ornate mirror which had been left behind by his predecessor. Digby had no idea where it had come from originally though he suspected it had been imported from Europe or some obscure part of the Orient. Way before the war. He didn't know exactly when, and if the man who trained him was aware of its history, he never bothered to share it.

Certainly, the old timer hadn't said anything positive about the mirror. Quite the contrary; he feared it and even swore it was cursed. He kept it covered with an old blanket and made Digby promise to leave it that way. That had changed over the years, but truth be told, using it scared the crap out of him, too, if not as badly now as it had the first few times.

He glanced toward it, hanging on the wall above a workbench. He kept a towel draped over it to keep the dust off. Whether that mattered to the inhabitant of the mirror he didn't know. He'd never asked. There were many questions he'd never asked.

Sometimes it was better not to know all the answers.

~*~

In a carefully hidden set of German command bunkers nestled in the wooded splendor of Bavaria, Axel Schmidt looked at the orders he'd been given for his new mission, one which had but two possible outcomes: disaster and suicide, probably both.

His thoughts were shaped in large part by the debacle known as "Operation Pastorius." In that ill-fated effort, a team of eight highly trained and well-funded saboteurs secretly entered the United States with the goal of blowing up factories, power plants, military installations and Jewish-owned businesses. Their success was intended to terrify the American population and force them to withdraw manpower and equipment from the war effort and put it to work guarding their homeland.

The plan could not have failed more miserably. Instead of spreading terror across the land, the mission whimpered to an end when the leader of the team turned himself in to the FBI. The other seven operatives were arrested, and all were put on trial and convicted. Two went to prison for life; the other six were executed. In Germany, they would have been shot. The Americans used their "electric chair." Axel's sphincter tightened to a pinprick at the thought.

While similar in nature to the failed Operation Pastorius, Axel's mission had a much narrower focus. The Americans were building a factory which would soon be churning out long-range bombers at an alarming rate. The massive aircraft would be flown by female pilots to bases near the war zone where they would be loaded with bombs and crewed by veteran airmen intent on laying waste to the fatherland. Axel's family had perished in Berlin, burned to ash along with countless thousands of other innocent civilians when the British and American bombers dropped their devastating loads on the unprotected populace below.

Der Führer himself had been rumored to say a few more such raids would force Germany to stop fighting. For Axel, that was unthinkable. The Americans had to pay for the misery and death they inflicted on his family, and that sentiment had propelled him to volunteer for the mission. He would have preferred to personally dole out retaliatory death and destruction, but he was enough of a realist to know that a covert operation had the capacity to do far greater damage than could one man, no matter how well armed.

The Americans had developed a high-altitude, high-speed airplane which carried a vastly bigger bomb payload than any other. The B29 could turn Germany into rubble; Axel and his crew were expected to slow down if not stop their delivery. The team would be dispatched onto American soil via U-boat as had their unfortunate predecessors. This time, however, the mission wasn't being planned by the craven leaders of the now-defunct *Abwher*. Every step of the complicated plan had been worked out by the *Schutzstaffel*, or SS, to which Axel had dedicated himself.

America *would* pay.

~*~

Stormy tried to brush some of the wrinkles from her skimpy outfit as she waited to see the *Clarion's* managing editor. A bony woman with gray hair and severe clothing had told her to wait, though she couldn't say for how long. The look she had given Stormy—or more accurately, Stormy's outfit—had screamed disapproval, though she settled for an obviously unneeded sniff. She claimed the staff had production deadlines to meet, and she couldn't be sure the managing editor, or anyone else, would have time to interview a potential trainee.

Stormy didn't even get the chance to correct the trainee reference. She was there for a real job. She'd had all the training she needed; she was ready to write.

Sitting in the empty room, she whiled away the time by filling out an employment application. She felt as if she'd gone through a hundred of the damned things since she received her college diploma, a handshake from the dean, and his mumbled good luck wish. He almost got her name right.

It was okay though; she was done with what her father called "higher education." She was on her own at last, free to pursue her dream. She never realized getting a paying job in the industry would be so hard.

"Miz Green?"

Stormy almost jumped to her feet but caught herself in time. No need to appear over-eager, though she knew the effort was hopeless. Her face always gave her away. Everyone said so.

"Mr. Sparks will see you now." The gray-haired stick figure smirked at her as she gestured for Stormy to follow, then turned and marched away. Stormy scrambled to catch up, chasing the real-life version of Popeye's girlfriend, Olive Oyl, down a hallway.

"He's in there," the woman said, aiming a skeletal digit toward a room that bore an atmospheric haze.

Is it safe?

"Hope you don't mind the smoke," said her gray guide. "Someday they'll pass a law about smoking in the workplace, and he'll be out of a job. Assuming he lives that long."

Stormy didn't believe Congress would go

along with anything like that; aside from the fact they were focused on a world war, there was simply too much money being made in the tobacco industry. Everyone in Hollywood smoked, or so it seemed. If opinions were based solely on what the movie stars did, everyone would think smoking was glamorous. Many of her friends in college smoked, but she'd only tried it once. That was enough. She'd heard of some who'd tried marijuana, too, but she figured if she couldn't handle tobacco, she'd never handle anything stronger.

"Well, c'mon in," said a voice from within the smoky room. "I'm not gettin' any younger."

Stormy eased into the cramped, messy room, most of which was occupied by a wide wooden desk. The speaker remained hidden from view behind a handful of yellow copy paper. She recognized the stuff from her time on the staff of her college rag.

"Siddown," he said. "Be with ya in a minute."

There were two chairs in the room. Mr. Sparks filled one of them, and a stack of files filled the other.

"Uh—"

"Hang on. I'm almost done." He dropped the paper on his desk and attacked it with a blue pencil, drawing a huge "X" on one paragraph and several lines through another. He circled a word here and there, drew some arrows and added a couple symbols she'd never seen before, then tossed it in a metal tray marked "Out." In the same motion, he pressed a button on the corner of his desk which summoned a runner. The boy, a couple years younger than Stormy, dashed in, emptied the "Out" box and departed without a word.

While Stormy observed the runner, Sparks observed her.

"Just set that stuff on the floor," he said, watching intently as she followed his instructions.

When finished, she handed him her resume and the partially completed job application. "I didn't have time to answer everything."

While he perused her paperwork in silence, Stormy glanced around his workspace. A dozen black and white photos and a handful of wooden plaques adorned the walls. She didn't recognize any of the awards, though some of the people in the photos looked familiar. Among them were the governor, a state court judge, who she was reasonably sure now occupied a cell in a federal prison, and some other supposed notables.

A poster featuring the face of Franklin Roosevelt bore a quote from his 1940 re-election campaign: "I'll say it again and again and again: Your boys are not going to be sent into any foreign wars." A feathered dart protruded from the left side of the president's forehead. Numerous tiny holes in the poster testified to previous assaults.

"Stormy, huh?"

"Yes, sir," she said, steeling herself for the inevitable snide comment about the notorious burlesque queen who performed under the name "Stormy Weather." She didn't have to wait long.

"I'm pretty sure there's a fan dancer by that name."

"I think the term 'stripper' is more accurate, but I assure you, that's where the similarity between us ends."

Sparks cleared his throat and lit up a Lucky Strike. His ashtray overflowed with snuffed out butts and burnt wooden matches. After taking his first deep drag, he smiled at her in a way that suggested a measure of respect. "So, you wanna be a reporter."

"Yes sir," she said, relieved that he hadn't said anything about a trainee position.

"We already have a trainee. You saw him a minute ago when he came in."

The room suddenly felt a great deal warmer than it had before, and the volume of cigarette smoke made her lightheaded. "Actually, I've already done some practice jobs. I'm ready for a real one."

He regarded her closely, paying significantly more time on her face and figure than on her resume. She suddenly wished she'd worn pants. And a parka.

After an uncomfortably long silence he

once again focused on her paperwork. "Says here you maintained a regular column on your school paper. Got any samples?"

"You bet," she said, digging into her portfolio. She had divided it by story types: news, features and opinion. She grabbed everything in the opinion section and handed it to him.

"Nice photo," he said, holding up the clipping to compare the headshot in it with her actual, in-the-flesh, flesh. "Very nice."

"Thanks."

"We don't use headshots in our opinion pages."

"Oh." *Crap.*

"But if the folks writing for us looked as good as you, I'd be tempted to change that." It appeared he wanted to say more, but once he started coughing it took him a good long while to regain his voice.

"Can I get you some water?" she asked.

"No," he said, red-faced. "I'll be okay."

He reached down beside his chair and retrieved a thermos jug from which he poured two fingers of something dark into a coffee mug. Stormy wasn't close enough to identify the fluid by smell, especially since the room reeked of cigarettes and other odors she chose not to think about.

"Which of these is your best?" he asked, holding up her columns.

"I think they're all pretty good," she said, "but the one I like the most is about problems with the nursing program. Those were—"

"This one?"

"Yes."

He handed it back to her.

"Which one do you like the least?"

She was trying to get a handle on his game, but had little confidence. "The one on women's sports, I guess."

He thumbed through them and finally held one up. "This it?"

"Yes."

He handed the rest back to her and started reading.

"I—"

"Shhh. Gimme a sec."

Trying not to do a slow burn or squirm too much in the straight-backed chair, Stormy waited until he finished.

"Not bad," he said at last. "A little overly dramatic, maybe, but not bad."

"Thanks." She managed to avoid adding, "I think."

"So, why do you want to work for the *Clarion*? Why not a big-time paper like the *Constitution*?"

"I'd love to work for a big paper," she said, "but from what I've seen, they only want writers with years and years of experience."

"And the *Clarion* doesn't?"

"I didn't say that!"

He smiled at her. At least, she thought it *might* have been a smile.

"Tell ya what," he said, "I'll take a chance on you. Your writing isn't bad. It isn't great, either, but we can fix that. What you need is seasoning—a little time in the saddle and exposure to some real editing. Before you know it, you'll *be* one of those experienced writers, and then I'll probably have to bribe you to stay here."

"You won't regret it," Stormy said, flushed with relief. "I promise."

"I'd rather you promised something else."

She blinked at him, her suspicions as taut as a harp string. "Like what?"

"Promise you'll continue to wear short skirts. Seems like everybody who works here is a couple hundred years old. Seeing a pretty girl in nice clothes will definitely improve the atmosphere around here."

Stormy paused, her mind racing. "Uh, okay.

But I confess, this is the only short outfit I own, and I probably won't get paid for—"

Sparks smiled and dashed off a note. "Give this to Audrey, she prefers 'Miz Banks' by the way. She's the woman who showed you in. It's an advance on your first paycheck."

I won't have to sleep in the car!

"Be back here at eight o'clock, sharp. I'll have an assignment for you. Screw it up, and you can return the advance before you leave in the afternoon."

"I won't screw it up," she said, forcing every bit of determination she could into her voice.

"Let's hope not," he said. "Now, skedaddle."

~End of excerpt~

Oh, Bits! is available now in e-book and paperback formats at your favorite on-line retailer.

Oh, Bits!